OMEGA FORCE
RETURN OF THE ARCHON

JOSHUA DALZELLE

©2014

Omega Force: Return of the Archon

By Joshua Dalzelle

Copyright 2014

*****

Edited by Monique Happy Editorial Services

http://www.moniquehappy.com

Chapter 1

Jason's lungs burned and his heart hammered in his chest, but he gritted his teeth and dug a little deeper for that last bit of strength he had left. He was sprinting over a rough dirt path towards a pink and orange tree line nearly a quarter mile ahead of him. Seeing that he was heading for a rise in the path, he quickly checked his speed via his neural implant.

Thirty-eight miles per hour.

Despite the horrific pain of the lactic acid burning through his muscles, he smiled tightly and concentrated on not going airborne when he crested the short hill. Timing his jump carefully, he leapt when he was halfway up and sailed over the crest of the shallow rise to come back down to a relatively soft landing on the downhill side, still at a full run. He could see his objective in front of him and put everything he had into the last two hundred meters. As his speed crept just a hair over forty miles per hour, he thrilled at the air rushing by and the light, fast strikes of his feet on the hard-packed ground. He flashed by two beings standing casually near the path and began to decelerate until he could safely slow to a walk.

Almost immediately after the breeze generated by his speed disappeared, he began to sweat profusely and pant heavily as he walked back to where the two beings were still standing, consulting their data pads. "How fast?" he asked, his words coming out between his gulping breaths.

"That was under five minutes for the entire course," the taller of the two said. "Simply astonishing." He had deep bronze-colored skin and was nearly eight feet tall, but two feet of that was all neck. "I've never seen numbers like this," he continued, talking to his colleague. "Have you?"

"I told you it would be impressive," Doc said, also consulting the data Jason's neural implant had sent them as he ran the course. "But not without some issues. Jason, your body's cooling capability is nearly maxed out. In fact, we're lucky it's not an especially warm day."

"You're telling me," Jason replied, breathing much slower as his body ramped down from the full-out assault on the obstacle course he'd just run. "But what are the chances I'll ever push myself that hard under normal circumstances?"

"You can't be serious," Doc deadpanned. "Do you want me to give you a list of times from the past year alone?"

"You're such a mother hen sometimes," Jason griped as he took a long pull off the water bottle Doc had given him.

"Dr. Ma'Fredich!" the other alien exclaimed. "I was unaware you were a mother!"

"That's not what he meant, Dalon," Doc said. "The captain here feels I fuss over them too much about their health. What he fails to realize is that if I don't, they'll run themselves into the ground."

"I'm afraid I still do not understand," Dalon said, his head bobbing back and forth as he considered the human's strange idiom. "But it's of no importance. I'd like to get back to the lab and finish analyzing the data from this run. Excuse me." The gangly alien strode across the grounds, his reverse-bent knees giving him a peculiar gait.

"In all seriousness, Captain," Doc began again, "we're at the very edge of what I can do to enhance your body through genetic manipulation. The only step beyond this is extensive cybernetic upgrades, which means we start chopping limbs off and stuffing your body cavity full of machinery."

"You paint such lovely images with your words, Doc," Jason said with a disgusted look on his face. "No … this will be it. I just needed that last little edge you could give me. You did really well. I would have never dreamed of even being able to complete that course before, much less in the time I did."

"I won't pretend to understand your motivations, Captain," Doc said as they began walking back towards the lab complex, "but I hope you're not putting yourself through this just to try and keep up with the other two."

Jason didn't answer as they continued on. The truth was that he did go through the procedure so that he wouldn't feel like he was the weak link when he was in the middle of an op with Lucky and Crusher, two of the most powerful soldiers and naturally gifted warriors he'd ever seen. He was able to compensate for his human body's shortcomings in expensive, powered armor, but that wasn't always a practical solution.

So six months earlier, he had asked Doc to do an extensive analysis and come up with a plan of attack to eliminate some of those weaknesses. Three months later, he and Doc, with the help of Crisstof Dalton, were given permission to set up shop in one of the preeminent genetics research labs on the world of Aracoria. The ConFed stronghold had the staff and facilities needed for Doc to begin modifying Jason's genetic makeup and perform the needed upgrades to his body. It was three months of unimaginable pain, hooked up to machines while he could literally feel his body morphing into something … else.

The culmination of that suffering had been a blistering time through a nearly impossible obstacle course with no ill effects afterwards. His skeleton had been again reinforced with organic, carbon-based materials. The muscle density and individual strand-strength had been increased by a magnitude of at least four. The gene that controlled his aging had been modified, as well as a host of other upgrades to his various systems, which would ensure that he ran at peak performance for some years to come. If he had felt less than human with the enhancements he had been given before, he felt positively alien now as he walked across the ground with a new spring in his step.

"I'm almost afraid to ask," Jason said after a moment, "but how is Kage?"

Since Jason was already going to be out of commission for months, Kage had asked if he could get his wetware upgraded to the newest state-of-the-art. What he hadn't realized was that in addition to integrating with a new neural computer, he also had to have a few genetic tweaks by Doc and the staff at the facility to make sure they bonded seamlessly. There was also the complication of removing the old computer that he'd had been carrying in his head that had a core that was nearly ten years old.

"That depends on who you ask," Doc said irritably. "As his doctor I can assure you he's making a phenomenally speedy recovery and is integrating with his new neural suite as we'd hoped he would."

"And if I ask him?"

Doc shrugged. "You should probably look in on him, Captain."

Jason sighed heavily. "Very well."

*****

"How's it going, buddy?" Jason said with exaggerated cheerfulness as he and Doc walked into Kage's room in the medical facility. It was not that Jason didn't feel a certain degree of sympathy for his diminutive friend, but Kage was an incessant whiner and a world-class drama queen and therefore it was difficult to say how much pain he was truly in.

Jason wasn't quite prepared for the sight in front of him. While his own recovery from his procedures had been arduous, the end results had quickly made him forget about the pain. Kage, however, looked to still be in the early stages of his own recovery. The little Veran was hooked up to a host of machines, some actually inserted into his brain through the cranium itself. Fluid-carrying tubes and electronic cables were also interfaced directly to the neural implant as it integrated with Kage's unique brain. Due to that brain's complexity and capabilities, the standard nanotech implants were of no real benefit. Instead, an invasive procedure to install a much more powerful interface was required. *Well, required for Kage's line of work.*

"Captain, is that you?" Kage said. Jason looked around in confusion. As far as he knew, Kage was still able to see and had even looked right at him when he walked in.

"Yeah, it's me," Jason said. "How are you feeling?"

"I'm dying, Captain," Kage whispered. Jason looked up at Doc, who only rolled his eyes and shook his head.

"The people here say you're going to be okay," Jason said. "You're just going to be very uncomfortable for a little bit longer."

"It's fine, Captain," Kage whispered again, ignoring Jason. "I've had a good run. If it wouldn't be too much trouble, could you take my body back to Ver and give it to the Overseers for the funeral rites?"

"Kage," Jason began before being interrupted.

"I wonder if it will hurt," the Veran continued. "Dying, I mean."

"Kage—"

"I wish my family knew about all the people I've helped out here."

"Kage, you're not fucking dying!" Jason snapped, pausing to pull in a deep breath and calm himself after the outburst. "You're going to be—" He was interrupted again by Kage, who reached out and stroked the side of his face with a clammy hand.

"I'm going to miss all of you," Kage said in a barely audible whisper. Then, without warning, he coughed a single, violent hack and a glob of yellowish, greenish … *something* … flew out of his mouth and landed on Jason's face with a wet *splat.* "Sorry," he whispered again and began to try and wipe it off with his hand. All he succeeded in doing, however, was smearing it all around Jason's face and over his now-clenched, closed mouth. Jason stood and angrily smacked his hand away. "Ow!" Kage squealed loudly.

Doc, having the good sense and requisite self-control to not even crack a smile, wordlessly handed Jason a soft cloth towel from the counter he was leaning against. Jason grabbed it and scrubbed at his face vigorously. Once he felt he had most of the slimy substance off his face, he went to the basin, still not relaxing the muscles in his mouth, and scrubbed his face with water as hot as he could stand. After drying off with another proffered towel, he turned, without looking at his friend, and walked out of the room.

"He's not actually dying," Doc said, following him out into the corridor.

"Oh, let's not rush to judgment," Jason said hotly. "There's still plenty of time for him to die."

"You may need to stand in line," Doc answered as they walked. "I think some of the nursing staff is plotting to kill him.

"To be fair, he is in a lot of discomfort. I wouldn't go so far as to call it actual pain, but the integration process can be quite disconcerting and he did have the previous core in his head for much longer than is recommended for that type of neural interface."

"If he's having this much trouble just getting used to the thing in his head, how long will it be until he's actual able to do his job again?" Jason asked with some concern.

"I'm not qualified to speak to that," Doc admitted. "I want to say that this is the hardest part, but I'm not fully certain either way."

"This is somewhat troubling," Jason mused. "We rely on him a lot more than I'd like to admit. It's a bit of a glaring weakness in our outfit, to be honest."

"There aren't many alternatives. Without Kage, we'd be forced to purchase an insanely expensive, less effective AI. Or ... another synth that's been specialized in code breaking and network intrusion. What are the chances we'd end up with another Deetz? While he's an enormous pain in the ass at times, Kage is one of the very best at what he does."

"You're not telling me anything new. It's why I've had to get his identity changed half a dozen times," Jason said. "Like you said ... he's a pain in the ass, but he's *our* pain in the ass. Let's get him through this and then he can tell us what he needs to get back to full mission capable." He left Doc so he could go check on Kage and made his own way back to the quarters he'd been occupying since arriving at the medical facility.

*****

Jason took the long way back to his temporary quarters, a circuitous route that led him back outside and along some footpaths where he could enjoy the beautiful Aracoria weather and the facility's stunning landscaping. If he ignored the sound of the air traffic overhead he could almost make himself believe he was back on Earth. The fact that this was a manufactured world that so closely resembled his own home boggled his mind a bit. There were some differences, of course. The atmosphere had a higher oxygen concentration, thanks to the terraformers still running as atmospheric conditioners, and the trace gas composition was different. But, in all the important ways, it was a pleasant reminder of home for the dispossessed human.

The fact he could reminisce so freely without feeling the pangs of homesickness reinforced in his mind that he'd made the right choice in staying where he was. He would have never been left in peace on Earth, and too many people depended on him now. His mismatched crew was closer to him than any family had been in his previous life. They lived together, fought with each other almost constantly, but any one of them would lay his life down for the others without hesitation. This gave Jason no small amount of pride when he considered that half the crew had no military background, although Kage had been a career criminal when they'd found him.

Sweeping his ident chip over the scanner, Jason stepped through the doorway into his quarters as the hatch whisked out of the way with a slight hiss. He tossed his stuff on the desk and made his way to the shower to get cleaned up, but the display on his com unit stopped him before he made it to the restroom. It was showing three separate times: local, *Phoenix's* time, and *Defiant's* time. The battlecruiser *Defiant* was currently just ending first watch. On a whim, he synced his com to the desktop display and punched in a slip-space com address he knew by memory.

He waited while the "Please Standby" message flashed on the screen for a few moments as he leaned back into the seat and ran his hands through his now-dry hair. He tried not to think of whatever it was that Kage had hacked into his face earlier. After a minute more, he reached for his com unit to break the connection; just then, the display lit up.

"Captain Burke," said the stunningly beautiful Captain Colleren with a smile. "I hope this is a social call and you're not in some trouble."

"No trouble, Captain," Jason said with a smile. "Just checking in to make sure you don't need us grubby mercs to come bail you out again." Her laughter was musical as she also leaned back in her seat and reached for what appeared to be a mug of tea.

"So how are things going? I can't really tell a difference from the neck up," she said. "I figured Doc would have made you unrecognizable by now."

"I asked for a more subtle touch," Jason laughed. "You can't really see it just by looking at me, but I'm as good as I'm going to get with all the parts I was born with."

"Was it worth it? It had to hurt."

"Yes, and yes."

"How is Kage?" she asked.

"He might not make it," Jason said, holding up his hand as she bolted upright in her seat. "No ... he came through the procedure well enough. But his behavior afterwards has made him the number one candidate to suffer an 'accident' while he recuperates. It probably won't even be me that does it."

"Oh, poor little guy," Kellea said. "Cut him some slack, he's not a big tough soldier like some of you guys. Speaking of … have you been in contact with the *Phoenix* recently?"

"No," Jason admitted with a tight voice. "I'm trying to maintain the illusion that I trust them with the ship and not check in every day."

"I was a bit surprised when you let them take it, if I'm honest," she said. "You know that Crusher and Twingo together without supervision may be disastrous."

"I'm hoping that Lucky will continue to be the voice of reason and not let them bully him into going along with a stupid idea," Jason said. "But keeping them here on Aracoria for months with nothing to do while Kage and I were getting upgraded would have been equally bad. Who knows what trouble they would have gotten into. Letting them take the job to train that Baron's security force made sense and will bring in a little cash."

"You have unfettered access to Crisstof's account when it comes to operational expenses and yet you still act like starving independent operators," she said, shaking her head.

"It's a good habit to keep up," he said with a shrug. "I'm sure they'll be fine."

"Who are you trying to convince?" she laughed at him again. "So, by the way, you never did tell me about the favor you owed Councilman Scleesz. You didn't have to assassinate anyone, did you?" Her tone clearly indicated she was teasing him, so he took no offense.

"I wish," he said. "Let's just say that his species' divorce proceedings require that documents be hand-delivered into the other party's hand with a witness present. His estranged wife was well aware of this fact and led us on a merry chase through the underbelly of The Portcha

Expanse for the better part of a month. That's not even an especially large region of space."

"Maybe you guys are losing your touch," Kellea said before looking off-camera for a moment. She looked back with a clearly annoyed expression. "I've got to head back to the bridge. We received clearance for docking a lot faster than I expected. Thanks for sending me a signal." She smiled hugely before reaching over and disconnecting the link.

Jason sat for a moment and stared at the screen as it reverted back to the main menu. The relationship between himself and Kellea had been progressing at a comfortable, if glacially slow, pace. There were some complications, of course, such as the fact they were two different species. Another was that they were routinely separated by no less than hundreds of lightyears at any given time. But they put no pressure on each other and were able to reconnect every so often thanks to the miracle of slip-space com nodes.

Since he and his crew had saved her life a little less than a year prior, she had let her guard down quite a bit and allowed him to see a side of her she would never show her crew or even her employer. He had no idea how far things would go between them, or if it would ever go further than exchanged messages and vid links until one of them met someone else, but he was happy with that. He went to scratch his nose, but instead punched himself forcefully in the face.

"Damnit!"

He still wasn't fully accustomed to the way his body now moved, and if he wasn't concentrating, it seemed to have a mind of its own. It would take his brain a bit to recalibrate itself to the increased speed and strength. He stood up, stretched his back out, and made his way to the restroom where he intended to take an obscenely long, hot water shower before grabbing Doc and maybe hitting up one of the local pubs in the nearby entertainment district.

Chapter 2

"How's he doing?" Jason asked for the fourth time.

"Captain," Doc said impatiently. "Please ... quiet." Jason went back to his seat in a huff. They were in a room in the lab section of the medical facility that was packed full of medical and computer equipment. Doc and his partner, Doran, were peering through the large window that made up the entire far wall. On the other side, hooked up to a host of medical machines, was Kage. His skull was now fully closed back up and the machines were hooked to him via passive connections only, a far cry from when Jason saw him with his head split open and full of wiring and tubing.

It had been two weeks since then and now Kage was putting his new neural implant through its paces. This was the second day of trials and the Veran was already drawing a crowd of astonished medical staff and technicians as he began to far exceed not only their test plan schedule but the generally accepted capabilities of the device itself. The training had started easily enough with the specialists asking Kage to simply ping a networked computer with his neural implant, but the Veran, true to his nature, had quickly broken out of the confines of the supposedly secure network and began wreaking havoc with the facility's systems. Why? Because he could.

As captain, one of Jason's most challenging tasks was keeping his crew out of trouble. They were all a little high-strung and bored easily, a serious problem when their ideas of entertainment ranged from petty theft to physical assault. Of them all, Lucky was by far the easiest to trust. Kage was far and away the worst. The smallest among them, he had a quick brain and an even quicker temper that manifested itself with him using his unique talents to make the person that angered him completely miserable. Toss in a gambling addiction for good measure and you had a volatile little package that needed near constant monitoring.

"He's already through the primary and secondary firewalls," one of the technicians reported. "I can't tell what he's doing now. He's somehow split his presence in the network into four separate entities that are attacking different nodes simultaneously. How can he do that?"

"Let's keep the speculation and conversation to a minimum," Doc said sternly. "You need to be focused on what he's doing or you'll miss it." There were a few more minutes of silence as everyone studied their displays, and Jason tried to find a comfortable position in a chair that was in no way meant for humans.

"That's impossible!" a technician exclaimed.

"Stop him! Shut the system down," another said, stumbling out of his chair and trying to reach the switches on the banks of computers. Jason stood and looked in on his friend through the window. The faintest ghost of a smile was playing across his wide mouth.

"He's outside the lab and on the public net! The hard lines are disabled, how is this even possible?"

"Captain," Doc said, "you should probably go in and tell him stop. He's had his fun and I think he proved his point. Tell him the testing phase is over. I'm not sure what he has in mind, but this *is* a ConFed enclave." Jason just nodded and stepped in through the door separating the two rooms.

"All right ... what are you up to?" Jason asked, standing at the foot of the reclined seat Kage was secured to. He received no response from his friend. "I know you can hear me." At this, one of Kage's eyes cracked open and an impish grin emerged.

"I'm just having a little fun," Kage said. "Nothing illegal or immoral. By the way, we have dinner reservations at that place we saw in Aracoria Center. The place at the top of the tower."

"Kage, that place is nearly a thousand credits a plate and it was booked solid for the next three months," Jason said in a pained voice.

"I took care of it," Kage answered. When he saw the look on Jason's face, he elaborated, "I didn't steal the funds ... exactly. I routed it from Crisstof's expense account that he has us tap for operational expenses. It will look like a fuel and service charge for the *Phoenix*."

"The *Phoenix* is four-hundred lightyears away right now, and you said this wasn't immoral."

"It isn't," Kage insisted.

"You're siphoning thousands of credits from Crisstof Dalton so we can go have a good time," Jason said sternly, crossing his arms over his chest. "That's stealing."

"We steal all the time," Kage said. "Besides, wouldn't it be nice to go there at least once? Just to say we did it?" Jason's admonition died on his lips as he considered Kage's words. *It has been a long few months.*

"You can guarantee Crisstof's bean counters won't figure it out?"

"You have no faith in me," Kage said in a mock-hurt tone. "It's handled, Captain. Now, can I get unhooked from all of this and go get cleaned up?"

*****

"How can we afford this?" Doc asked in a hushed voice after a prissy, olive-skinned alien ushered them to a private table in the upper level of the venue. The entire outer ring of the floor slowly revolved, affording them a three-hundred and sixty degree view of Aracoria Center as they ate.

"It was just—"

"I have a special 'Captain's Fund' for things like this." Jason cut Kage off. Doc had made his opinions on Kage's creative accounting very clear over the years.

"How special?"

"Relax, Doc," Jason lied smoothly. "Just some slush funds I picked up from things like selling off my outdated armor." Doc was about to protest again when he saw a tray loaded with expensive drinks and delicacies move past on its way to another table. The life of a mercenary didn't present him with many opportunities to enjoy the luxuries of the life he had left behind as a preeminent geneticist.

"Well, if you're sure we can spare the credits," Doc finished lamely as his eyes followed the tray. Jason knew he had him, so he let it drop and began keying through the interactive menu that had been placed in front of him.

It was nearly three hours, and six courses, later and all three of them were leaning back in the plush seats, watching the city of Aracoria Center drift by. Jason recognized at least three high-ranking committee members also dining on the private floor and had to wonder exactly how much cash Kage had skimmed off the top of their operational account to cover it. His com unit's persistent beeping shook him out of his post-meal lethargy as he dug the small device from the pocket of his expensive suit pants. He read the message twice and compared it with local time before clearing his throat and addressing his friends. "Kage, go ahead and pay up. Let's head back and all of us grab a good night of sleep."

"We have something pressing to do tomorrow?" Kage asked, his feet propped up on the empty chair across from him.

"The *Phoenix* is due to make landfall midday tomorrow."

Chapter 3

"Here they come," Kage said, pointing to the sleek shape of the DL7 gunship descending out of the traffic pattern and towards the designated landing pad where Jason, Doc, and Kage were waiting, their bags stacked neatly in a pile on the tarmac. The ship continued down in a lazy arc that would put it over the landing spot in a few minutes.

When it was still nearly a quarter mile away, the gunship jerked to a halt, her nose bobbing slightly as she settled into a hover. The *Phoenix* stayed there for nearly thirty seconds as the three crew members on the ground looked at each other in confusion. Jason was about to pull out his com unit when the ship began moving again, spinning around so it was facing the opposite way and reversing towards the landing pad on repulsors only. A moment later, the landing gear dropped with a few loud clunks as the ship continued its backwards march towards the pad.

Jason's eyes narrowed in suspicion as the ship stopped at a hover ten meters above the tarmac before gently lowering down and settling onto her landing gear with a few groans and pops. Now convinced that something was amiss, he waited for the drives to spool down and the main ramp to open so he could interrogate his crew.

"Captain!" Twingo shouted with a huge wave as he walked down the ramp. "You look great! How did it go?"

"What did you idiots do to my ship?" Jason asked bluntly. There it was. A quick shifting of eyes and a pause in his gait.

"What do you mean?" Twingo asked in a strained voice. "What did you hear?" That was all he needed. Jason marched off without another word and began inspecting the hull as he walked around the perimeter of the landing pad with Twingo jogging beside him to keep up. "I mean ... there was nothing other than the usual bumps and bruises. You know?"

"No, Twingo, I don't know," Jason said, his eyes never leaving the *Phoenix* as he walked. "All this ship was required to do was transport Crusher and Lucky to Telamar Station. Why would there be any bumps?"

"Well ... there are numerous navigational hazards one may encounter at any given time while moving a vessel through space. Interstellar travel is a dangerous game, as you've said so many times yourself," Twingo was talking very fast now that Jason had cleared the starboard flank and was walking around the pointed nose.

"What the hell is this?!" Jason's bellow echoed across the tarmac loudly enough that some of the ground crew working on the next pad over looked up. All along the *Phoenix's* port flank were the unmistakable scorch marks of plasma cannon hits.

"What is what?" Twingo asked, making a show of looking up and down the hull. "Oh, that? That's nothing, Captain. Just some discoloration from high-energy discharges."

"Would these discharges have been in the form of plasma bolts fired at my ship?" Jason asked. Not waiting for an answer, he turned and bellowed across the tarmac again, "Lucky, Crusher ... get your asses up here!"

"Captain, there's no need—" Jason held up a finger to silence his friend as Lucky and Crusher came shuffling up from around the starboard engine nacelle.

"OK," Jason began in a calm voice. "I want to know who shot up the side of the ship. I want this information in a concise and factual manner. Who wants to go first?"

Twingo and Crusher looked at each other a moment before the latter decided it was every man for himself.

"This is the first time I've seen any of this, Captain," Crusher said, gesturing expansively to the scorched hull. "I must have missed it when he picked us up. What happened, Twingo?" The big warrior had strategically placed himself next to Jason during his performance to give the illusion he was on his side. Jason wasn't fooled in the least, and it wouldn't be the first time the pair had tried to play him. Twingo's mouth dropped open and he stared at Crusher in shock. Apparently this wasn't part of their pre-arranged plan.

"You son of a—"

"Somebody better speak up," Jason cut Twingo off, trying to keep control of the situation while simultaneously trying to maintain his anger. Or at least the appearance of it. He could now clearly see that the blast marks were little more than superficial and hadn't actually damaged the hard alloy of the hull. It meant they were more than likely goofing off and it had gone too far, but he still wanted to know what happened and who the ring leader had been. This was precisely why he hadn't wanted to turn the gunship over to them in the first place. "Do I have to do this the hard way?" Jason asked with a weary sigh.

"What way would that be?" Twingo said, taking a step back apprehensively.

"Lucky, what happened?" Jason asked the battlesynth. Lucky's shoulders drooped a bit. He clearly had hoped he wouldn't be dragged into the mess, but his captain had just asked him a direct question. He looked helplessly at

Crusher and then Twingo, hoping they'd bail him out. When they didn't, he turned to Jason.

"The blast marks are from an outdated anti-aircraft battery that utilizes accelerated plasma discharges, but the ship was not engaged in combat operations when it happened." Jason stared the synth in the eyes, waiting for more. It was clear Lucky hoped he could get by with the barest amount of information.

"Keep going," Jason said flatly.

"We had concluded our mission and were preparing to leave when a group approached us at the spaceport with a business proposition," Lucky began. "They told us about an annual race the locals run within the system. It was mostly local ships but it was open to outside registration."

"I think I see where this is going," Jason said, rubbing at his scalp. "Twingo, would you like to redeem yourself and pick the story up since you left your crewmate flapping in the breeze here?"

"The prize money for first place was huge." Twingo picked up the story, dropping his act. "The course was across the system and had waypoints you had to cross, many of which were within the atmosphere of the various planets and moons.

"We checked the other ships in the race. There were about fifteen, and none looked like they could match the *Phoenix* in this type of flying. We figured it would be a sure thing."

"Two points," Jason said, stopping the tale. By now Kage and Doc had walked up and were staring at the scorch marks themselves. "One, you are a barely proficient pilot. Certainly not someone I would want flying my ship in a race. Two, did it ever occur to you that you were being hustled by the local crowd?"

"It did," Twingo said. "And I wasn't flying. Anyway, like you said ... this was a local hustle. We put up the entry fee and right away we could see the locals ganging up on the outsiders to put them out of the race early. So we didn't bother being creative and just ran the course at full power. There wasn't anybody even close when we crossed the final waypoint on the way to the finish, but they'd set up that ancient anti-aircraft battery. We took three glancing blows on the port side but were quickly out of range."

"So who was flying?" Kage asked.

"I flew the *Phoenix* during the race," Lucky admitted.

"You?" Jason asked, shocked. "I expect this sort of nonsense from these two, but I had hoped you would have been the voice of reason, Lucky, not helped them out. And when did you learn to pilot?"

"It was clear they were going to enter the ship in the race regardless of my protests," Lucky said in his quiet, dignified manner. "I surmised our best chance of a positive outcome, which meant returning with the ship intact, would be with me piloting. I have been utilizing the simulator mode on the bridge during my night watch in order to expand my skill set." Jason struggled to find fault in his friend's logic, but came up empty.

"So you got hit with an outdated gun they'd set up as a fail-safe," he said. "So you're out the entry fee and whatever it will cost to clean up the hull?"

"Well ... not exactly, Captain," Twingo said uncomfortably. "We actually won. The *Phoenix* outran the next closest ship by nearly six hours. They didn't want to pay up at first, but Lucky and Crusher were able to secure our winnings."

"How much?"

"Three hundred thousand credits, give or take a few thousand." Jason just stood and stared at Twingo, certain he had misheard the number. That was nearly twice as much as the contract they'd been filling was worth. After a moment he just shook his head.

"Did the payout for your actual mission cover operational costs and end up deposited in the treasury?" When he received a few affirmative nods, he continued. "So here's how this is going to work ... the cost of fixing my hull is coming out of your winnings. The remaining will be split evenly between the three of you."

"You're letting us keep it?" Crusher asked in shock.

"You earned it, you keep it," Jason shrugged. "But I don't expect anything like this to happen again. This was a foolish risk you took with the ship just for fun and games."

"Yes, Captain," came the chorus of relieved replies.

"Now get with the dockmaster and get to work," Jason said, pointing to the hull before walking off towards the ramp. He hadn't seen the ship in months and was almost afraid to see the state it was in on the inside.

Chapter 4

The *Phoenix* lifted off from Aracoria nearly seven hours after she had landed, her port side sporting a splotchy, mismatched coating from the hasty repair. After negotiating the convoluted air traffic control system, then the orbital traffic control system, they were finally free navigating away from the planet at a brisk pace, all of them eager to leave such a heavy ConFed presence behind them.

Jason was letting the computer do the flying for now. Although he was much more in control of his reflexes and strength compared to when he first underwent the procedures, the muscle memory from hours and hours of stick time would now be out of whack. He had a four-day slip-space flight coming up, so there was plenty of time to log some significant simulator time and recalibrate himself. He was also looking forward to sparring with Crusher during the flight. Despite being asked repeatedly, Jason had shrugged off his enhancements as somewhat insignificant, wanting to give his friend a nasty surprise later. Whenever they had trained before, Crusher's vastly superior strength was almost impossible to overcome. While he held no delusions that he was now somehow equal to the Galvetic warrior, he did think he might be able to get the drop on him in the opening seconds of a match.

"So," Kage said from the copilot seat, "where to?"

"Set a course for the Colton Hub and we'll see what we can find going on there," Jason said.

"Oh boy," Kage muttered sarcastically. "When we're trying to avoid getting knifed in a back corridor, we can look forward to severe gastrointestinal distress from all the fine eateries there."

"It's not that bad anymore," Twingo said from the engineering station. "Since the cartel that was running it got wiped out by the ConFed last year, the new ownership seems to be making a real effort to make it suitable to sustain life. I heard they even replaced the atmospheric filters."

"We're not going there for a vacation," Jason reminded them. "We'll be staying as long as it takes to pick up a lead on another job or find out where the action is, and then we're out of there."

"Why do all of our shady dealings take place on rundown, decrepit space stations?" Kage complained loudly. "You'd think a nice beachfront resort would work just as well. Course laid in and ready for you, Captain."

"I personally like the decrepit old stations," Jason said as he engaged the slip-drive. "Harder for the authorities to sneak up on us and there's the excitement that goes along with being outside any official jurisdiction."

As per their usual habit, once the ship transitioned into slip-space, the crew began to disperse to find something to do other than stare at the darkened canopy. Soon he was left alone on the bridge with Lucky, who was standing near the hatch like he normally did.

"So other than the race, how did the job go?" Jason asked him.

"Quite well, Captain," Lucky said. "We were able to make the security force proficient in the concepts of protection detail, small unit fighting, and general infantry principles."

"You'd think they would have already been able to figure that part out," Jason mused. "Don't they have a military?"

"Their military is comprised entirely of autonomous drones. They are a somewhat pacifist species," Lucky explained. "Although they have not completely rejected war, they are unwilling to fight it themselves."

"Seems you would have some feelings about that."

"Unrelated, Captain," Lucky corrected. "The drones in use are not sentient."
"Gotcha," Jason said as he began setting his station up for a simulator session. "So why don't they just hire mercs or outside security? Why did they need to train a homegrown detail at all?"

"They are additionally fiercely xenophobic. They would never concede to their ruler being protected by another species. It was quite a contradiction, I will admit." Lucky said.

"Sounds like an exceedingly unpleasant species to be around," Jason said as the canopy cleared to show them flying over an unnamed mountain range on an unnamed planet. In truth, they were still in slip-space, but the computer was utilizing the canopy display and bridge grav-plating to create a flight simulator of unparalleled fidelity. "Let me guess ... along with these charming traits, they were also insufferably smug about their own superiority."

"An astute guess, Captain," Lucky confirmed. "Many felt themselves to be experts in hand-to-hand combat. It took Crusher almost twenty minutes to dispel that misconception. It was a trying mission, to say the least."

"So what made you interested in learning to pilot this bucket?" Jason asked, changing the subject.

"You are the only proficient combat pilot on the crew," Lucky said. "While Doc, Kage, and to a lesser extent, Twingo all have the ability to fly the ship, none are able to do so in a tactical situation."

"Is that the only reason?" Jason prodded.

"I find it to be a satisfying experience."

"You can say it, Lucky," Jason laughed. "You thought it looked fun so you decided to give it a try ... and it was fun."

"That is as good a term as any," Lucky admitted. "And yes, piloting the ship during the race was as *fun* as I had hoped it would be after all my simulation time."

"Well then, hop into the copilot seat and we can take turns running though these sims," Jason said. "This first one is mostly intra-atmospheric and the terrain randomizes after each run. We can do this for a bit and then start adding targets."

After an hour, Jason was impressed with how naturally Lucky adapted to the ever-changing simulations. Two hours after that and he was hard-pressed to keep ahead of him.

Chapter 5

"Oh, holy shit, that smells bad," Jason choked out as the ramp descended. The air from Colton Hub wafting into the cargo bay was enough to make his stomach do a back flip. "Okay ... we all remember the rules, right? No unnecessary fighting, stealing, or cheating. Actually, don't do any of those things at all."

"Don't worry about me, Captain," Kage said in a muffled voice as he covered his nose and mouth with his smaller pair of hands while the other two waved at the air in front of him. "I'm not going out there. I'll be here enjoying the filtered and recirculated air aboard the ship if you need me." As he turned and left, Doc also followed him back into the ship without a word.

"This has got to be brutal for you," Twingo said to Crusher. "It smells like raw sewage in here, and your sense of smell is so incredibly delicate." When Crusher just turned to stare at him, he pressed on. "Does it bother you that in order to smell something, tiny particles of it actually need to go into your nose and embed into the receptor? Just think, that means when you smell—"

"Twingo," Jason snapped. "Leave him alone." In truth, Jason also would rather not think about what may be pulled into his body with each breath he took. He considered going back for a rebreather for a moment, shrugged it off, and descended the ramp with the remaining three of his crew in tow.

The *Phoenix* was parked in a hangar that had three other similarly sized ships fanned out across the deck, each parking berth sharing the one hangar door. Jason was always uneasy leaving his ship hooked up to an external docking arm if he was leaving for any length of time under the best of circumstances, but the looks of the docking complex branching away from Colton Hub had convinced him to pony up the credits for a hangar berth.

The station was a huge, sprawling facility that, like most platforms over a century old, looked like a hodgepodge of ill-conceived and hastily completed construction efforts. What made it unique was that it wasn't anchored in a star system, it sat motionless in interstellar space. It had started as a refueling depot a few hundred years prior when the larger ships didn't have the legs to make it across the Colton Expanse, a region of empty space that sat between the core worlds and the fringe settlements, without exhausting their fuel supply.

Once the big ships had slip-drives that were as efficient as the smaller, faster ships, the station fell into disuse and, inevitably, the criminal element moved in. A lack of any governmental oversight in deep space helped that immensely. The most distinguishing physical feature of the station was the "crown" of mangled, jagged alloy at the top. That was all that remained of the section that once housed the actual refueling arms. As legend had it, a frigate-class ship escaped a firefight by jumping into slip-space, unaware that their real-space flight systems were damaged. When the ship exited slip-space, it was on a collision course for the station and ended up shearing off the entire top section, killing all on board both the ship and those station decks.

Jason personally thought that entire story was bullshit. Who jumps into slip-space unaware that they have no ability to navigate their ship? Given the shoddy maintenance everywhere else on the station, and coupled with the fact most starships used liquid hydrogen for fuel in their anti-matter reactors, he figured the refueling booms were most likely detached by a massive explosion down in the pumping station that used to be housed right where the "crown" now sat.

Regardless of how true the story was or not, it did serve as a reminder that there were dangers on the facility that didn't necessarily relate to the bottom feeders that inhabited it. They were just one faulty seal away from explosive decompression at any time aboard the dilapidated hulk. It was certainly a motivating factor in trying to scrounge up a lead on a job and get back aboard the pristinely maintained gunship.

"So what are we looking for?" Crusher asked as he looked at the passing foot traffic with disdain.

"The usual," Jason said, also keeping an eye on the crowd. "Someone who doesn't belong." Crusher simply grunted at this and continued his scrutiny as they strolled along the main promenade. The tactic had been Jason's idea originally, something he had picked up from being deployed in third-world hovels and observing human behavior. It was surprisingly simple; look for people who stood out for the wrong reasons. For starters, they would have the wrong clothes for a station inhabited by cutthroat pirates and smugglers. Then there was the look that seemed to transcend all species in their situation: the slow dawning of realization of the sheep that wanders into the lion's den.

These types had usually exhausted all options and were now looking to outside help to solve their problem. Omega Force had picked up contracts on at least a dozen occasions where they were asked to ferret out packs of raiders or narco-gangs that were terrorizing one small settlement or the other. Often these infestations simply had to be eradicated, something Jason and the boys were more than happy to help with. After being the small town bully for so long, many of these groups were hopelessly unprepared for the level of violence the small mercenary crew would bring to bear. The smart ones ran. Those that didn't were no longer around to cause any further trouble.

Jason's "lost sheep" method worked so well, in fact, that they were even funneling taskings to Crisstof's group for the times when a little bit of political pressure would be far more effective than a thermobaric warhead. Given the predatory nature of mercenaries in general, he figured he was doing them a great service by identifying them first. Some of the crews he was walking among wouldn't hesitate to kill off the problem, take what they had, and then take everything the contract holders had as well.

They walked past the usual smattering of beggars and con artists before coming upon a dirty and emaciated little girl of a species Jason thought he had seen before, but couldn't name off the top of his head. She was holding a scrawled sign that read, "Please help. Family stranded. Have credits." He stopped and looked down at her while her eyes darted fearfully between Crusher and Lucky.

"How did you get stranded?" Jason asked her in Jenovian Standard.

"The ship we were on left us here when we all got off while it was being repaired," she said quietly. "There are six of us and we just need to get back home."

"Where are you from?"

"Um ... Kellariss-2," she said. The hesitation didn't go unnoticed.

"Wow, you're a long way from home," Jason said. "Where were you going?"

"I don't know," she said plaintively. "My parents just said we have to leave. Can you help us?"

"Maybe. Where are your parents?"

"Back in one of the service corridors that lead to the auxiliary docking complex. My mother is not well and they didn't want to stress her by bringing her to the main galleria," the girl said, already standing and folding her sign up.

"Let's go talk to them and maybe we can work something out," Jason said, gesturing for her to lead the way.

"Captain," Twingo called, "I'm going to head down two levels to where all the scrap hawks hang out, see what I can find."

"Okay," Jason nodded. "Lucky, go with him." The battlesynth broke off and followed Twingo thorough the crowd on their way to see what hardware may be available for trade or outright purchase. Jason knew Twingo just liked poking around the shops and talking to the other engineers. Most of the parts were recovered salvage and not anything Twingo would ever consent to installing on "his" ship. As the pair left, Jason noticed the little girl's mouth compress into a tight grin as she turned and headed off in the other direction. "Stay loose," he muttered to Crusher over his shoulder as they followed her away from the main bulk of the crowd.

"Always."

They wove their way off the promenade and down a side corridor that looked like service access to the shops. They moved past all of this and Jason watched his guide walk quickly and confidently through the litter-strewn passage. After a few hundred meters, she veered off to take another, smaller passage that curved downward into the lower levels. He was keenly aware of the walls closing in as well as the dim, sputtering light barely cutting through the gloom.

The smells of industrial lubricant and hot electronics wafted over him as they pressed further into the tight service tunnels. They hadn't seen another being for at least five minutes and were now well away from any of the main gathering places on the station. He switched his ocular implant over to a mix of mid-wave infrared and low-light amplification as the weak lighting seemed to become more sparse the further they went. Behind him Crusher was *chuffing* as he drew in the scents around him to analyze his surroundings. The little girl, now silent, looked over her shoulder more and more often to make sure they were still following before slowing her pace.

"So ... where is your family is staying?" Jason asked conversationally.

"I'm not sure where they went," she said softly.

"Are you about finished with this game?" Jason asked. "For future reference, children don't usually know about auxiliary docking complexes, but not the world they're travelling to." The childlike mannerisms dropped immediately, and the alien reached up under her tunic. Jason drew his own sidearm in the blink of an eye and leveled it at her.

"Don't. So, how many victims have you lured down here with this little con you're running?"

"Wouldn't you like to know," it laughed, the voice now deeper and gravelly. Jason tilted his head in surprise at the sudden change. "Now!" the alien shouted.

Before he could react, a section of pipe swung down on his wrist, sending pain lancing up his arm and his blaster clattering to the floor. From behind the nearest support columns, a burly sqroro, a heavy-grav species, and a heavily muscled saurian came at him from both sides, the sqroro still holding the pipe.

He was dimly aware of Crusher snarling and the sounds of a struggle behind him as he ducked the pipe being swung at his head. Something was wrong though. They seemed to be moving too slowly and his ears were filled with the sound of rushing air. As the pipe whizzed overhead, he sent a tight punch out to the sqroro's thick torso and was surprised when he heard a gasp of pain and saw the alien dropping to a knee. Jason planted on the ball of his right foot and pushed off, driving forward while bringing his right fist around, aiming for the sqroro's head before he could get back up.

There was the crack of his fist connecting with the other's head and then the heavy alien was flung down the corridor to where he lay, bleeding profusely, likely fatally, from the horrific head wound. *There's no way I hit him that hard.* Before he could turn to get a bead on his other assailant, an impossibly strong, scaly arm snaked around his neck and pulled his head up while the saurian's other hand tried to reach the top of his head to pull it backwards. Jason couldn't get the angle to bring his elbows into play to try and dislodge his attacker, so he leaned back and literally ran up the wall of the tight corridor, using the saurian for leverage.

When his body was parallel to the deck, and with the saurian still hanging on for dear life, Jason launched himself backwards with all the strength he could muster. Again, he was unprepared for the results. He launched them backwards through the air with such force that when they hit the far bulkhead there was a sickening crunch and the arms around his neck went slack. He rolled over and came to his feet to see where Crusher was.

The big warrior was holding another wriggling saurian at arm's length, staring at Jason with a slack-jawed look of shock.

"Uh, Crusher," Jason said. "Are you going to do anything with that one?"

"Huh?" Crusher asked. "Oh ... yeah." He planted the alien on the deck and shoved him hard into the far bulkhead. When the dazed saurian came back at him, Crusher met him halfway with his elbow, delivering a devastating blow to the head that dropped the alien instantly. Jason bent, retrieved his blaster, and looked around.

"I know you're still here. I can see you," Jason called out. He couldn't really, but it never hurt to bluff.

"I'm not armed," the scratchy voice said as the "little girl" stepped from around a column. "If you knew this was a trap, why did you follow me down here?"

"It's sort of my thing," Jason said. "Can't have you running free and preying on helpless travelers." The alien laughed uproariously at that.

"Do you have any idea where you are? All there is here is predators. Do you plan to take us all out one by one?"

"Nah, you were just convenient," Jason said. "So ... about those other victims. How long have you been running this spider trap?"

"Long enough to have my appearance altered to look like this," the alien said. "It's not like we waylaid anyone important. Just broke settlers and freighter crews too dumb to stay up on the main levels. Look, I've got quite a bit of loot hidden away. Maybe we can work something out."

"These settlers and spacer crews," Jason drawled, "I'm guessing they weren't allowed to go on their way once you relieved them of their property."

"What do you think?"

Jason didn't bother answering. He raised the blaster and fired straight into the alien's chest, sending it rolling over backwards twice before coming to a stop in a crumpled heap. The acrid smell of burnt flesh assaulted his nostrils as he turned to look at Crusher.

"These three are dead too," he said, still looking at Jason oddly. "We should probably get out of here."

"No argument there," Jason said, tucking his sidearm into its holster at the small of his back. "Let's see if the upper levels have a pub that serves anything that wasn't actually made on this shithole."

*****

"Why do you keep staring at me?" Jason said more forcefully than he meant to. Crusher simply leaned back in his chair, giving no indication his captain's tone had offended him.

"So what exactly did Doc do to you?"

"Mostly a continuation of what he'd already been doing," Jason answered defensively. "Just a little tune up on the muscles and reflexes."

"No."

"What do you mean no?" Jason said with a frown.

"What do you remember about that little tussle back there?" Crusher asked, ignoring his question.

"Nothing special," Jason said, "they seemed like amateurs. Are you thinking we should have let them go?"

"No, I couldn't give a shit about killing a handful of lowlife murderers like that," Crusher said with a dismissive wave. "You killed both of those idiots so fast that I barely had time to grab the third and check to see how you were faring. That's why I was still holding him ... I had no time to do anything else. Those lizards weren't a pair of pushovers either; their race is closely related to Korkarans. But it's not just the fact you split a sqroro skull open with one punch or launched yourself through the air hard enough to kill the other one. It's the speed you moved at. It didn't feel unnatural to you?"

"I did feel like I was off-balance the whole time," Jason admitted. "I just figured it was the adrenaline surge. All Doc did was max out the potential my body already had. There was no DNA splicing with a Galvetic soldier, or anything like that, if that's what you're asking."

"There must be something in your evolution, some switch that allows you to turn it all on like that when in a fight," Crusher mused. "Otherwise you'd be vibrating in your seat and you'd have crushed that glass already. Interesting. You've become a very dangerous man, Captain."

"I've always been dangerous," Jason said with a wink, wanting to lighten the mood. Crusher laughed and raised his own glass in a mock salute. Crusher's words had made him think about the unintended consequences of having his genetic code messed with. He didn't want to tell his friend that it was likely his "fight or flight" response that had kicked in, nor did he want to bring up that it was a bit unpredictable.

They were sitting on a balcony well above the main galleria in one of the more high class establishments on Colton Hub. Jason knew there was an obvious joke there, but in reality the pub wasn't half bad. The glasses were clean, the air was filtered, and the liquor was vintage and off-world. All in all, not a bad little place. It was like a little island oasis in the middle of a sewage desert. Jason's com unit beeped twice, breaking him out of his reverie.

"Go for Burke," he said into the device.

Lucky's voice came over the speaker. "*Captain, I have ensured Twingo is safely aboard the Phoenix and the ship is locked up. Where are you and Crusher?*" Jason told him how to get to the bar and which table they were sitting at. "*I will be there momentarily. Lucky out.*"

"Probably shouldn't tell him about our adventure in the tunnels," Crusher said, draining his glass and gesturing to the serving girl with a clawed hand. "It'll hurt his feelings he got left out."

"Good idea," Jason agreed. Lucky was so stoic that it was often easy to overlook that he had a full range of emotions and was actually quite sensitive to perceived insults from his friends. Fifteen minutes later, the battlesynth strode over to their table, which was thankfully tall enough that he could stand by it without looming over them, and greeted each in turn.

"I take it we have no additional passengers?" he asked.

"Nah," Jason said. "It was a scam. Trying to fleece us for credits. The usual deal in this place. What was Twingo up to? I'm surprised he didn't come back with you."

"He was very excited about some of the things he was able to procure in the lower levels," Lucky said. "It looked like refuse to me, but he paid handsomely for it." Jason winced.

"I knew his winnings were going to burn a hole in his pocket," he said, taking a sip as the other two puzzled through the meaning of the phrase. "He couldn't help himself. Every stop we make he's going to buy more and more junk until we can't even get into the engineering bays."

"Most of the items were small, Captain," Lucky assured him, "but I agree that he will likely continue to make impulse purchases until he is out of credits."

"Bah," Jason grunted, "let him collect garbage. I'll just start throwing it out the airlock when he's asleep like I did last time." He paused mid-drink as both his friends' heads snapped in his direction. *Shit.*

"I *knew* that was you," Crusher accused. "Months and months he pissed and moaned about that. All the accusing stares across the galley table. The searching of our quarters when he thought we weren't around. I should have known."

"I was aware the entire time," Lucky said.

"How?" Crusher demanded.

"Who is the only person who has the command authority to order the computer to loop the internal sensor feed so it appeared nobody had entered Engineering?" Lucky said.

"This is all ancient history," Jason said, trying to hurry the conversation along. "I would appreciate a certain amount of discretion, gentlemen."

"Discretion is gonna cost you extra," Crusher said, taking a long pull of his drink.

"Naturally," Jason said sourly. He waved the server over and ordered another strong drink. Now that Lucky had arrived, he felt fairly secure in kicking back and blowing off some steam as he watched the horde of beings rush around below them. Many of the shops never closed as a constant stream of incoming ships made it unwise to close down for station "night hours" and miss out on all the potential business.

The more he watched, the quieter and more introspective Jason became. All the bustling below him … like so many ants scurrying around, as loud and boisterous aliens jostled each other to get the best deal on this meaningless trinket or that. *Maybe ants is the wrong comparison … they actually look like a group of humans during an after-holiday sale. Sad.* He grabbed his drink, his fourth since Lucky arrived, and leaned back into his chair to rejoin the conversation with his friends. Since he was facing the entrance to the bar, he had a better view than the other two of new arrivals. Three beings stood in the entryway now, scanning the crowd and paying especially close attention to the three of them. They also looked impossibly familiar. He squinted and tried to focus his blurring vision, trying to dismiss what he was seeing.

"That's it," he announced loudly, sliding his glass to the middle of the table. "I'm done."

"Really?" Crusher asked, surprised. "Seemed like you were settling in for a real bender."

"That was the plan, but it's getting too weird," Jason said, slurring his words slightly between the hard consonant sounds. "I'm looking at you here at the table, which is where you should be … but there are two other Crushers over by the door. And something that looks like a half-human, half mini-Crusher. Maybe this shit is laced with something?" As he made an elaborate inspection of his glass, the other two turned to inspect the newcomers.

"Your initial assessment was partially correct, Captain," Lucky said. "There are two Galvetic warriors and a female gelten walking towards us."

"What's a gelten?" Jason asked.

"It's the actual name of my species," Crusher said tightly, turning to face the approaching trio. "Galvetor is the name of our homeworld."

"Ah," Jason said. The fact that, like him, most species had a name for themselves and another for their homeworld and/or star system was somewhat confusing. Most identified with their homeworld after they'd been in space for a few generations, while others preferred their species name. Kage called himself a Veran because he was from the Ver System, but Jason was sure his kind had another name for themselves. Jason still referred to himself as human, though Earthling would work just as well. The fact two warriors like

Crusher were approaching their table finally penetrated his awareness and gave him a little jolt of panic. "Oh shit," he said, eyeing their progress through the crowd.

"Let's not jump to conclusions," Crusher rumbled. "They may not be looking for a fight." They waited until the lone female gelten stood at their table, the two warriors a step behind and flanking her on either side. Now that they were close, Jason could see that, while still intimidating, they were both at least four or five inches shorter than Crusher and looked to be giving up fifty to sixty pounds to his friend.

"You will tell me your name," the female demanded imperiously. Her voice was beautiful, strong and melodic, but the edge to her tone made Jason tense up.

"My name is Crusher."

"I will have your real name," she demanded again, all but ignoring Jason and Lucky.

"You will get only a warning, old woman, and then you will be on your way," Crusher snarled in a sudden display of ferocity. "I've no time to waste on the likes of you."

"You will not speak so to the Caretaker, outcast trash!" one of the warriors shouted, moving towards Crusher. Things were going to shit quickly. Crusher stood to meet the challenge and the whine of Lucky switching to combat mode cut through the chaos. The female gelten, the *Caretaker*, calmly raised a hand. Shockingly, everyone seemed to heed her signal and froze in place.

"You will calm yourself," she admonished her warrior, "or you will remove yourself from this room."

"But, Caretaker!" he spluttered. "How can you let this renegade speak to you in such a manner?"

She sighed, turning back to the table. "Because he is Lord Felex Tezakar, the Guardian Archon of Galvetor, and he may speak as he wishes," she said quietly, locking gazes with Crusher. There was a clatter as both warriors dropped to their knees, placing their foreheads on the floor and prostrating before Crusher.

"Tell them to get up," Crusher growled. "They're making a scene."

"You know that I cannot do that," the Caretaker said. "Only you can command them." The snarl that emanated from Crusher convinced Jason that he was about to strike the woman. Instead, he turned to the two warriors.

"Rise," he said simply. "Quickly! Off the floor, you fools." Both warriors climbed to their feet but kept their eyes downcast, refusing to meet Crusher's gaze.

"Please forgive us, Lord Archon," the one who had threatened him said. "We thought you long dead. Never would we raise arms against you."

"So," Jason said conversationally, "anybody care to fill Lucky and I in on what the hell is going on?"

"We should get to the ship, Captain," Crusher said. "And as quickly as possible."

Chapter 6

"Hey, Captain," Twingo called over his shoulder. He and Kage were hunched over something in the cargo bay that looked, at least to Jason, like a twisted chunk of space garbage. "What's new?"

"We've got some guests if you two would like to stop playing in the trash," Jason said. Both of them spun around, then walked over to where Lucky and Crusher were also coming up the ramp, followed closely by their guests from Galvetor.

"Guys, these are—"

"Oh, shit!" Kage suddenly exclaimed as he spotted the two additional warriors. "There are three of them now." He actually turned and looked like he was going to flee back up into the ship, but Twingo reached out and grabbed his collar.

"Calm down, damnit!" the engineer said through clenched teeth. "You're embarrassing us."

"What the hell is wrong with you?" Jason ground out before turning back to where the others had stopped to observe the commotion. "Don't mind him," he said with a smile. "He just gets a little excited. Anyway, as I was about to say, this is … you know, other than *Caretaker,* I have no idea who any of you are."

"Caretaker is simply an informal title," the female gelten said with a slight smile. "A term of familiarity and respect, if you will. My name is Connimon Helick. The warrior to my right is Morakar Reddix and his younger brother, Mazer Reddix, is to my left. We are not a species particularly obsessed with formality, Captain. You, and your crew, may simply address us by our given names."

"Simple enough," Jason said. "This is my engineer, Twingo, and our excitable code slicer, the one with two extra arms, is Kage."

"Greetings all," Connimon said with a nod of her head. "Captain Burke, while I look forward to filling you in on why we've sought you out, I feel that it would be prudent to launch as quickly as possible. I can't be sure, but we may have been tracked."

Jason sighed heavily, getting a sinking feeling he was getting involved in something he would rather not. Again.

"Very well," he said. "Kage, Twingo … go up front and get us flight prepped and cleared for launch. I'll be up shortly."

Twingo turned to look longingly at the pile of trash on the bay floor. "Captain, I was sort of in the middle of—"

"Now!"

"Right."

"Connimon," Jason said carefully, "while we're not necessarily a danger-adverse group, what assurances do you have that I'm not taking my ship and crew into a war?"

"I have none, Captain," she answered bluntly. "But if you care for Felex at all, this is something you will find worth the risk."

"Who is Felex?" Kage asked from behind him. Jason didn't answer; instead he simply turned and glared at him.

"Fine," Kage huffed, "I'm going." Jason watched him until he had made it all the way up the stairs to the mezzanine that led to the crew entry hatch. When he turned back to suggest they also enter the ship, he saw that Crusher (he still couldn't think of him as Felex Tezakar) was standing near the ramp, arms crossed, with an openly hostile expression on his face.

"Crusher," he said. "Go ahead and close her up, I'll take our … guests … up to the bridge to get settled in for departure." Without a word, Crusher turned and smacked the controls to close up the ramp and pressure doors hard enough that Jason was surprised the control panel wasn't torn from the pedestal. Wisely choosing to ignore his friend's abuse of his ship, he turned and ushered the rest of the geltens up the steps and through the ship.

*****

"There's one thing I love about Colton Hub," Kage said as he scanned the surrounding traffic. "Once we clear the doors, we're free navigating and no pain in the ass departure control to argue with. By the way, we're on a collision course with that light-freighter. Range is fifteen thousand kilometers."

"I've got him," Jason said, nonplussed as he continued to swing the nose of the *Phoenix* around to line up with their mesh-out vector. "Keep scanning for anybody taking an unhealthy interest in us. By the way, Connimon, how did you get to Colton Hub? Are you leaving a ship here?"

"We paid for passage aboard a freighter of ill-repute," she said simply. "The voyage was … unpleasant. This is an impressive vessel, Captain."

"Thanks," Jason said absently. Her story of flying in aboard some random smuggler's scow raised more than a few flags in his mind. Their decision to go to Colton Hub had been a spur-of-the-moment choice when they had flown off of Aracoria. There was no possible way they could have known their destination, much less their arrival time and where they'd be on the massive deep-space station. He filed those concerns away for later when he would have a chance to sort out exactly what was going on.

There was another concern he had with two Galvetic warriors standing on his bridge. Although smaller than Crusher, he had no doubt they could be a deadly duo if things turned violent. It was fortunate he had a trump card in his hand that could nullify the advantage of even two Galvetic warriors. He subtly turned to Lucky and scratched his ear with three fingers, a seemingly meaningless gesture that the battlesynth would recognize as part of their prearranged signals: keep an eye on the two heavies and be ready for anything.

When he turned back to the forward canopy, he caught Connimon looking directly at him. Her mouth twitched up in a small smile and she shook her head, as if in amusement, before turning back to the terminal she was sitting near. *Damn, she caught that and she's only just met us. The brothers may not be the most dangerous passengers after all.* All the terminals not in use by crew members were displaying a generic flight status for the benefit of their guests. There was nothing to see outside the canopy in interstellar space save for a few random uninteresting points of light against the black.

"We've got a fast mover coming around the station, Captain," Kage reported. "I can't identify a class or type, but they came from the far docking complex."

"Do they look like they're tailing?" Jason asked, advancing the throttle up further.

"We're the only ship on this vector and they're coming around awfully fast on what looks like an intercept—"

He paused, frowning. "They're gone."

"What do you mean, *gone*?"

"I mean they've disappeared from the scope," Kage said. "I'm running full active scans and they didn't stop, explode, or turn back … they're just gone."

"Sensor stealthing?" Jason asked Doc in disbelief.

"It would appear so," Doc said doubtfully. "But …"

"But we've never seen anything outside of the ConFed Spec Ops Section that has that sort of tech," Crusher finished for him.

"I'm getting ghosts of returns along their projected flightpath," Kage said. "They're definitely trailing us, but don't look like they're making any move to overtake us."

"Twingo, do we have full power?" Jason asked.

"We're ready for anything," Twingo affirmed. "What do you have in mind?"

Jason didn't hesitate or second guess himself. "Full combat mode!" he barked as he swung the *Phoenix* around to head back the way they had just come and slammed the throttle down to the stop. "Kage, prep a tachyon burst bomb." The gunship shot back towards the station, accelerating into the traffic patterns that were drifting lazily to and from the docks arms. The com began squawking warnings and queries the closer they came, but the crew ignored them. "Are they coming about?"

"Confirmed, Captain," Kage said. "I've detected their drive coming up to full power as they're attempting to turn and pursue. Looks like their stealth tech is imperfect at best and they're flying an underpowered drive."

"All good things," Jason said, threading the gunship through the traffic as she continued to accelerate. He wanted to get around to the other side of the station before their pursuers. Even though it was difficult, it was possible to track a ship through slip-space depending on the level of technology and the skill of the crew. He'd rather not find out the hard way they had both. "Program a series of short dummy jumps," he ordered. "We'll drop tachyon charges at each."

"How many?" Kage asked, his hands flying over his navigation panel.

"Five."

"That's going to be expensive," Kage muttered.

"Sure will be," Jason agreed as the *Phoenix* shot over the "crown" of Colton Hub and through the traffic around the docking arms. A few plasma shots were fired their direction, one even splashing against the shields, as they streaked by. Jason chuckled and shook his head. *The universal constant about the galaxy's bottom feeders: if you don't understand it, shoot at it.*

"We're clear," Doc reported, "you can engage the slip-drive any time."

"We've shaken them, but not for long," Kage said. "They've dropped their stealth while they're navigating through traffic. When we passed, it spooked everyone and ships are flying out in all directions."

"Engaging now," Jason said, squeezing the trigger to release the first tachyon charge before smacking the control to send them streaking out of the system. As the coronal discharge of dissipating slip energies faded away, the first tachyon charge triggered, flooding the area with tachyon particles and blinding anyone's sensors who may have been trying to track the gunship's exit.

"So," Jason said as he carried his mug of chroot back to the galley table, "do we think it was a random coincidence that a sensor-stealthed ship was tailing us away from Colton Hub?"

"Of course not," Twingo snorted. "But who were they following? Them, or us?"

"That's the million credit question," Jason agreed. "So … were you followed to Colton Hub? And if so, how did they know which ship you boarded to leave?"

"We were not tracked," Connimon said. When she offered nothing more, Jason let out an exasperated breath.

"This will go much quicker if you would volunteer information and maybe even go so far as to say why you were there, why you were looking for Crusher, and why you're on my ship."

"My apologies, Captain," she said, nodding to him in a sort of half-bow. "I certainly do not mean to be vague, but when I tell you what we've been through you may forgive me for not immediately volunteering information to beings I've only just met."

"By all means," Jason said sardonically, taking a seat. "Proceed." While Connimon's manner was exquisitely courteous and even a bit deferential, he didn't trust her, and Crusher's immediate reaction to seeing her was decidedly not a happy one. In fact, his friend was still standing somewhat apart from the group, glowering at their passengers. If Connimon was offended by Jason's tone, she did not let on as she began her story.

"I can surmise that we were not tracked to Colton Hub because we've been there for over seven months," she said, pausing at the looks coming at her across the table.

"You spent *seven months* on that death trap," Kage said. "Why?"

"We were waiting on you," she said simply. "We'd been attempting to track your movements, but that proved impossible as you were far too elusive. In our investigation, we learned that Colton Hub was one of the places you would frequent more than once or twice a year. So, as unpleasant as it was, we made arrangements to stay there until you arrived. In all that time we were never followed or paid any undue attention. Given that, I must conclude that the ship we recently escaped from was tracking you for its own reasons."

"Tracking is certainly the correct term," Jason said. "It was dumb luck we saw them at all. For all we know, they could have been following us all the way from Aracoria." As soon as he said it, the rest of the crew tensed up.

"Are you suggesting ConFed Intel has renewed its interest in us?" Doc asked tensely.

"I'm suggesting nothing," Jason said quickly. "Let's just stick to what we know for now. Connimon, please continue."

"We were first made aware of your arrival when you, Felex, and Lucky were walking through the galleria. Mazer lost track of you when you split up and we were unable to reacquire you until the three of you entered the establishment on the upper level.

"Even then we were unsure if the gelten on your crew was truly Felex. We had only rumors and eye-witness accounts to go on. Even when we saw him there was some doubt. Years apart from us have changed him some. It was then that we approached your table."

"Who is Felex?" Doc asked, raising his hand as he did so.

"Ah, shit. I forgot to tell you—" Jason began before Morakar cut him off.

"The warrior you call *Crusher* is in truth Lord Felex Tezakar, the Guardian Archon of Galvetor," he said in a hushed but intense voice. He was staring at Crusher as he spoke. Doc's mouth dropped open and he also turned to look at Crusher.

"I take it you recognize the name?" Jason asked.

"I remember the rumors when Felex disappeared," Doc said, somewhat awed. "But Galvetor is so closed off that nothing had ever been confirmed. I can't believe I never put it together."

"How is it you know so much about our internal politics?" Connimon asked.

"I'm a geneticist," Doc answered, pulling his eyes away from Crusher, who had remained brooding and silent, to face her. "Early in my career I was given permission to visit Galvetor to study the warrior caste of your people. What you've been able to do with such archaic methods is nothing short of miraculous. No offense intended."

"No offense is taken," she said with a slightly indulgent smile. "Our way is not as fast as your gene splicing and DNA manipulation, but our results speak for themselves. Galvetic warriors are the most feared fighters throughout the known worlds." Lucky, who had been resting a hand on the table, began ticking his index finger loudly against the composite surface.

"We are aware of your kind, battlesynth, but we do not subscribe to the theory that a warrior can be manufactured," Connimon said.

"Perhaps a demonstration some time," Lucky said politely. "When you have more warriors available, that is." He looked pointedly at the Reddix brothers after his last comment, causing Jason to hide a smile behind his hand and the two warriors to look at each other with apprehension. Being so openly challenged was apparently something they were unaccustomed to.

"Let's try and stay focused," Jason said. "You've explained how you found us, sort of, but not why. Staying on that shithole station for over half a year … it's got to be something important."

"Yes, Captain," Connimon said quietly, "it is quite important. Your people need you, Felex. Galvetor is on the brink of civil war and the warrior caste is no longer willing to stay neutral. Your return would—"

"There will be no going back for me," Crusher snarled, coming forward so quickly that Mazer and Morakar braced themselves. "I was banished from my home! Sent away like some beggar only to be captured, sold into slavery, and almost killed! I was told then that the only way to save my people was to accept disgrace and never come back!" His voice had risen to a deafening roar and Jason was becoming seriously concerned. He was about to signal to Lucky to be ready, but Crusher wasn't finished.

"Now you tell me to save them I must return? I have no people! I'm a renegade, damned to wander the galaxy with no home. You've wasted your time, Caretaker," Crusher thundered. "There is nothing here for you!" As his last words left his mouth, he swung his massive fist down in a savage overhead strike into the table right between where Jason and Kage were sitting. Predictably, the table exploded into shards of hard composite, and drinking glasses went flying. Ignoring the blood flowing from the wound the sharp edges of the broken table had caused, Crusher stormed out of the galley towards the armory, snarling a challenge at the other two warriors as he did so.

Twingo and Doc had wide-eyed, startled expressions as they looked at each other. Kage's face, on the other hand, was frozen into a visage of absolute terror.

"Captain," Twingo said in a cracking voice. "Shouldn't you check on Kage? He looks like he's locked up."

"In a moment," Jason said calmly. "I'm currently trying to keep from pissing myself."

Chapter 7

After Crusher broke the galley table in half, Jason had the other geltens confined in starboard berthing while he tried to regain control of the situation, if he ever even had it in the first place. It had taken them a moment to get Kage sorted out, and then Jason ordered the others up to the bridge to keep them busy while Lucky stayed on the main deck to head off any potential issues with their unwanted guests.

He was currently in a heated discussion with Lucky. Heated on his part, of course. Lucky remained predictably stoic.

"Why should I go in there? *You're* his closest friend."

"And you are his captain," Lucky countered. "He will want to know that you are still backing him up."

"That goes without saying," Jason said with a dismissive wave.

"But he may not realize that," Lucky pressed. "That was an uncharacteristically violent display of emotion from Crusher. He will want your assurances."

"Great," Jason grumbled. "If you hear a loud, girlish scream that is suddenly cut short, don't bother running in. Just come and get what's left of me and toss the remains out an airlock."

"Of course, Captain," Lucky said agreeably, drawing an irritated glare from Jason.

He stepped lightly from the main deck down to the port engineering bay and around where he could get eyes on the armory door. It was closed, but unlocked. Taking a deep breath, he walked up and keyed the door open, unsure what would greet him.

It was rather anticlimactic. Crusher was on his knees in a sitting position, his hands resting lightly on his thighs, eyes closed, and his shoulders rose and fell with his slow, steady breathing. Jason recognized this as a kind of meditative position the big warrior would go into if he wanted to calm himself or simply slow his bodily functions down after a workout. He'd also seen him do this prior to combat, however, so this was either an attempt to stay calm or it was simply a precursor to a horrifically violent confrontation.

"Hello, Captain," Crusher said, his voice soft and steady.

"Hey," Jason said, sitting on one of the benches. "So, that was some display back there."

"I apologize for the table," Crusher said, still not opening his eyes. "I will pay for it out of my personal account."

"I'm not concerned about the table," Jason said. "My only concern is that you're okay. You're usually more in control than that."

"Did you come here to get my side?" Crusher asked. "I assume you've already talked to the Caretaker."

"I did not. I confined them to berthing after you left the galley," Jason said, beginning to relax now that it appeared Crusher was completely in control of himself again. "Honestly, I don't care about their side. And I'm not here to pump you for information either. I'm interested, of course, but if you choose not to share that's your business. I've trusted you with my life since we started all this together and that hasn't changed. You give me the word and we'll drop those three off on the nearest habitable rock and be done with the entire thing."

Crusher's eyes opened slowly and he stared at Jason a moment before speaking.

"Thank you, Captain," he said finally. He rose in one fluid motion and sat on a bench opposite from Jason. "The situation won't be resolved that simply, I'm afraid. I'll need to hear the details, of course, but Galvetor has been on the brink of a civil war for some time. If it's over the usual argument, I'd imagine one side or another has gained some sort of advantage that makes them think they can break the stalemate."

"Civil war over what?" Jason asked. "Isn't Galvetor intentionally isolated?"

"Which brings us to the source of the conflict," Crusher said. "There is a small but vocal group that feels it's time we begin to exert our influence. Their movement is growing and they've convinced more than a few players that we have the means by which to become a major power on the galactic stage."

"Your warrior caste," Jason guessed.

"Yes. Thanks to millennia of tradition, Galvetor has a powerful, willing army of shock troopers that would be an absolute terror if unleashed on their neighbors."

"They wouldn't just strike out militarily would they? The ConFed won't allow you to begin invading neighboring star systems," Jason said slowly.

"No," Crusher sighed. "It would be the threat of violence from the legions that would extort our trading partners into favorable terms. Given that our closet neighbors are not only relatively peaceful, but also master ship builders, I wouldn't think it would be long before Galvetor was fielding a powerful fleet to go along with their army."

"Don't take any offense at what I'm about to say," Jason said carefully, "but isn't this all a little … simplistic?"

"Yes and no," Crusher said. "I'm giving you the broad strokes, but you're right … we're not a politically sophisticated people. That may be due to our isolation or it may just be a character flaw."

"I suppose we should finish our discussion with Connimon and then you can decide from there what you want to do," Jason said after a long moment of thought.

"Agreed," Crusher said, standing up. "So far she's given no particular reason why they've taken the trouble to track me down."

Twenty minutes later they were all reassembled in the galley, seated at the second table, smaller table, with Twingo and Kage conspicuously absent. The gelten contingent all wore studiously blank looks peppered with occasional glances at Crusher. Jason watched it all with great interest. Crusher was the only member of his species he'd ever seen, so the way they treated him with deference while simultaneously seeming to genuinely fear him gave Jason some further insight as to who Crusher, or Felex, really was. As per their agreement when they'd left the armory, Crusher took control of the meeting.

"Now that we've all had time to cool our tempers," he began, "I'd like to know why you've come to find me. Tread wearily, Caretaker, for I will tolerate no lies." Jason's right eyebrow lifted a notch as Crusher seemed to switch between his usual, familiar manner of speaking and an odd, stilted formality.

"As we were discussing, Galvetor is on the brink," she said, holding up a hand to cut off Crusher's protest. "I know, Felex … this conflict has been brewing so long that it has a feel of normalcy to it. Maybe it's even slipped into the background of everyday life. The vast majority of our citizens feel it's just the harmless wrangling of politicians that, in the end, will impact their lives very little.

"My first indication that things may have changed was the concerted effort to have you removed. You were far too influential and a traditionalist; the legions would never have budged with you still in place as Archon. It was a surprise to everyone when you accepted exile without much of a fight."

"I had little choice," Crusher said. "The legions had made it clear they would resist any overt effort to remove me. Had I not stepped down, there was no doubt it would have led to a violent conflict between us and Galvetor Internal Security."

"That was the thought of the senior leadership as well," Connimon confirmed. "We gravely miscalculated, however, and in the time of your absence the oversight committee has been staffed with interventionist sympathizers."

"The oversight committee is a strictly civilian council that observes the warrior caste and acts as a liaison between the legions and the capital on Galvetor," Crusher said to Jason. "During the wrangling between isolationist and interventionist factions within the civilian government, both sides try to stack the deck in their favor in the oversight committee in case the worst was to happen."

"You mean if this little political cold war turned hot, the side that had the most influence over the legions would have a huge advantage," Jason said.

"Essentially, yes," Connimon said. "But with Felex as Archon, none of this would have mattered. Not a single warrior would have marched without his consent. It was the main reason he was forced out; neither side liked the level of influence he exerted on such a powerful force."

"Especially not when they wanted it for themselves," Jason said, nodding in understanding. "So this title … Archon … you were the presiding military officer within your ranks?"

"It's not quite what you would call a 'general' in your own experience," Crusher explained. "I was, am still, I suppose, the spiritual, political, and military leader of my people. I know I'm making it sound like a cult, but being a Galvetic warrior isn't something you volunteer for. You're born into it and have little choice of being anything else. As such, our society is a bit different than the volunteer military force of your peers that you enlisted in." This was the first time since they had met the geltens in Colton Hub that Crusher had fully admitted that what Connimon said of him was true. Her slow nod of agreement seemed to say she took this as a small victory.

"What do you mean that you still are?" Jason asked in confusion.

"He cannot be removed from his position while he is still alive," Connimon answered. "Felex's death would need to be confirmed before the process of elevating a new Archon could begin. As an exile, he was far more useful; so long as he was thought to be alive no other could claim his place and cause them similar problems."

"I'd imagine there was also the added benefit that the legions, a militarily organized group, had a bit of a power vacuum with their Archon suddenly gone," Jason said, thinking aloud. "This would allow the council to step into that leadership role and strengthen the opposition's grip on the warrior caste just that much more."

"Very good, young captain," Connimon said with some surprise. "You seem to have some grasp of the psyche of our warrior brothers."

"I know militaries," Jason corrected. "And I've found that the similarities run deep, even across different species. Was I correct in hearing that there are no female warriors? I suppose there's something obvious I'm missing ... but how do you keep the race alive?"

"Despite the physical differences, there is actually very little genetic difference between geltens and the warrior sub-race," Doc said, speaking up for the first time since they'd reconvened. "A warrior child is always male, but can be born to what we would refer to as 'normal' geltens. Although the gene that determines this is carried by the female, a mating couple with a warrior male greatly increases the chances."

"Yes," Connimon said. "Since warrior offspring are rare, one out of every few hundred, it is a great honor for the family when it happens."

"We're getting a bit far afield here," Crusher said, exerting control over the wandering conversation. "What exactly do you need of me?"

"We didn't seek you out to antagonize you," Connimon said. "As I've said repeatedly, Galvetor is on the brink of war and the legions look as if they are ready to pick a side. Then there is the fact that senior leadership within the ranks have been rounded up and imprisoned."

"On what charges?" Crusher demanded.

"Anything they can make stick. Sedition, conspiracy to overthrow the government, misappropriation of funds." Connimon shrugged. "The list has been varied and predictably ridiculous, but thanks to the justice system the legions operate under, the conviction rate has been nearly one hundred percent."

"Where are they being held?"

"They've been taken to Galvetor itself," Connimon said. "They were deemed too dangerous to leave on Restaria."

"Restaria?" Jason asked.

"It's the second habitable world in our star system," Connimon said. "Generations ago, the warrior caste agreed to live there after the last civil conflict on Galvetor. There's something else, Felex … they took Fordix. His arrest and imprisonment was what made us leave and seek you out."

"We also felt it was only a matter of time before the Caretaker was also falsely accused and locked up in a cage," Morakar said quietly from his end of the table. Crusher's shoulders were bunched up and his fists were clenched. Jason knew his friend well enough to know that he was barely in control of his temper.

"Caretaker," Crusher began in a calm voice. "If you would, please give me some time to discuss all of this with my crew."

"Of course," she said with a bow and led the other two warriors from the galley and back to port berthing where they'd already spent some time.

"This is a lot to take in," Jason remarked dryly. "So who is Fordix?"

"The short answer is that he was my mentor," Crusher said. "It goes much deeper than that, however. He was more like a father to me."

"So what do you want to do?"

There was a pregnant pause while Crusher contemplated Jason's question.

"I don't have much of a choice," Crusher said quietly. "I'll need to travel to Restaria at the very least to determine what is really going on. Even though I know her well, I don't discount the possibility that Connimon has her own agenda."

"OK," Jason said simply. "I'm putting the *Phoenix* at your disposal for as long as you need her. You'll be both tactics and operations on this trip, so we'll be taking our lead from you."

"I won't insult you by trying to talk you out of this," Crusher said, "so I'll simply say: Thank you."

"If you are in exile, how will we safely travel to your homeworld?" Lucky asked, getting down to business.

"We won't be going to Galvetor," Crusher said. "We wouldn't be able to land the *Phoenix* there anyway. Instead, we'll fly directly to Restaria and begin operations from there. While I'm technically not supposed to be on either world, the reality is they expected me to simply slink away into the wilderness of our world. The legions don't use up a lot of space and the bulk of Restaria belongs to nature."

"So why didn't you?" Jason asked. "Just go camping, that is."

"Pride," Crusher said. "While I willingly accepted my sentence, I wasn't happy about it. I asked to be dropped off on a frontier world, convinced I would thrive among the weaker species. I wasn't prepared for the cunning of the galaxy's criminal element. After a year or so of bouncing around, I was drugged and chained and presented to Bondrass as a gift to settle a debt. You know how that turned out."

"Is there any place we can safely land? Other than a spaceport?" Jason asked.

"There is," Crusher confirmed. "Here's what I had in mind ..."

Chapter 8

The *Phoenix* had changed course and increased speed and was streaking though the ether of slip-space towards the Galvetor System. Jason sat in the pilot's seat, trying to absorb as much information as he could on Crusher's homeworlds in the short amount of time he had. Information on Galvetor was slim on any public nexus, but Connimon had uploaded some files to the *Phoenix's* main computer that filled in a lot of the gaps.

The split culture of the geltens was fascinating. Jason had yet to encounter a people with such a divided personality. The warrior caste had been developed over centuries and centuries of careful selective breeding until the unique traits of Crusher's kind began to emerge. The blunted snout, the vestigial crest on the forehead, the exaggerated sensory organs around the head, and even the sheer size and strength were all traits missing from Connimon. To Jason, she simply looked like any other bipedal alien with dark, almost black skin.

They'd inadvertently developed the most powerful warriors in the known galaxy, if one were to discount Lucky's creators giving life to the battlesynths, and when those warriors reached the zenith of what was possible as a species, their world no longer needed or wanted them. They were an army without a war. The general consensus was that the warrior class was too dangerous to live among the normal citizenry and a concerted effort to remove them from Galvetor began in earnest. Predictably, the warrior class, whose only crime was to be born different, pushed back against them. Hard. Bloody conflicts forced the government's hand and a solution needed to be found, and quickly.

Oddly enough, the star system had a second perfectly good, habitable planet that had no prime species. Given the geltens' isolationist, almost xenophobic, nature, the planet had never been colonized. After a short negotiation, the legions agreed that they would inhabit the second world, Restaria. It was also agreed that any warrior child born on Galvetor would be sent to Restaria to begin his education and training after his first year of life.

Jason leaned back, absorbing the condensed history lesson he'd just read through. There were some parallels that could be found between the Galvetic warriors and some of Earth's ancient warrior cultures, but the geltens had taken the idea to extremes. The most obvious of these would be the Spartan army in the fifth century B.C., soldiers trained from infancy to stand head and shoulders above their contemporary peers.

"Now this is interesting," Jason murmured to himself, scrolling up through a different file.

"What's interesting?" Kage asked as he walked onto the bridge, chewing loudly on what looked like a peanut butter and jelly sandwich. Jason had programmed the childhood staple into the *Phoenix's* food processing unit, and the rest of the crew quickly became borderline addicts.

"What have I told you about eating on the flight deck?" Jason asked pointedly, ignoring his friend's question. Kage stuffed the entire remaining half of the sandwich into his mouth and began slowly chewing it, his cheeks puffed out and synthesized grape jelly dribbling out of one corner. He wiped all four hands on his shirt and held them up for inspection. Jason shuddered, mildly disgusted. "That's a technicality," he said. "Just sit down and wipe your mouth off."

"So what was interesting?" Kage said after he'd managed to choke the sticky sandwich down. Having nothing to rinse it down with, however, he was struggling to work his mouth to get the words out.

"I was wondering how the Galvetic Legions were such an effective fighting force given that they remain isolated with almost no real-world experience," Jason said, doing his best to ignore the sounds coming from the copilot's seat. "You can't train in a bubble, no matter how capable your soldiers are. It looks like they knew this as well. I'm reading a whole dissertation on tactical experts and elite military units that have been invited to Restaria, sometimes under the pretense of training exercises, other times to participate in games. But in all these cases, the Galvetic warriors were able to use what they learned and adapt their tactics. This is incredible … without fighting a single major engagement, they've somehow made themselves into the preeminent infantry unit in the galaxy."

"But how useful is that in modern warfare?" Kage asked, pulling up the same documents at his own station. "I mean, even a thousand Crushers isn't a whole lot of good when you're getting bombarded from orbit by starships."

"Sheer firepower doesn't always win wars," Jason said. "From my own experience, I can tell you that there's never a substitute for well-trained, disciplined, and motivated soldiers."

"So you're saying that a ConFed battle wagon makes orbit, turns the surface of a planet into molten slag, and somehow a group of ground pounders will make a difference?" Kage asked scornfully.

"You're talking about something else," Jason argued. "The point of war is to achieve a political objective or capture territory. You're talking about annihilating an entire planet."

"For some species that is war," Kage said.

"Not in this area of space," Jason retorted. "At least not that I've seen."

"Whatever," Kage said, losing interest. "Let's just agree to disagree."

*****

"Here are the pass codes for the first watch station," Connimon said, passing a data pad to Kage. He accepted and began configuring one of the *Phoenix's* com transponders to transmit the provided codes.

They'd popped back into real-space outside of Galvetor Prime's heliopause. Since their ultimate target was Restaria, Connimon said their best bet would be to sneak into the system and not bother with any attempted subterfuge that would be required if they were to enter the normal traffic of the system. To that end, she had promised to provide the bypass codes that would allow them to fly right by the defense monitoring stations without triggering an alarm.

Jason plotted his course and speed to match Connimon's instructions as Doc worked at the port sensor station to manage the ship's countermeasures suite. With any luck, they'd make it all the way to Restaria's atmosphere without being detected. After that, it would be up to Jason to hide the ship in the ground clutter of the undeveloped world from anyone who may observe their entry.

"Codes are entered," Kage said. "Will I get any confirmation from the station?"

"No," Connimon said. "But you will know if the codes weren't properly entered or received. The station will send out an automated hail that needs to be answered properly within thirty seconds or a general alert will be issued to the fleet."

"What sort of fleet presence are we talking about?" Jason asked, feeling more than a little foolish he hadn't asked before now.

"Two corvettes and three squadrons of fighters," Connimon said with a half-smile. "Calling it a 'fleet' may be a bit of a conceit." Jason breathed a sigh of relief. The small force fielded by the geltens wouldn't be much of a threat to the *Phoenix* as she could easily outrun any, or all, of them. "However," Connimon continued, "we often have ConFed cruisers or expeditionary ships that come through the system and even enter orbit over Galvetor itself."

"That's unfortunate," Jason said with a frown. "And you permit this?"

"It is the primary reason we have such a light space force of our own," she said. "We have neither the will nor the inclination to fly a large combat-ready fleet. The ConFed wants us as a member planet in order to gain some level of access to the legions. It's a game we both play that is mutually beneficial."

"What happens when one day the ConFed Council decides you're no longer worth protecting?" Kage asked.

"Then we will do what we must," she said. "We will enter into alliances and ensure our people are protected. There are others who have made overtures to such alliances, including the mighty Eshquarian Empire."

Something clicked in Jason's brain at the mention of the Eshquarians. The one little detail that had been nagging at him was how the Caretaker knew that this crew, this ship, was where Crusher had ended up. They had performed a service for the Eshquarian Empire—and were paid handsomely in the form of a rebuilt *Phoenix*—a few years ago. The mission had almost cost them all their lives, and in the aftermath the prime minister had gotten to know his crew quite well. He decided to throw it against the wall and see if anything stuck.

"So, in your talks with the Eshquarians ... I wouldn't imagine we came up, did we?" he asked casually. "I mean, if you were trying to keep tabs on someone as important as your Archon, it would be natural to ask a favor of a government with an extensive intelligence network. It would also be an easy favor for them to give since they knew exactly which ship a large Galvetic warrior may be serving on." Doc and Jason were both watching Connimon and caught the narrowing of the eyes and pinching of her nose. To her credit, she met Jason's challenge head on.

"Yes, Captain," she said evenly. "We were made aware of your role in thwarting what would have been a devastating terrorist attack. And yes ... we asked them to poke around and see if they could find any leads on Felex's whereabouts. Imagine my surprise when we were provided high-resolution images of your adventures there, including one demolished hospitality suite." Kage giggled at that as Jason simply nodded and went back to flying the ship.

"Thank you for the honesty, Connimon," Jason said. "How you knew which ship to track down to find Crusher has been a point of concern for me since you came aboard."

"Distrustful," she replied with no trace of being offended. "That is not a bad trait when men's lives depend on the decisions you make."

"How long until we make orbit?" Crusher demanded loudly as he clomped onto the bridge. Morakar and Mazer were right behind him, both moving slowly and the latter of the two limping noticeably.

"Training?" Jason asked.

"In a way," Crusher confirmed. "These two wouldn't spar with me for some reason. They were, however, wildly curious about the hand-to-hand capability of battlesynths."

"And?" Connimon asked eagerly.

69

"Let's just say your warriors learned a valuable lesson in humility and overconfidence," Crusher laughed. "Lucky was mostly toying with them so there aren't any serious injuries."

"They both fought the mechanical soldier?" Connimon pressed, looking at her two companions with a frown of disapproval.

"Yes," Crusher replied. "And at the same time."

"It was not possible how fast it moved, Caretaker," Mazer said softly. "It was astonishing. The speed, the strength … it threw me across the entire width of the cargo hold while simultaneously engaging Morakar." Jason frowned at that.

"Lucky switched to combat mode inside the ship?" he asked Crusher.

"Nope," the warrior said with a huge grin. "He was operating at standard speed and strength. Like I said, he was just playing around. By the way, Mazer, it *is* he. While it may not make sense to you, Lucky identifies gender specifically to male. I wouldn't make the mistake of insulting him by calling him *it.*"

"No, Lord Felex," Mazer agreed quickly. Jason had noticed that over the course of the flight to Restaria, Crusher had become more and more comfortable with his old name and title. He had even begun to command the other two warriors around. While this may have just been his friend sliding into old and comfortable habits, Jason was getting a sinking feeling in his stomach about what this mission could mean for the future of Omega Force.

"It's almost party time, Captain," Kage reported. "We just cleared the last listening post and we have a clear sky all the way into Restaria. I'll give you vectors on the navigational hazards we have in orbit and then you can fly your own approach."

"Sounds good," Jason said, settling into the pilot's seat and syncing his navigation display with Kage's. "Everybody, if you would please find an unoccupied seat and strap in we'll begin what is hopefully a boring landfall on Restaria. Crusher, did you give Kage the planetary coordinates for our primary and secondary landing sites?"

"He should already have them," Crusher confirmed. He then motioned to the other two warriors who were lounging in the seats next to him. "I'd actually strap in as he says. Our landings are sometimes … vigorous." Jason ignored the pointed insult and began configuring the *Phoenix* for atmospheric entry.

Restaria was a lush, green world that shared an overlapping orbit with Galvetor. While the two planets were always on opposite sides of Galvetor Prime, the system's star, they did have almost identical climates. This wasn't unheard of, but it was unusual. What made the pair truly unique, however, was that life had developed simultaneously and nearly parallel on the two worlds. So while the plant and animal species weren't necessarily the same, the building blocks they were made from were. This meant geltens could easily inhabit one planet or the other. It was an unheard of luxury for developing species to have a pair of inhabitable worlds, but it was one the geltens had never fully taken advantage of.

There was an advantage to the fact that Restaria had only recently been colonized. Nobody had polluted the upper orbits with junk and there weren't any crowded entry lanes. Jason swung the *Phoenix* smoothly onto a vector that would bring them in right over the equator and allow him to swing north to his primary landing site from there, using the mountain ranges as cover in case his entry was detected. Crusher had told him nobody lived along the equatorial belt.

As on Earth, it was hot and steamy and his people preferred higher, cooler climes.

"Here we go, everybody," Jason said. His words were unnecessary since they could clearly see the planet outside of the canopy, but he felt the need to keep the tradition of annoying his friends with obvious statements alive and well. The ship began to rock slightly as she bounced down into the first thin layers of the upper atmosphere. Soon, the deck was vibrating, and thin, white plasma streamers could be seen forming along the leading edges of their shields. Jason angled the nose down a few degrees and allowed the airfoils to bite into the comparatively dense stratosphere as they streaked over the equator, leaving a fiery wake in their passing.

"There was a passing satellite that could have observed us if it was looking at the surface, but it's made no transmissions in the time it took to reach the horizon," Doc reported.

"We aren't being hailed or pinged," Kage said. "It looks like we might have gotten in clean."

"On the contrary," Connimon said. "We were detected and tracked the moment we reached upper orbit. The last octet in the final pass code I gave you was a signal to Restaria that we would be making atmospheric entry shortly."

"If you had a clearance code all the way to the surface why didn't we just fly to our landing site?" Jason asked irritably.

"There are goings on here that we would rather Galvetor not be aware of," Connimon said, shooting Crusher an uncomfortable look. "This hides us from their long range scans as well as giving us plausible deniability if you're discovered. After all, why would you be sneaking around if we were allowing you to be here?"

"I see," said Jason as he angled his course north and advanced the throttle. As the *Phoenix* roared through the mountain range, he continued to bleed off altitude until the big gunship was hugging the terrain. He glanced up long enough to see his passengers were becoming increasingly uncomfortable with the flight, alternating from looking out the canopy in terror and looking back at him in concern. *Apparently a dislike of flight is a racial trait.* He smiled humorlessly and pushed the speed up even more as they streaked over the surface.

"We're coming up on Alpha LZ," Kage reported after another few hours of flight.

"Copy," Jason said, throttling back power and angling the nose up a bit to bleed off some speed. He reached over and cycled the landing gear, looking over the landing site on his sensor display. Everything looked clear so he brought power all the way back and let the *Phoenix* settle into a hover thirty meters over the clearing. "Descending, stand by for touchdown."

He eased the power back on the grav-drive until he felt the landing gear impact the ground with a gentle bump. There were a few groans and pops from the *Phoenix* as she settled all her weight on the three landing gear struts until Jason's indicators greened up and told him they were completely down. He leveled the ship and began securing the primary flight systems as everyone else unbuckled their restraints and walked around the bridge, stretching legs and backs that had tensed up during the low-level flight through the mountains.

They were fifty kilometers away from the nearest legion settlement and had landed in a treeless basin that would conceal the gunship from any casual passersby.

Jason kept the reactor power up and the drives in standby; while this made the *Phoenix* easier to detect, it also meant if they needed to leave in a hurry she'd be ready.

"Let's get out of here," he said. "How far to our pickup?"

"We have a ten kilometer walk until we reach the rendezvous point," Connimon said. "We'll be picked up by soldiers from the 7th Legion, the same unit Mazer and Morakar serve in."

"Very good," Jason said. "Let's get on the move."

Had Jason not been worried about landing on a potentially hostile planet and leaving his ship sitting in an unattended clearing, the walk through the Restaria wilderness would have been quite pleasant. The trees towered over their heads a couple hundred feet above them, blotting out the midday sun. The flora under their feet crawled along the forest floor, not getting enough light to become overly large, and a soft breeze whispered through the enormous trunks. For a moment he was transported back to Earth, walking through the sequoias and generally enjoying a simple existence.

"Are we heading back to the 7th Legion's base?" Crusher asked as he walked along beside Jason.

"No," Mazer said hesitantly. "The base may not be safe. Galvetor has informants and spies everywhere. We'll be going to a safe house in Ker."

"What's Ker?" Jason asked quietly.

"The third largest settlement on Restaria," Crusher said. "It is a place not many outside the warrior class care to venture."

"Why is that?" Kage asked from behind them.

"It is a city that exists in the overlap of four different legion territories," Crusher said. "The 7th, 11th, 21st, and the 4th all butt up against the city limits. Two of these legions aren't exactly known for their tolerance of outsiders, especially *normal* geltens."

"So … I guess the next obvious question would be if they don't like outsiders of their own species, what are they going to do with five aliens?" Twingo asked.

"We will need to take precautions," Crusher admitted.

"That doesn't exactly fill me with confidence," Jason muttered as they trudged off through the woods after Connimon and her warrior escort. The forest suddenly seemed a lot less pleasant to him than it had a moment ago. There was a legitimate worry; he still had no idea why they were even there and now they were marching right into a possibly dangerous situation depending on how intolerant the legionnaires actually were.

His next thought was that the relationship between the warrior class and Galvetor was a lot more complicated than he'd been led to believe. Mazer's talk of outsiders and spies, both used in a derogatory sense, made Jason think the rift between the cultures may be wider and the resentments deeper than Crusher or Connimon wanted to admit. This also led him to ponder what Crusher meant by legion territories. He had assumed some sort of centralized leadership, but now he had the impression that the legions were loosely connected outfits that competed with each other and didn't necessarily cooperate or agree. He voiced this to Crusher as they walked through the forest.

"That's what I meant when I said that Archon wasn't exactly a ceremonial position," Crusher answered with a smile. "I was the face of the warrior class on Galvetor and wasn't affiliated with any particular legion, but had influence over all."

"Influence? Not actual command authority?" Jason asked.

"No. Out of respect and tradition they followed my lead, but they were never required to do so by threat of punishment," Crusher said. "We are a confusing group at times. While fiercely loyal to our commanders, even to the death, we resent any outside pressure and rebel with little provocation."

"I'm beginning to see what may have precipitated the decision to … relocate you to Restaria," Jason said carefully.

"While that's true, be careful about voicing that opinion here in the open," Crusher warned. "We've carefully constructed the deception to ourselves that moving here was our choice. Words like relocate, exile, or banish aren't especially popular here."

"Thanks for the heads up," Jason said. "While we're walking, perhaps you could brief the others on any other social faux pas."

"Did you have anyone in particular in mind?"

"The usual suspects," Jason said wearily.

"Right," Crusher agreed before raising his voice," Twingo, Kage … I need to talk to you two for a moment."

"What for?" The insolent response from Kage surprised nobody.

Chapter 9

As the airtruck whisked along, its repulsors making the transition from rough dirt path to paved street seamless, Jason craned his neck to see past the two huge warriors in the front seat to get his first view of Ker. The airtruck was an open-air affair that had two benches lining the cargo bed, not unlike the M939 five-ton truck that he'd been around during his time with the Air Force. If the M939 hovered a meter off the ground and had a forcefield to protect the occupants from the wind and weather, that is.

He didn't know what he'd been expecting. A rough, Old Western-style town, perhaps, or maybe even a battle-scarred hovel. But Ker didn't fit any preconceived notion he'd formed of what a settlement of a warrior culture would be like. It was stunning in its artistic beauty. The only comparison he could draw to an Earth city would be possibly Prague, but Ker had no evidence of a violent past scarring its streets and buildings. Even the size surprised him as he'd expected more of an outpost than a legitimate city as he was seeing now.

"Outsiders aren't entirely unheard of, but try not to draw undue attention to yourselves as we drive through the city. It's not likely you'd be stopped or harassed, but let's not risk it," Morakar said as the driver slowed the airtruck down and turned onto one of the perimeter roads to avoid driving through the city center. The air of Restaria was crisp and fresh, even this close to Ker, and the weather was beautiful. Despite the fact that they were in a mildly dangerous situation given the gelten warriors' predilection towards open hostility towards outsiders, and that he had no idea what they were actually doing on Restaria, Jason couldn't help but enjoy the drive through open streets of the city outskirts.

While he was busy gawking at the monolithic, gothic construction of the city, he began to take notice of the geltens themselves. Again, he had to admit, with no small amount of shame, that he had been too quick to judge his friend's culture and people. There were no cage matches to the death in town squares, no bands of swaggering warriors in full combat regalia, and no brutish behavior of any sort that he could see. They were colorfully dressed in a wide array of styles, albeit most of them sleeveless, and were clumped together in small groups laughing, eating, enjoying street performances, and generally taking in the day. There was an upbeat vibrancy to the city so that it seemed to hum with positivity.

"Not what you were expecting, was it?" Crusher said with a smug smile.

"Well … I, er," Jason floundered. Crusher let him go a moment longer before holding his hand up, laughing softly.

"This is our sanctuary," he explained. "We can come here and remember that despite our differences we're still geltens and have the same appreciation for art, music, and community as our cousins on Galvetor." He looked around, breathing in deeply. "Make no mistake, though," he continued. "Any one of these legionnaires is capable of horrific violence in the blink of an eye if provoked. This is also considered neutral ground and fighting between legions is not only rare, but punishable."

"What legion are you from?" Twingo asked.

"I was selected to be raised as an Archon in early childhood, so I don't really identify with any one of them, but with all of them," Crusher said. "But when I was brought here from Galvetor, I was selected by the 7th to be trained, so I always have an affinity for that unit."

"Which legion are you and Morakar from?" Kage asked Mazer.

"The 7th," he said proudly. "We have carried the honor of Lord Felex hailing from our unit, as well as—" He trailed off and looked quickly at Crusher, and then away.

"You can say it, Mazer," Crusher said. "You also bear the shame of my exile."

"I would not insult you, Lord Felex," the other warrior said, turning back to him. "But these have been hard times for the 7th, and for Restaria as a whole. Galvetor blusters and makes threats against us, and the imprisonment of Fordix was an affront to us all."

"It's what we're here to sort out," Crusher assured him. Jason wasn't so sure.

"What would happen if they caught you here?" Jason asked.

"It would not be good," Crusher admitted. "Galvetor would issue a warning, and then likely come here to enforce their ruling. After that—" He splayed his hands to indicate he wasn't sure what the final outcome would be.

"After that, we go to war," Morakar said darkly. "No more ground will be given to the bureaucrats and politicians." Crusher remained silent, but looked meaningfully at Jason. It seemed Connimon had been accurate about that part at least: the relationship between the two worlds was dangerously strained.

The airtruck pulled off the small feeder street it had been traveling on and down an alley between two large buildings that looked to be constructed of stone blocks the size of delivery vans. They slid to a stop near what appeared to be a loading dock and sat silently while the driver pulled out a com unit and began talking. It was some minutes later when the driver turned to Connimon. "You may go in now."

"If you'll all follow me," she said, climbing out of the back of the airtruck. They all climbed out after her and walked, single file, towards a narrow staircase near the edge of the loading dock that led down into the sublevels. There were no signs or markers near the stairs, and they would likely be overlooked by a casual observer. Following Connimon down into the depths beneath Ker, Jason had a momentary pang of anxiety. If she was leading them into a trap, there would be no room to maneuver or fight. He quickly dismissed his worries; if she planned to have them attacked, it could have happened at any time leading up to the airtruck dropping them off, and in a much more discreet location than the third largest city on the planet.

When they reached the bottom of the staircase, there was a door to the left of the landing that was already standing wide open and a dim light spilling out from within. Connimon passed through the doorway without hesitation, as did Mazer and Morakar and Crusher behind them. Jason looked over his shoulder to ensure Lucky was close behind him before walking in himself.

Beyond the door was simply a long corridor that sloped down and to the right, leading them even deeper beneath Restaria's surface until they passed through a large archway and into what looked like a sparsely appointed reception area ... and it was occupied. No fewer than twenty Galvetic warriors were milling around when the group walked in, hushing all conversation as they did so. All eyes were on Crusher as he walked confidently to the middle of the room and looked around. All the warriors were wearing a wide, red sash from right shoulder to left hip that Jason guessed was some sort of identifier. Not exactly subtle.

"This way, Lord Felex," a booming voice said from a doorway near the rear of the room. Without a word, everyone turned and went towards the door. "Only members of the order are permitted," the voice boomed again as a large Galvetic arm loomed from the crowd, intent on grabbing Jason's shoulder. It was met with a lightning fast armored hand that latched onto it at the wrist. The warrior who owned the arm traced his gaze along the metallic one until he was staring into the unblinking eyes of a pissed-off battlesynth.

"You will refrain from touching the captain," Lucky said simply. The warrior wrenched his arm free and turned to face Lucky, three more warriors coming to stand behind him, drawing weapons as they did. Jason was still looking at the warrior who'd reached for him when he heard a *pop/whine* from behind him; he could see the red glow of Lucky's eyes reflected in the eyes of the warriors facing him as the battlesynth switched to full combat mode. In such cramped quarters this was going to be messy.

"Enough!" Crusher thundered. "Lucky, stand down." What happened next surprised all of Omega Force, but especially Jason.

"I do not take orders from you, Crusher," Lucky said harshly, even angrily, the smell of ozone permeating the air as the power coursed through his weapon systems. "I will stand down only when I have assurances the captain is safe and not before."

"Oh, shit," Jason heard Twingo mutter from the back of the room. "This is going to be a bloodbath." Jason risked looking around the room and saw that Morakar and Mazer were nowhere to be found, and Connimon was watching the spectacle with an alarming look of detached disinterest. All of this happened in the blink of an eye and Jason knew if someone didn't defuse the situation it was going to escalate quickly. With so many weapons in such a cramped space, he had no illusions about surviving the engagement.

Crusher, having gotten over his shock at Lucky's rebuke, also seemed to grasp the danger.

"Legionnaires," Crusher said, "At ease!" The response was immediate. The four facing Jason holstered their weapons with lighting speed and stepped to the side, arms locked to their sides and standing at a rigid attention. In fact, all the warriors in the room were locked up, forming into lines of four or five. Lucky looked around the room and, when he was certain that Crusher had control over the soldiers still standing at attention, secured his own weaponry and the angry red glow faded from his eyes as he stood down from full combat mode. Crusher nodded to him before addressing the warrior who was standing at the door. "What did you mean by members of the order only?"

"Just as I said, Lord Felex," the warrior said, looking straight ahead as he did. "Your companions may wait out here, but they will not be permitted to pass through this door."

"That is your final say on the matter?"

"It is."

"Let's go," Crusher said to Jason, walking back the way they'd come. "We've wasted our time coming here." They had almost made it back to the archway when, amid the sharp gasps and groans of despair, Connimon's voice rang out.

"Lord Felex," she said harshly. "Why did you agree to come here if you just abandon us at the slightest inconvenience?"

"You don't need me, Caretaker," Crusher snarled back. He pointed to the warrior who was still standing watch at the door. "He appears to be making the decisions here. Have him fix your problems." They were nearly to the door that led to the staircase when she caught up with them.

"Felex," she said, now almost pleading, "please wait." Crusher spun on her, teeth bared. She shrank against the wall and went to spin away, but Crusher slammed his palm into the surface in front of her, cutting off her retreat.

"I watched you allow that situation to spiral out of control," he growled. "I don't know what game you're playing here, but I will not have my crew insulted or endangered. Not for you, not for anyone. No matter how long I've lived among aliens in the fringe worlds, I am *still* Felex Tezakar ... I'll tear your throat out and leave your body to rot in this alley without a moment's hesitation if you get in my way." Jason's right eyebrow went up a notch as he watched the exchange, not sure if he believed what he was hearing.

Connimon, however, did believe it as her body began to tremble and she looked at Crusher for the first time with genuine fear in her eyes. "I meant no disrespect to you or your crew, my lord," she said. "But how could I, the Caretaker, walk in front of a living Archon and give the appearance I was in charge? They would have not only ignored me, but that action alone would have stoked their anger. Have you forgotten what it is to lead on Restaria?"

"I have not," Crusher said, leaning away from her and allowing her some space. "I had hoped to avoid it, however. The brutality and savagery of it all ... my time away has made it seem so senseless."

"We are who we are, Felex," she said. "If you're to help us, help Fordix, you will have to remember who, and what, you are as well."

"Captain?" Crusher asked, leaving the final decision up to Jason.

"Let's go see what is really going on here," Jason suggested. "We can always walk away at any time. But I don't think we should risk everyone in case this goes sideways again. Lucky, I need you to stay here with Doc, Twingo, and Kage. I'll keep a channel open on my com unit and you can monitor us from there. It goes without saying, but if you hear screaming and shooting don't let that door stop you."

"I will be standing by, Captain," Lucky acknowledged. Jason had found that giving Lucky orders he didn't like went smoother if he offered an alternative like the open com channel. It allowed him to do what he wanted without the battlesynth hovering over him. Most of the time.

"Follow my lead," Crusher said to Jason. "Try not to act shocked at what is about to happen." Before Jason could ask what the hell he was talking about the big warrior was already striding down the corridor. When they walked in, the warriors were still there, babbling animatedly amongst themselves. The moment they appeared in the archway all of the conversation ceased.

Crusher strode purposefully towards the door and the warrior standing guard. As he reached the door, he drew back his fist and delivered a crushing blow to the warrior's face, sending him flying back into the stone wall as blood erupted from the deep pressure cut that appeared. Before he could slump against the floor, Crusher grabbed his arm to hold him up and came down with another vicious hit to the side of the head. He threw the warrior, who was now convulsing, to the floor and turned to the rest of the room, blood dripping from his still-clenched fist.

"Is there anyone else here who would like to tell me where I can and cannot go?" he roared at them. "The next of you who questions me will die. *He* got off easy because I'm feeling generous. You! Open this door, NOW!" The warrior he pointed at lunged for the handle and nearly tore it off while trying to get the door open. When the heavy wooden door swung open on its hinges, Crusher shoved the warrior back out of the way. "My friend and I are going in," he said.

"Do any of you wish to challenge this?" Though none of them looked away in fear, none of them stepped up either. Crusher motioned for Jason to follow him and went into the next room.

The room was large and vaulted, but the only thing in it was a single table with three Galvetic warriors seated along one side, staring at them as they entered. Crusher walked into the center of the room and stepped into the light where they could see him. They sprang from their seats and locked into attention, staring straight ahead.

"Who are you supposed to be?" Crusher asked.

"We are an order that arose in your absence, Lord Felex," the center warrior said. "We maintain the balance between the legions and Galvetor."

"Interesting," Crusher said, his voice indicating he thought it was anything but. "Nice to see I was so easily replaced. So what do you call yourselves?"

"We are the Archon's Fist."

*****

The three Galvetic warriors in the chamber identified themselves as the Praetores of the Archon's Fist. Jason wasn't sure what rank they may have held in their respective units, but as Praetores they were laying claim to the highest rank in the Galvetic Legions. But the more the trio talked, the more Jason got the distinct impression that, no matter the noble intentions at the beginning, the Archon's Fist was more of a cult than a military unit. A cult that had Crusher as its surrogate deity. He only hoped that Crusher being here, in the flesh and mortal, would dispel some of that.

"The arrest and imprisonment of Fordix, without a trial I might add, was an affront. It was meant as an insult and a reminder of our place," said Fostel, the elder of the three and the one they seemed to defer to.

"Do you have any reason why they would do this?" Crusher asked, leaning back in his seat. "This makes no sense to me. Even if they skipped a trial, which is within their power under extreme circumstances, they are required to provide a reason and a body of proof."

"What sense does it have to make?" demanded Zetarix. From Jason's impression he was the more hotheaded of the group and was often butting in with rash, and mostly unhelpful, comments. "Galvetor has harbored a deep resentment towards us for centuries. With Lord Felex gone, they have finally worked up the nerve to do something about it."

"This is where we disagree," added Mutabor, the third Praetore. "Like you, Lord Felex, I can't see any logic in Galvetor's actions of late. While it is true that without you our voice in the capital is muted, practically nonexistent, for them to move against us doesn't have any obvious benefit for them."

"Why must you apply logic to their blind prejudice?" Zetarix asked. "Has it occurred to you that—" He broke off instantly when Crusher raised his hand.

"Connimon spoke to me earlier of two factions in the capital," he said. "That there were some underlying reasons that one or the other would be trying to gain control of the legions."

"The Caretaker has some funny ideas," Zetarix scoffed. "She is an able administrator, not a warrior."

"Which may be exactly what is needed," Mutabor argued. "She is also the only one on this entire planet who freely travels to Galvetor and interacts with the government there on a personal level."

"Praetore Mutabor has a point," Crusher said wearily, "and to be honest you're all giving me a headache. I refuse to believe that Galvetor has suddenly upped and decided to wipe out the warrior class one day. Especially considering that we're one of the main reasons they're allowed to enjoy their private planet free of random invasions and interference." He took in a deep breath before continuing. "Who really has a handle on what is going on here?" The three Praetores looked at each other a moment before one of them spoke up.

"Fordix," Fostel said. "He was the one who had informants and connections on Galvetor and beyond."

"You didn't think any of that was pertinent information?" Crusher demanded loudly. "Please tell me that old fool wasn't a part of this little club you have going on here." Although Crusher seemed to miss it, Jason perked up when Fostel talked of Fordix having contacts that were beyond Gaveltor.

"He's the one who approached us, my lord," Mutabor said. "This was his idea. He said with you gone that we had to be ready to unite the legions."

"And it's also the obvious reason he was captured and imprisoned without trial," Crusher said, rolling his eyes. "His informant was either part of a trap or was captured himself. Why was I not made aware of this the moment I walked in here?"

"We know what he means to you," Fostel said. "Take no offense to this, Lord Felex, but we're also well aware of your impulsive nature. We couldn't afford to lose you too if you and Omega Force tried to blast into the prison and free him without talking to us first." Jason, who had only been partially listening, snapped his head up.

"Yes, Captain Burke," Mutabor said. "We know of your unit and Lord Felex's place in it. Your, and his, exploits have been a point of special pride among us: you can exile the Archon, but you cannot take away his honor or sense of duty. The battle of Shorret-3 is told to our young trainees as an example of what can be possible, even in a hopeless situation, by even a few warriors with heart."

"Don't remind me," Jason said with a shudder. "So answer me this ... if you're aware of our operations even as far back as the Eshquarian affair then why the need for secrecy? I would think Crusher would be welcomed home with a parade, or at least allowed to land the ship in an actual spaceport." Jason had almost called the secret order nonsense, the theater of the absurd, but despite what he saw as a flair for the melodramatic, these were still powerful and deadly fighters. It also wouldn't do him any good to insult the people he would likely need later on this op, wherever the hell it ended up.

"I'm still in exile," Crusher answered, turning to him. "Landing the *Phoenix* here, a ship they likely have a description of, would only cause trouble. While many are loyal to traditions and to the Archon, their first loyalty is to Galvetor. They would see it as their duty to apprehend me or to alert the capital ... and they'd be right."

"So what will we do now, my lord?" Zetarix asked.

"We haven't much of a choice," Crusher answered. "We'll do that rash thing you were so worried about ... we'll break Fordix out of Casguard Prison."

Jason groaned.

Chapter 10

"So what's the story?" Twingo asked Jason when they were alone. Connimon had arranged for a suite of rooms within the building under which the secret meeting place of the Archon's Fist was. Apparently it was not only a sort of administration center but living quarters as well.

"This is about to turn into a cluster fuck of epic proportions," Jason said, leaning back in his chair and accepting a beer, or beer-like drink, from his friend.

"That good, eh?"

"I'm serious, Twingo," Jason said. "I would never walk out on Crusher, or ask him to abandon something he feels so strongly about, but we have absolutely no idea what the hell is going on here. We're used to rolling into situations blindly, but this is absurd."

"What did you find out in their secret clubhouse?" Twingo asked.

"Only that they know less than we do and Connimon knows more than she's letting on. I get the feeling she's feeding out information to manipulate the situation to her liking, but the others don't take her seriously anyway so it doesn't really matter much," Jason said. "This Fordix supposedly knows what's at the heart of the unrest on Galvetor, but he's in jail. So, of course, we're going to try and break him out."

"We've done that sort of thing before," Twingo argued.

"Twice. We've only done it twice and both times with the benefit of airtight intel from Crisstof and logistical support from the Diligent," Jason said.

"Speaking of which, did you let them know where we were heading?"

"Shit. No," Jason admitted. "I'll call them when we get back to the *Phoenix*. I don't trust any of the com nodes here, at least not enough to enter the *Defiant's* codes into."

"You gonna call Kellea out here to run interference for us?"

"No," Jason said, swallowing the last of his beer. "Crisstof has no influence here and the *Defiant* would just draw attention since it has no reason to be in the system."

"So what do you think of the geltens?" Twingo asked, finishing off his own drink.

"Ker was a bit of a surprise," Jason admitted. "I had thought I'd completely misjudged them based solely on Crusher when I first saw it, but in the end they didn't disappoint. Crusher caved in the face of one of the warriors in there just to reestablish the authority of his position, and this was even among a group dedicated to who he is. But there's a brutal simplicity to a warrior culture that I can appreciate."

"Yeah ... it should be a grand adventure for you and Lucky. Not so much for the rest of us," Twingo said sourly. "Another thing I just thought of ... who is giving the orders right now? That little scene in the antechamber between Crusher and Lucky was a bit tense. Crusher holds a very high position here, but you're the captain of our merry little band ... so who's in charge here on Restaria?"

"I'd be lying if I said I hadn't thought or worried about it," Jason said, getting up from his chair. "Get some sleep, buddy. I have a feeling the next few days are going to suck."

*****

"Jason … how in the six hells do you get yourself wrapped up into these situations?" Kellea Colleren asked in a pained voice.

"You guys have six hells? We have one. Or nine, depending on who you ask," Jason said. "Although—"

"I'm serious," she said sternly. "Galvetic politics are dangerous. If they catch you meddling around, they'll kill your entire crew without a second thought or any due process. We'd be powerless to stop them as they have no interest in outside interference."

"I know, Kellea," he said, the next sarcastic comment dying on his lips. "We'll be careful. If we can get Fordix out of custody we may have a chance at seeing what we're really up against. If it gets too wild I can always pull the plug." She looked at him dubiously for a moment.

"You've mentioned that option many times, and yet I've never seen you walk away despite the numerous times you should have," she said with a resigned sigh. "Crisstof will want a full debrief afterwards … assuming you survive."

"Assuming that," Jason agreed. "Anyway, I'm just giving you a heads up on what we're doing and where we're at. I'll try to keep you apprised as we go along, but only if I have a secure connection."

"Understood," she said. "We're a week away from your current position, but we'll always have a strong com connection."

"Sounds good," Jason said. "We'll talk again soon."

"Be careful, Jason," she said quickly before cutting the connection. He sat for a moment in the *Phoenix's* com room, staring at the now-blank screen. The others were down in the cargo hold and armory gearing up for their upcoming mission. He was taking the time to reach out to

Kellea and ensure the *Phoenix* was properly locked down once they were away. The plan they had tentatively agreed upon required they leave the gunship behind as they traveled to Galvetor, a prospect he wasn't thrilled about, but could find no way around. His ship would likely not be given clearance to land, and an unaffiliated warship dropping in usually made security forces nervous and tightened up response times.

"Computer, lock out main memory core and prepare the ship for defensive posture alpha-one-one," he said.

"Please confirm command code," the computer said.

"One-eight-six-delta-four-four-one-seven."

"Please confirm final command authorization."

"Denver Broncos, 1969 Yenko Camaro," Jason said. There were a few beeps and warbles from the console before he received confirmation.

"Confirmation accepted," the computer said. "Defensive posture alpha-one-one will commence after final departure. Computer memory core is now secured and locked; any tampering will result in core destruction."

Jason hopped out of the seat and walked out into the main corridor of the command deck, colliding with Connimon as he did.

"What are you doing up here?" he demanded harshly.

"My apologies, Captain," she said with a nod. "I didn't mean to startle you."

"You didn't startle me," Jason said, trying to soften his tone. "I just don't like anyone wandering the command deck on my ship without my knowledge."

"Of course," she said. "I came to inform you that we're ready to begin mission planning and briefing in the cargo bay." She walked back down to the main deck as Jason watched from the doorway of the com room, a frown still creasing his face.

"Computer," he said, "rotate command codes to secondary protocol."

"Please confirm command authorization," the computer said. Jason repeated his uniquely Earthling command authorization and shut off the consoles before heading to the cargo bay himself.

Chapter 11

"Now that we're all here, let's get started," Morakar said as Jason descended the steps from the crew hatch mezzanine to the cargo bay deck. Even with the secretive nature of the order, Crusher made it clear he wanted to let only essential personnel in on the plan to spring Fordix from Casguard. He also quickly put down the loud dissent that arose when he informed them that Jason, Lucky, and Kage would be joining the strike team. The leadership felt it should be an all-gelten operation and that outsiders would just get in the way. Crusher knew that the unique skills of his crew would be needed, but rather than explain that, he simply commanded their silence and obedience.

Jason knew that things worked differently on Restaria, in the Legions, and especially where the Archon was concerned, but he was becoming increasingly worried about the shift in Crusher's demeanor. He was thrilled his friend was back among his people and shocked, as well as proud, to learn what he was to them, but he could feel the tight cohesion of his unit beginning to slip. Relationships and discipline that had been honed over years together and countless hours of live operations were shifting as Crusher's tendency towards command began to reassert itself. It wasn't that Jason's ego was so big that he felt threatened, but he knew what happened when there was confusion about the chain of command. This was a worst case scenario: Lucky and Kage would follow Jason without question, while the gelten contingent would only listen to Crusher. He hoped their careful planning would negate this fundamental flaw in their team's structure.

"Why are we meeting in here?" Zetarix said, looking around the *Phoenix's* hold with undisguised disdain.

"This is the only truly secure location on all of Restaria," Crusher said. "If word of this leaks out and compromises the mission, we'll know it was one of you."

"I'm not sure I appreciate the insinuation, Lord Felex," Fostel said. "What's to say it isn't any of your people?"

"Because we have no motivation to betray you," Jason said, looking the older warrior in the eye.

"And because the integrity of Omega Force is absolute," Crusher finished forcefully. "The Archon's Fist, however, is a huge question for us. While I may appreciate what its intention is, you cannot guarantee the order has not been infiltrated. The fact that I still have an unclear picture as to what the hell is going on between Galvetor and Restaria only heightens my distrust."

"Let's get back to the op," Jason suggested. "Morakar?"

"Thank you, Captain Burke," Morakar said with a nod. "In order to get close to Casguard Prison we will, of course, need to get to Galvetor undetected. This means we won't be able to take something obvious like a legion shuttle or this fine warship. Instead, we've procured a standard supply shuttle and made the necessary modifications for a discreet infiltration."

"What sort of mods?" Twingo asked.

"Scanner masks to hide how many lifeforms are aboard as well as any weaponry," Mazer answered. "Upgraded engines and layered armor added to the inside of the hull."

"Do you mind if I take a look at it?" the engineer asked.

"Of course not, but time is short," Mazer said with a frown.

"I won't need long," Twingo mumbled, already making notes on his data pad.

"We also have a current transponder code that will allow us to land at Cessell Spaceport, which is only fifty kilometers away from the prison," Morakar continued. "Our necessary, and more illicit, equipment is already on Galvetor with a sympathetic contingent on the homeworld."

"What the hell?" Jason interrupted. "We're parking our getaway ride right next to the scene of the crime?"

"We'll get picked up for sure," Kage piped up. "They'll lock that spaceport down first thing."

"If I may continue," Morakar said in a pained voice, "we will not be using the shuttle for exfil, and it is meant to be found.

"We will move directly from Cessell City to the former mining settlement of Kessmett, which is near the northern ice plains. There we have a fully operational tactical spacecraft that has been equipped with the best sensor-stealthing technology we could afford. That will get us, and Fordix, back to Restaria where the Archon's Fist stands ready to keep us hidden as we plan the next phase of our operation based on what information Fordix gives us."

"Why hasn't Fordix briefed you on this information before now?" Crusher asked.

"Your mentor, while sympathetic to our cause, has never fully aligned himself with our order," Morakar said. "He said it was for our own protection. His frequent travels to Galvetor and interaction with the government made him paranoid. He was sure he was being watched and feared that even casual contact with us could compromise the entire movement."

"He was probably right about that," Crusher conceded. "Although I can't believe the relationship with Galvetor has become so contentious that they would have the intelligence service keep tabs on an elder statesman like Fordix."

"We never believed they would have you exiled," Mutabor said quietly, the first time he'd spoken during the entire brief. Crusher just nodded and gestured for Morakar to continue.

The briefing lasted for another hour as all the team members asked questions and committed the details to memory. Jason was not happy about the lack of time to rehearse or prepare, but the Praetores insisted that there was no time to delay. Their fear was that, even in a prison of mostly non-warrior geltens, Fordix's life could be in danger. The same forces that were able to bypass the Galvetic justice system and have him imprisoned could no doubt reach out and have him quietly executed as he slept in his cell.

*****

"Looks like you're good to go, Captain," Twingo said as he pulled off a set of heavy work gloves. "They did a decent job of the upgrades and I was able to fix the issues they were having with the power generators and the flight stability systems. They put so much additional armor near the cockpit that it was a bit nose heavy."

"Power generators?" Jason asked, eyeing the shuttle skeptically. "So you're saying—"

"Yep," the engineer confirmed. "This old bucket still used the engines to provide system power to the rest of the ship. No standalone powerplant. Nothing to worry about though on a flight this short through such well-traveled spacelanes."

"While true from a technical standpoint, I'm not sure being picked up by a Galvetic patrol ship will be helpful with three aliens and a political exile onboard," Jason pointed out.

"True," Twingo conceded. "So why are Doc and I stuck here?"

"Why would I need you along?"

"Well, if this Fordix character is hurt Doc would come in handy," Twingo said.

"I didn't just ask about Doc," Jason said as he continued his walk around the small intrasystem shuttle.

"I'm a good luck charm," Twingo said. "Things tend to go much more smoothly if I'm along."

"Really? I've never noticed that," Jason said. "In fact, I'd say the last two major screw ups were directly attributed to you."

"Yes," Twingo admitted, "but we were still able to successfully complete the mission. That's where the luck comes in."

"You're not going," Jason said. "I need you here."

"Doing what?"

"Not being in the shuttle," Jason said. "What do you have for me, Lucky?"

"I completed the gear inspection as you requested, Captain," Lucky said as he walked up to the pair. "My own sensors were unable to detect anything that should not be there."

"What's this?" Twingo asked. "Distrustful of our new friends?"

"Distrustful is a strong word," Jason said, "but no, I trust nobody that isn't Omega Force at this point in the operation."

"Which is a good thing I installed three different passive trackers on this bird that the *Phoenix* can activate remotely and track," Twingo said.

"Clever," Jason said approvingly.

"Like I said … lucky," Twingo said, pointing at himself with his four thumbs.

"What?" Lucky asked as he walked up.

"No, I was saying … eh, never mind," Twingo said.

"Did I miss something?" Lucky asked as the engineer walked away.

"Yes, but nothing important enough to repeat," Jason said. "Let's go get the others and get this show on the road."

*****

The small transit shuttle was surprisingly nimble as it rocketed up through Restaria's atmosphere, even with the additional weight the tech crews had added in armament and armor. Jason flew up and through the thermosphere towards their intersect point for one of Restaria's standard transfer orbits. He accelerated along the designated vector before the computer picked up the planet's nav system beacon and took over. This particular shuttle didn't allow him to retain manual flight authority like the *Phoenix* did, so he just sat back to enjoy the ride.

There had been some heated debate about who would fly the shuttle. Crusher said Jason was the obvious choice and the most skilled pilot in the group, but Mazer thought Morakar should do it since he had been the mission planner and team leader up to the moment Crusher was brought back into the fold. In the end Jason presented it to the group in a manner that made it look like he was accepting piloting duties as a favor to Morakar so the latter wouldn't have to deal with inconsequential details like babysitting the flight computer of a cargo shuttle. Morakar made a show of thanking Jason for his generous offer, thus saving face in front of the group that had gathered around the discussion.

"We were just accepted by the nav system so it looks like our credentials are still good," Jason announced, kicking the seat release with his foot so he could back it away from the console and swivel around to see everybody. "Now it's a long and hopefully boring flight until Gaveltor's traffic system picks us up."

"Any chance our credentials won't pass scrutiny there?" Mazer asked.

"Practically none," Jason said. "When I entered our destination of Cessell Spaceport, there was a handshake between the two systems before it was accepted. If there was an issue on that end it would have kicked us out of the pattern here and alerted your fleet." Since Restaria and Galvetor shared such similar orbits, with the former's apogee extending out several hundred thousand kilometers further than the latter's, the usual procedure was to depart one and essentially begin decelerating immediately, slowing while the other came around Galvetor Prime and caught up. It was a bit more complicated than that, but the end result was that a flight that would take the *Phoenix* less than ten minutes was going to be the better part of fifteen hours.

"I can't believe we're still using this ridiculous system to get between planets," Crusher grumbled.

"If we were a government or military flight we wouldn't be," Morakar corrected. "We'd have access to one of the new grav-drive shuttles and just make a direct flight. But with the limited amount of traffic that isn't accommodated on scheduled ferries there hasn't been much of a demand that the government upgrade the system or loosen the restrictions on privately operated grav-drives."

"I wasn't aware of that," Jason said with concern. "Will we be searched when we land at Cessell? If flights like this are so rare, a bored official may send out a customs team when we touch down."

"This is a scheduled flight," Mazer said. "We simply swapped transponders with the shuttle that normally runs the route and cosmetically altered this one to match."

"What's the other shuttle running?" Jason asked.

"Diplomatic mail," Morakar answered. "There are still items that need a witnessed signature or are too sensitive to transmit over the nexus, so controlled copies are flown between the two planets. It's an antiquated method, but the bureaucrats on both sides seem to enjoy the perk of a private service."

"All things considered, I would say it is fortunate they do," Lucky said from the back of the cargo hold. Even though the shuttle was shielded against lifeform scans, Lucky's unique physiology had concerned Jason. Twingo mounted a crash seat against the rear bulkhead, near the engines, and assured him that any chance of the battlesynth being detected would be negated by the propulsion system's interference.

The conversation tapered off as each began to review their own role in the upcoming mission, running the details of the briefing through their heads over and over. There were only six people in the spacious shuttle: Crusher, Morakar, Mazer, Lucky, Kage, and Jason. Of those six, only the members of Omega Force had ever seen any actual combat. Even though this wasn't a combat op, exactly, it was still the first true operational experience the pair would have seen. Jason was also concerned about the fact none of them had ever even so much as performed a dry-run with the pair of warrior brothers and had no idea how they reacted to stress or the inevitable moment when the plan fell apart and had to be improvised. *I guess we'll burn that bridge down when we get to it.*

"That's Galvetor," Mazer said after an extended silence. The drone of the engines in the cabin had lulled everyone except Lucky into a drowsy half-sleep as the shuttle hummed merrily along the orbital plane.

"Where?" Jason asked, rubbing his eyes and sitting up.

"There," Mazer said, pointing at a bright prick of light moving much faster than the other stars visible through the canopy. "It won't be long before we're picked up by their orbital traffic control system."

"Are we likely to be contacted for a verbal confirmation of cargo or destination?" Jason asked.

"No," Mazer said. "The system is completely automated. There is only a minimal crew in the operations center in case of catastrophic failure, but the system requires no controller interaction."

"A smuggler's dream," Kage murmured

"Hardly," Morakar laughed. "The punishments far outweigh the risks. We're a fairly isolationist society and only deal with a few approved brokers for our imported goods and services. There are no illicit shipments or sales to Galvetor."

Jason and Kage looked at each other a moment before both broke out in a hearty laugh.

"Whatever you say," Kage said, still laughing.

"What do you mean?" Morakar said darkly.

"He simply means that criminals are the most enterprising people you'll ever meet, especially when it comes to a closed market like a planet that restricts free travel," Jason said. "We smuggled ourselves to Restaria, we're now smuggling you to Galvetor, and we'll then be smuggling Fordix off of that planet. I can say with certainty that there is an underworld of Galvetor that is serviced by someone willing to take the risk for the pay."

"You're talking about narcotics," Morakar said. "You're operating under the assumption geltens are prone to such vices."

"It may not be widespread due to your strict control, but it's there. It always is," Jason said.

"As a people, we're not prone to such weaknesses," Crusher declared, drawing incredulous looks from his three crewmates.

"Really?" Kage asked. "So how is it I've had to go and steal a cargo load lifter on no less than three occasions to get your drunken carcass back to the ship?"

Crusher glared at the Veran, but made no effort to answer him either.

"Let's settle the chatter," Jason said. "We're beginning our braking maneuver. Shouldn't be long before we hit Galvetor's upper atmosphere."

He got his first good view of Crusher's homeworld as the shuttle closed quickly on the planet, allowing itself to be captured by its gravity and slung into a high holding orbit. The traffic control system automatically began firing the thrusters to slow their velocity and allow them to descend to a lower transfer orbit before holding them for their turn to enter the atmosphere.

It was another full hour before the braking thruster fired once again to deorbit the shuttle. As the ship began to rock and bounce in the increasingly dense atmosphere, the interior began to heat up noticeably. Jason was surprised at this and hoped that this was just a design flaw and that the techs hadn't stripped away too much of the shuttle's original shielding to make room for the enhanced armor. They had been flying through space fairly close to Galvetor Prime; if the thermal shielding was compromised or lacking, he had to assume the radiation shielding wasn't much better. He put the thought out of his head and watched the altitude continue to decrease as the orbital control system brought them in across the largest continent on the planet.

He got a beeping alert from the navigation panel letting him know the automated system was about to relinquish control of the ship. After he spun around and locked his seat in position, he acknowledged that he was ready and waited for the indicators to green up. It was another fifteen minutes before he got the final trilling alert and the manual controls for the ship were activated. He kept it along the designated flightpath towards Cessell City and allowed the atmospheric friction to scrub off the excess speed as they streaked over Galvetor.

The planet was stunningly beautiful, much like its sister, Restaria. The major population centers seemed to be well-planned and spaced in a manner that was harmonious with the natural lay of the land instead of at odds with it, something you often saw on developed planets where the prime species tried to bend nature to its will. The geltens seemed to embrace their home and lived upon it as unobtrusively as possible. He mentioned this to Crusher.

"Some of that is our nature, some just practicality," Crusher answered. "Our ancient ancestors revered the planet and believed it had a soul and a consciousness. Some still do hold this view, actually. Our civilization was built around that belief and, thanks largely to a small population, we had no need to change this. By the time we began to industrialize, we were already well aware of our impact on our environment and what the consequences would be to disrespect that."

"Why the small population?" Jason asked. "That seems unusual for such an advanced species."

"A natural checks and balances that's a holdover from when we roamed the planet as wild nomads," Crusher said. "Just one of our evolutionary ancestors required a large amount of range, and those ranges didn't overlap between males. So gelten pregnancies, while more than sufficient to propagate our species, are far more rare than in others."

"Must be nice," Kage said. "I was one of twenty-eight siblings. Being hungry was a near constant on my world."

"Twenty-eight?" Mazer asked in disbelief.

"Our evolutionary history is quite different than yours," Kage said with a smile. "My ancestors were hunted for food. We didn't have the luxury of single births if we were to survive. Now there are so many that Ver is more or less a slum and we're desperately trying to colonize surrounding space." Jason filed away that little insight into Kage's previous life and motivations for being what he was. Hunger is a powerful motivator when it comes to deciding between slaving away on an overpopulated world for next to nothing or striking out and taking a chance at a life of crime.

Jason let them blather on. He was not immune to the pre-op jitters and the meaningless conversation was an easy distraction. Besides, he was the only person doing anything as he flew the designated glidepath that would put him at an altitude of fifty meters just outside the spaceport limits where he would be required to wait for final clearance to land from a live controller at the port itself.

It was forty-five minutes later when he had Mazer negotiate their landing with the port controller as the others continued to argue in the background about the next inane subject in their near constant bickering since they made orbit. He looked back in annoyance, but held his tongue as the landing pad and clearance code appeared on his nav display. He settled the shuttle down to an altitude of ten meters and began a slow crawl across the tarmac, the ship sluggish and unresponsive as the maneuvering thrusters fired at a near-constant rate to keep them moving. When he was finally over his designated pad, he deployed the landing skids and set the shuttle down with a slight bump and grinding of metal against tarmac.

"Slick landing, Captain," Kage called up from his seat. "When's the last time you flew something this small?"

"It's been awhile," Jason admitted. "First time landing something without struts and wheels in a long time too; the fixed skids aren't very forgiving. So where is our guy?" His last question was directed at Morakar.

"He will be negotiating the entry gate even now," Morakar said confidently. "He will have been waiting for the shuttle to overfly Cessell." Jason shrugged and went back to shutting down the flight systems.

"This place really must have sparse traffic if he can pick out a single shuttle overflying the city." Once he had shut the engines down, and switched the accessory bus over to battery power so they still had lights and ventilation, he left the cockpit and flopped down casually in the seat on the far side of where Crusher sat. But before he did, he cranked the air handler blowers up to full blast, creating a wall of white noise that forced everyone to raise their voices to continue talking. "We're really exposed here," he whispered near his friend's ear. Crusher just nodded in the affirmative, also looking out the canopy with a tense expression. His punishment for even being back on Galvetor would be severe, and likely fatal.

"Here's our contact," Mazer called out, pointing at an enclosed airtruck that was lumbering across the tarmac towards them. It had the same markings on it as their disguised spacecraft.

"Not a moment too soon," Jason said. "Mazer, shut off the marker lights and the rest of the systems. Kage, pull the flight data recorder and hit the boxes with that pulser."

"On it," Kage said. Mazer turned and began killing the power to the rest of the ship. They would pull the data recorders to ensure that when the ship was discovered it would be harder to backtrack, and as an added insurance Kage was going to hit all the avionics modules themselves with a device Twingo had fabricated for him: a directional EM gun that shot an intense burst of electromagnetic energy into the device it was aimed at. It would kill any redundant backup memory the unit may have as well as any other clues stored within the box. A competent investigator would probably still be able to track down where the shuttle had come from, but by the time they did the team would be long gone. *Well … hopefully.*

There was a bump as the airtruck backed all the way up to the side of the shuttle, its open rear door making direct contact with the cargo hatch. Mazer and Lucky covered the door as the others tensed up. There came a tapping at the door that seemed random at first, but was actually a specific pattern that was repeated four times. After the fourth iteration, Lucky stood down and Mazer popped the release on the hatch, sliding it up out of the way.

"Lord Felex Tezakar, Guardian Archon of Galvetor, I greet you," the gelten standing in the hatchway said formally, sinking down to his knees.

"Rise," Crusher said impatiently, "we cannot risk the time for such things. I greet you in turn, soldier of Galvetor." This seemed to satisfy the gelten who, while not a member of the warrior class, was still bigger than any human Jason had ever seen.

"I am Meluuk," he said. "If you and your team will get into the vehicle, we will quickly be away." With that Meluuk climbed back into the cab of the airtruck and waited as the team climbed into the bed and sealed the hatch on the shuttle behind them. Once they were all settled, the airtruck pulled smoothly away and made it through the gate without incident.

Chapter 12

The ride through Cessell City was boring. That was mostly because they were stuck in an enclosed cargo bed and were unable to see anything, and partly because the repulsors the airtruck rode on made for a ride without any real sense of movement. This meant Jason couldn't get a feel for how far they had traveled from the spaceport. He knew the exact distance from the pre-mission brief, but he always preferred independent verification. While his own neural implant was having trouble calculating the distance traveled, he knew Lucky's internal systems would have no such issue. In fact, he knew that if the battlesynth detected any deviation from the prearranged course, he would alert them immediately. So he quit fretting about the things he couldn't control and settled back for the remainder of the ride.

When the airtruck finally pulled to a stop and the door opened, Jason found himself inside a large industrial flat, one of the ubiquitous shells that seemed to dot the periphery of any major city. But, in what he came to recognize as the gelten flair for the artistic, the interior of the building wasn't bare steel girders and corrugated outer walls. Instead, sculpted stone columns rose up to support the roof and the walls looked to be made of enormous, square bricks that were hewn from solid stone. Even the floor, a smooth permacrete, was inlaid with swirling patterns of colored stones. Jason shook his head in wonder that anybody would take the time to design and build what was essentially a warehouse in such a manner.

"This will be the operations center, as Connimon no doubt already told you," Meluuk said. Jason noticed that the gelten's arms were massively overdeveloped, far more muscular than any non-warrior he had met so far. After seeing the look of awe on his face as he watched Crusher,

Mazer, and Morakar walk around the area, he thought he understood why. "It is an honor to have you all here. If there's anything you need, don't hesitate to ask."

"We've had a long flight," Morakar said. "It is currently early morning, local time, and we should all get some rest."

"Of course," Meluuk said, almost bowing before stopping himself. "If you'll follow me I'll show you to where we've prepared temporary barracks." They all followed the tall gelten deeper into the warehouse until they came to a pre-fab structure that was free-standing near the southwest corner of the building. The unit was complete with sleeping quarters, showers, and their equipment laid out in front of their bunks. "I will be standing watch while you sleep."

"You won't be the only one," Jason said, looking over his shoulder at the gelten. "Lucky."

"Of course, Captain," Lucky said, turning to make his way out of the temporary barracks. When he had left, Meluuk turned to Jason.

"I've never had the honor of meeting an actual battlesynth," he said. "Or any synth, for that matter. Is there anything I should be aware of?"

"Don't piss him off," Kage said as he flopped down on his bunk. "He'll tear your arms off."

"Ignore him," Jason said. "Lucky is a soldier. Treat him with the according respect. He's also my crewmember, a personal friend of Lord Felex, and a free-thinking being. He's not a machine or a tool to be ordered around."

"I wouldn't dream of giving him insult, Captain Burke," Meluuk said, still eyeing Kage uncertainly.

"Good," Jason said, patting the other on the shoulder.

"Feel free to engage him in conversation," Crusher called. "He likes to meet new people, but he's a little shy. You have to be persistent to get him out of his shell." This time Meluuk actually did bow before leaving the barracks and pulling the door closed after him. Jason waited a few beats before speaking.

"You know Lucky's going to kick your ass for that, right? Meluuk will follow him around and drive him insane the entire time we're sleeping."

"That's the idea," Crusher said with a smile. "It's what he gets for selling me out about the race when we picked you up on Aracoria." Jason opened his mouth to argue, thought better of it, and went to his bunk to lie down. Mazer was already snoring by the time he kicked his boots off and stretched out. Tomorrow night the mission would hit the operational stage and there would be no easy way to turn back. Although even if he wanted to call it off now it would be problematic. They were dependent on the sympathizers here to get them off-world and the *Phoenix* was on the other side of Galvetor Prime with no way to call it in if he got into trouble. As he drifted off to sleep, his last thought was that he may be using the powerful gunship as a crutch, always depending on her speed and firepower to bail him out of situations he had planned poorly for. Maybe that was why he was so apprehensive now.

*****

Jason's neural implant told him he'd been asleep for seven hours. He hadn't authorized it to try and link up with the local nexus over operational security concerns, so he wasn't aware of what the local time was. He rolled out of his bunk, restless after so much sleep. When they were aboard the *Phoenix* and there was no real day or night, he tended to take a series of two or three hour catnaps throughout the day. He found it broke up the monotony a bit and allowed him to be up for significant portions of both watch shifts.

All the warriors were now snoring loudly and Kage was making a weird, warbling sound in the back of his throat, so Jason slipped on his boots and padded quietly out of the barracks. The warehouse was still dimly lit and the lack of windows made it impossible to tell if it was day or night, but he assumed it had to be mid-morning given when they had arrived. He saw Meluuk walking the perimeter and strode off towards him. Lucky was nowhere in sight.

"Good morning, I think," Jason called as he approached.

"It is indeed and good morning to you as well, Captain Burke," Meluuk said.

"Where is Lucky?"

"He went out to inspect the neighboring buildings a few hours ago to ensure that they were empty as they are supposed to be," Meluuk said. "He should be back soon."

"Is it wise for him to be out there?" Jason asked with a frown. Getting caught before they even started wasn't what he had in mind when he signed on for this mission.

"There is little risk," Meluuk said. "This area has practically no surveillance and his sensors would be able to pick up someone, or something, hiding in one of the adjacent flats better than our own visual search would have." Jason couldn't fault his logic so he let the matter drop.

"Can I ask you what may be a personal question?" he asked.

"Certainly," Meluuk said somewhat hesitantly.

"This is my first time around any geltens other than Crusher … Felex … and I notice that you're much larger than anyone else I've seen that isn't in the warrior class," Jason said. "Is this something natural, or from conditioning?"

"I am somewhat taller than the average here on Galvetor, but my size is also from near constant training," Meluuk said with a hint of pride in his voice. "The day is coming when the classes won't live separately, as if we were different species. When that day comes I want to be ready."

"For what?" Jason asked. "Surely this abolishing of the class division wouldn't result in a war. Would it?"

"You misunderstand me, Captain," Meluuk said with a patient smile. "When I am permitted, it would be my greatest honor to apply for entry into the Legions. I was not blessed with the warriors' strength and abilities from birth, but I hope to overcome that through hard work." A few things clicked in Jason's head and confirmed his suspicions when he saw the awe Meluuk seemed to regard the other warriors with. "So allow me a question, Captain. You've served with Lord Felex since his exile?"

"Not quite," Jason said. "We were both captives at one point and had to rely on each other to gain our freedom. Neither of us had reason to trust the other, but we succeeded and got along well enough together so we all decided to make the arrangement permanent."

"Is it true what I've heard about your Omega Force? That you and Lord Felex fight for the oppressed?" There was a desperation in Meluuk's voice that Jason picked up on. The hero worship of Crusher in some circles had almost reached cult status and his real actions while away from Galvetor had become legend. He was gaining valuable insight into the gelten psyche the more he was around them, and a lot of what he was learning explained some of Crusher's more unpredictable behavior.

"It's our primary mission," Jason affirmed. "There are a lot of beings out there who are powerless to defend themselves. That's where we come in." He could see Meluuk swell with pride. His next question was cut off as Morakar emerged from the barracks.

"Is there anything to eat in this hovel?" he practically bellowed.

"At once, sir," Meluuk called back, hustling away towards the stacks of equipment cases and work benches. Morakar nodded to Jason and then began walking off the perimeter of the building for himself.

"Captain," a voice said from behind him, causing him to jump.

"Damnit, Lucky!"

"My apologies, Captain," Lucky said. "I did not mean to frighten you."

"You didn't frighten me."

"You jumped, as if in fear," Lucky said in his deadpan delivery.

"What do you want?" Jason said irritably.

"Nothing in particular," Lucky answered. "I completed a search of the surrounding area and found nothing of concern. My scans revealed that, aside from Meluuk's vehicle, there has been almost no traffic to this area recently."

"That's good," Jason said. "I'm trying to take it on faith that they know what they're doing, but I keep reminding myself they've never been in a live operation and covert isn't exactly their strong suit."

"Agreed."

"So what do you think of the geltens, Lucky?" Jason asked after a moment. "Now that we've spent some time around a group of them."

Lucky considered the question before answering. "They live in a world of extremes," he said. "They are capable of incredible feats of architecture and artistic expression, and also horrific levels of violence and savagery. Despite their reputation as hardened warriors, they are an overly emotional species, which may explain my earlier observations. It also makes them prone to melodrama and hyperbole in their interactions with each other."

"That's along the lines of what I was thinking," Jason said with a nod. "You've said it a bit more succinctly, of course."

"Of course," Lucky agreed, drawing another annoyed look form Jason. The pair stood around until Mazer and Crusher made an appearance, leaving only Kage in the barracks still asleep. *Not the least bit surprising.*

"Crusher," Jason called. "Wake Kage up, we need to get started on preps for tonight's recon." Crusher just smiled and turned to move back into the makeshift building. As Jason expected, there was soon what could only be described as a ruckus.

"What the hell!" he heard Kage scream, but before that there was a loud clanging of metal on concrete. Afterwards there was the maniacal laughter of a Galvetic warrior. As Jason and Lucky approached the group, Crusher emerged from the barracks with a beatific smile splitting his face.

"I take it you didn't just shake him awake?" Before Crusher could answer, an infuriated Veran stormed out of the barracks, although a being less than one hundred and thirty pounds didn't "storm" out of anywhere with much authority. He was pointing an accusing finger at Crusher with one hand while trying to pull up his pants and fasten them with the other three.

"Captain, this asshole kicked my bed across the bay while I was still in it. I want him punished," Kage declared dramatically.

"What would you have me do?" Jason asked, trying not to laugh at his friend.

"What?" Kage asked incredulously. "I don't know. You're the captain … think of something."

"I'll give it serious thought," Jason assured him, trying to give him his most earnest "Captain" expression. Kage just stared at him a moment before walking away, muttering to himself.

"Crusher, why do you insist on tormenting him just before we need him to perform a vital role in a mission to keep us alive or out of a prison?" Jason asked.

"You know … I'm not sure," Crusher admitted before slapping Jason on the shoulder. "Let's grab something to eat and get this final brief out of the way."

Chapter 13

"I know this prison is a few hundred years old," Jason mused while looking though his binoculars, "but why does it still look like it? I don't see much in the way of improvements."

"Casguard was designed for the warrior class when we all still lived on Galvetor," Mazer explained, looking through a pair of similar enhanced binoculars. Both pairs were equipped to view in multiple spectrums and provide analysis of anomalous readings.

"That doesn't really answer my question," Jason said. The pair were sitting in a generic aircar on a seldom used side road that overlooked the prison a mile and a half away. They had popped off some panels to make it look like a breakdown to the unlikely passersby. While Jason's presence would be difficult to explain, it wouldn't raise much suspicion as Galvetor did have its contingent of alien guests. If Crusher were to be seen and recognized, however, it would be disastrous not only him but for the entire mission.

"If a warrior is sentenced to this place, his honor dictates that he serves out that term with dignity. Nobody would dream of trying to escape. In modern times, the facility is used to house mostly normal geltens. The walls and cells are more than enough to hold them," Mazer explained. Jason was glad he was partnered up with the younger brother this night. Morakar was a bit more harsh and brooding than Mazer, not necessarily a bad thing but not exactly pleasant company for a night of boring recon of a stationary target.

"That makes sense," Jason said. "But even then, other than a couple of guard towers, I don't see much in the way of surveillance on the outside."

"Isn't that better for us?"

"Yes, but I've long ago learned to distrust things that look too easy," Jason said, continuing to sweep the complex and memorize the details. He knew the interior was much more secure than the outside looked from their multiple intel briefs. The cells were arranged in rows and had heavy steel bars that even Lucky would be unable to simply bend out of the way. The floors along the walkways were also pressure sensitive and individual footsteps were tracked when the cells were all closed and locked; even an increase in walking speed from one of the guards would trigger an alarm and bring more into the area. There were also autonomous, airborne bots that patrolled the entire cellblock in random patterns and would look in on occupied cells to confirm bio signs and scan the room with lasers to ensure the physical dimensions were the same from lockdown.

"We'll stay another hour and then move to our next position," Mazer said, moving to keep an eye out for approaching vehicles and letting Jason concentrate on the prison. The next thirty minutes passed in comfortable silence before Mazer spoke up again. "I say this with no intent of giving insult," he began, "but is Kage as … flighty … as he appears?"

"He's just excitable," Jason said a bit defensively. "He's solid though. We've been in more than a few scrapes we thought we weren't going to walk away from and he's come through every time."

"Good enough for me," Mazer said with a shrug. "I will admit to you, Jason, that I'm nearly overcome by jealousy of you."

"Me?" Jason said, surprised. "I can't imagine what for."

"We train from the time we're children to the time we die to be the best individual warrior we can be," Mazer said. "While we organize ourselves into legions, we're very much in competition with each other and want nothing more than to apply what we've learned in real combat, but for generations we've done nothing but train. There's a certain ideology that is also imparted to us, and it's very much embodied in the mission you and your crew have taken on without being asked.

"The thought of travelling between the stars, finding individual injustices to rectify, and all through that fighting beside Lord Felex as an equal." He heaved a huge sigh before looking at Jason with a slightly sheepish grin. "I know I'm probably romanticizing it and that there are challenges with the life you lead, but it's a pleasant daydream I distract myself with."

"Sometimes you need a new perspective to realize how fortunate you are," Jason said after a moment. "It's easy to forget how unique our position really is sometimes when you live the mundane day to day routine. The bickering, eating ship food for months on end, no privacy, annoying friends, no gratitude from those we help … you get the point."

Mazer just laughed. "A small price to pay, my friend," he said. "Trust me."

"Well, I think we've exhausted all possibilities at this location," Jason said. "I think we can confirm the intel claiming a lack of external presence at night. This place reeks of complacency."

"We'll be doing them a service," Mazer said as he started the vehicle. "The excitement of tomorrow night will be the highlight of their careers."

"That's one way to look at it," Jason laughed as he stepped out to replace the body panels they'd removed earlier. They sped back down the hill to the first vehicle swap point in a series of drops that would eventually get them back to the warehouse they were squatting in. Along the way, Jason had nothing to do but reflect on how badly things could go wrong the next evening.

*****

The next evening everyone was assembled and already geared up by the airtruck. The temporary barracks and remaining equipment had already been packed up and removed earlier in the day and Meluuk had scrubbed the area clear of any evidence they'd ever been there.

"Are we ready for this?" Jason asked simply, looking around at the major players. He received an affirmative response from everyone. "Good. Let's load up and get to it."

They all piled into the airtruck and waited as Meluuk climbed into the driver's seat and eased them out into the early evening air.

They rode in silence for the hour trip it took to get to their first waypoint: a food prep service that had the contract for Casguard Prison. Meluuk backed up to an unlit corner of the grounds and killed the repulsors on their airtruck. It was another twenty minutes before another large airtruck, emblazoned with the company logo, pulled out of the gated staging area and eased to a stop in front of them, blocking off the view of them to any curious employee who happened to be walking through the yard. The driver of the airtruck climbed out, nodded to Meluuk, and made a big show of inspecting the front, right repulsor pod.

"We're on," Crusher said, pulling the hood of his specialized suit over his head. Jason followed suit and the pair climbed out of the vehicle. They slunk across the short distance and slipped up to the rear quarter of the cargo area. Crusher turned and kept watch as Jason opened the hinged access panel that led into the airtruck's chassis. The area normally contained redundant running gear required by Galvetic law for safety in case the primary drive failed. On this particular airtruck, it had been hollowed out to provide an area big enough for Crusher and Jason to lay side by side in.

Jason slapped Crusher's shoulder and motioned to the opening. The big warrior contorted his body and slid foot-first into the opening and scrunched himself up against the opposite side. Jason entered afterwards in the same manner and then pulled the panel closed after him.

"This is cozy," Crusher said as they felt the airtruck lift up and pull out of the food service company yard.

"Yeah," Jason said. "If this goes to shit we don't have a lot of room to do anything other than get shot."

"You worry too much," Crusher said. "They'll pull you out and detain you. They'll shoot me."

"You think these suits will actually work?" Jason asked after another few minutes.

"Sure," Crusher said without much conviction. "The scanners at Casguard are over eighty years old and the gate checks are mostly just to satisfy procedure." Each of them was wearing a specialized suit that was supposed to mask their bio signature from the scanner embedded in the tarmac at the prison's gate. There was also a specialized liner installed in the compartment they were in that would help that out. The trick was not to completely blank out the sensors and create a dead space that would be equally suspicious. This was one of the parts of the operation that Jason had to trust to the geltens, and he wasn't happy about that. He would have much preferred to have Twingo set up the truck and test their suits.

As it turned out, the gate inspection would be the least of their concerns. The vehicle didn't even come to a complete stop. It slowed down, was apparently recognized and waved through, and accelerated through the gate far too fast for a detailed scan with such antiquated equipment. There were some more stops and starts before the airtruck finally came to a halt and they could feel the repulsors power down and the vehicle settled down to the ground. A minute later there was a bang, then two more sharp bangs on the sheet metal.

"Thirty seconds," Jason whispered, counting down the time in his head. When he reached thirty he grabbed the handle and eased open the body panel they had entered through, pulling his hood off so he could see now that the sun had fully set and darkness had fallen. The airtruck was in a dimly lit parking area, backed up against a brick retaining wall, exactly as they had planned. The driver could be heard talking boisterously with two of the guards as they went through shift change and prepared for the evening lockdown.

Jason slid soundlessly from his hiding place and helped Crusher do the same, supporting his friend's bulk as he slid his legs out of the hole and under him. He slowly closed the panel and followed Crusher away from the vehicle as they crept along the wall at a quick but deliberate pace. They were heading for a storm drain at the center of the walled-in parking area that was right up against the retaining wall. Thankfully their luck held and the intel was still accurate, as the holes that used to contain the bolts anchoring the grate were missing and looked to have been for some time. Jason looked around while Crusher squatted down and effortlessly lifted the grate, which must have weighed at least two hundred pounds, and placed it off to the side.

"Go," Jason whispered. Wordlessly, Crusher squeezed his way down through the opening, his shoulders scrunched up and still barely fitting. Once he was down, he clucked his tongue twice. Hearing the signal and still looking out across the parking area, Jason stepped off the ledge and dropped into the gaping black maw, trusting his friend to arrest his descent.

Crusher caught him by the waist and slowed his fall to a silent, soft touchdown in the cylindrical runoff sewer. "Ready?" he asked. Jason nodded once and crouched down in front of his friend. "Go!" Crusher whispered harshly. Jason leapt up, his newly augmented body easily clearing Crusher's shoulders and propelling him high enough to grab the lip of the drain. He felt Crusher grab his feet and maneuver up underneath him so he was standing on the big warrior's shoulders. Once he felt the double tap on his right foot, he reached over and picked the grate up. Just as silently as Crusher had lifted it, he carefully maneuvered it back into place and settled it into its recess in the pavement. He paused for a moment and listened to the continued diversion their driver was providing with his loud and bawdy joking with the guards before letting go of the drain grate and hopping forward, allowing Crusher to once again catch him and lower him without making a loud splash in the shallow water.

"Good to go," he whispered. Crusher nodded once and started moving deeper into the drain towards the main complex of Casguard Prison. Jason took a quick look around before turning and following him at a distance of ten meters.

After creeping along for another one hundred and fifty meters, they came to another drain. This should be the one that led up into an outbuilding that contained one of the six emergency generators around the complex. According to their intel, it hadn't been opened for anything other than cursory annual inspections in over a decade, and even then it was only to ensure no equipment had been stolen.

"Looks quiet," Crusher breathed almost soundlessly. He motioned for Jason to repeat the procedure they'd used to replace the other grate. After leaping up on the big warrior's shoulders Jason immediately noticed a problem.

"Shit!" he whispered down to Crusher. "The fucking bolts are still in place."

"This is the right generator shack, isn't it?"

"It has to be, it's the only one on this side of the complex," Jason whispered back. "Watch out, I'm coming down."

"So, now what?" Crusher asked after Jason was back on the floor of the sewer pipe.

"We need that equipment," Jason stated simply.

"Can you force it with your new muscles?" Crusher asked, only partially joking.

"Not a chance," Jason said. "Maybe Lucky could if he braced against something. Those bolts are at least an inch in diameter and there are four of them."

"I thought something like this might happen," Crusher said. "Hang on." He then began pulling components out of the waistline of his sensor-stealthing suit and assembling them. "I never fully trusted Morakar's network here on Galvetor, so I brought just a tiny bit of insurance." He handed Jason a compact laser cutting torch. The unit looked fairly capable, but with a woefully inadequate power supply. He would have maybe ninety seconds of cutting time.

"You could have mentioned this earlier before I compressed my spine," Jason said with clenched teeth. "And we weren't supposed to bring anything with a power source through the main gate."

"So are you telling me that little holdout blaster in your waistband is non-powered?" Crusher asked blandly.

"We're not talking about me," Jason said loftily. "Now get ready to hold me up there again. I need to figure out how well this little torch is going to cut through that grate."

Once he was back up on Crusher's shoulders, he inspected the problem carefully. There was not enough power to cut through the individual rungs of the grate and he would rather not make it too easy for the investigators to determine how they'd gotten into the prison. He brushed along the edge of the heavy iron flange that the grate was bolted into.

"Take your time," Crusher muttered. "It's not like you haven't gained a ton of weight lately or anything."

"Quiet," Jason said. "I'm thinking."

"I don't believe we have that kind of time, Captain," Crusher said. Ignoring him, Jason pressed the tip of the torch right up against where the grate met the flange and activated it. The acrid smell of burning metal filled the confined space and the sound of the beam sizzling seemed shockingly loud. He fired the beam a total of four times before slipping it into his waistband, thankful that the laser cutting tool didn't heat up like a plasma torch at the tip. He pressed against the grate and found that it was still holding fast.

"I've cut through the bolts between the grate and the flange," he whispered down, "but it's still stuck. I think it may be rusted together."

"So what do we do? Wait for it to rust the rest of the way through?"

"No, asshole, we'll need to put enough pressure on it to pop it loose," Jason ground out. "This means your legs and my arms. I'll lock my knees and you push up with your legs at the same time I do with my arms. Hopefully we have enough strength to push it off."

"Sounds like I'm doing most of the work," Crusher grumbled, but bent his legs so that Jason could lock his knees. "And … push!" At his command, Jason began to push up against the grate, straining his shoulders and triceps against the immense pressure Crusher was putting against him with his powerful legs. The grate held fast, so the pair dug down deep and pushed harder. The pressure against his feet and knees was excruciating, but Jason gritted his teeth and put everything he had into rotating his arms up against the grate.

POP!

The drain grate let loose and, thanks to the enormous force the two were putting on it, went flying up with so much velocity that Jason lost his grip and it went careening around the generator shack with a deafening clang. "Shit!" he exclaimed and grabbed the edge of the hole to pull himself up through the opening and grab the errant chunk of iron.

"Captain! Get back down here!" Crusher said, still trying to stay somewhat quiet. Jason ignored him and grabbed the grate, stopping by the locked doors to listen. If he heard anyone coming he was prepared to dive back down into the hole and replace the drain, hopefully leading to a curious poking around for the noise and not a general alarm raised. If they came in and the drain grate was lying across the room, the mission would be scrubbed and they would lose their only chance to get Fordix out. While he was still not completely clear on why they needed to do that in the first place, a job was a job and it was worth doing right.

After a tense five-minute wait, Jason relaxed and made his way back over to the open drain. "Still down there?" he called.

"Where else would I be?"

"Just get up here," Jason shot back. "We're clear and we're also losing time." He stepped back so Crusher could leap up and get a hold of the edge and pull himself through. This drain was wider than the previous so he had no issue pulling his bulk up and into the room. Once he was in, they went behind a dusty equipment rack and found what they were after: two large duffle bags.

They quickly and efficiently pulled out their gear and inventoried it before stripping off the skintight sensor-stealthing suit and donning their tactical gear complete with load-bearing vests and personal weaponry, although the latter was on the light side compared to what they normally carried. The biggest weapons they had were high-capacity stun rifles that were designed primarily for riot control situations. The prison guards were not their enemies nor were they technically combatants; they would not be shooting their way out if they were caught.

Once they were geared up, Crusher went over to look at the drain flange as Jason maneuvered the grate back over to the edge. "Nice job cutting all the way through the bolts, Captain," Crusher said sarcastically. Jason peeked over his shoulder to see what he was talking about. Sure enough, two of the bolts, at opposite corners, hadn't been cut all the way through. Each had retained about an eighth of an inch and that was what had held the grate down. Though the heat had weakened the steel, there was still enough left to hold the grate fast.

"Hmm," Jason said. "Sorry about that."

"Apologize to my knees," Crusher said. "Here, hand me the bags." Jason began handing him their discarded gear and Crusher threw it down the drain before jumping back into the sewer himself. Jason took a final look around before hopping back down as well. He had fully expected Crusher to grab him again, so he wasn't ready when he continued to fall and crashed into the floor of the sewer with a bone-jarring impact that made his teeth slam together.

"Hmm," Crusher said, "sorry about that."

"I seriously think I may shoot you before this is over. Now get me back up there so I can replace the damn grate, you big baby," Jason said.

Once the petty paybacks and foolishness was over, the pair got back to business and moved quickly up the pipe towards their next objective. The prison had been built primarily to house the warrior class, but had been staffed by normal geltens, so there were some provisions put in place that allowed the much stronger soldiers to be managed and subdued without risking the life of a prison guard. One such provision was a tunnel system that ran the length of the first level of each cell block and served as a secure holding area that could be flooded with knockout gas, or the lights could be cut off and the labyrinth would double as a convenient solitary confinement. What made it unique was that the floors of the applicable cells could be retracted into the wall and the prisoner would have no choice but to simply fall into the tunnel.

When the system had first been described to Jason, it seemed to him an incredibly convoluted solution to a problem that could be solved by jamming a stun stick through the bars. Connimon had told him they had tried that method, but the strength of the warrior class, as well as their resistance to non-lethal weaponry, made it a dangerous proposition. Not only that, but when one of them became violent they released a pheromone that would get the others wound up. Soon you'd have an entire floor of warriors trying to tear the prison apart. So they devised a solution that allowed them to evacuate the cell the moment one of them became agitated.

The plan was for them to access this now-unused tunnel system and extract Fordix through it when they learned he was being held on the first floor. After their experience with the drain in the generator shack, however, Jason wasn't entirely confident a mechanism that hadn't been used in over a century was still going to work. But they had no contingency plan on this one. Fordix had to be extracted in a manner that didn't expose the fact that Crusher was back on Galvetor. It was the main reason why Jason had insisted that only he and Crusher go into the prison. They'd done this sort of thing countless times before and he didn't fully trust the other members of the cult-like order they were now helping.

It took them the better part of an hour to find the section of the pipe they were looking for. Using a handheld sonar device, courtesy of Kage and Twingo, they found a section of the wall that was only two feet away from another, smaller auxiliary drain that would lead up into the tunnels.

"Let's pick up the pace," Crusher said worriedly, looking at the mission computer on his wrist that showed local time as well as mission-elapsed time.

"We're fine," Jason said patiently. "If we start rushing we'll make mistakes. If we're caught this will be all for nothing. Worst case scenario is we spend an extra night down here. We've already provisioned for that." He switched the sonar to high resolution mode and outlined where would be the best place to cut an access hole with the least amount of material removed. The tunnels were centuries old and while they looked strong enough, he didn't want to chance a cave-in.

Once he had his area outlined with a luminescent marker, he went into his pack and pulled out a much more powerful laser cutter, essentially a stripped-down version of the one he used to breach starship hulls. He placed the device firmly against the smooth wall of the pipe and let it determine the power needed based on the depth of the material. When it beeped twice at him that it was ready, he activated the beam and slowly worked it along the line he'd drawn. The smoke and noise were significant, but they were now well away from any external drains and deep under the structure of the prison itself.

Once he completed the perimeter cut, he made two more cuts, sectioning the piece to be removed into quarters, and then shut the beam down. He looked and nodded in satisfaction that there was still a seventy-percent charge on it.

"I beveled the cut outward as best I could," Jason said. "We should be able to push the sections into the next pipe over."

"I've heard that before," Crusher said and reared back to kick one of the quadrants. He put all his weight into the kick and so was unprepared when the piece flew out of the hole with almost no resistance. There was so much velocity on his kick that his leg also followed the section and he found himself off balance and with one leg now stuck in the wall. "What the hell did you do?"

"There must be high silica content in the soil here," Jason remarked, running a hand along the smooth, polished surface of the inside of the hole. "The laser turned the inside of the cut almost to glass."

"How fascinating," Crusher grunted before kicking the remaining three sections clear. "After you," he said with a flourish. Jason grabbed the cutting tool and sonar device and crept through the hole on his stomach, emerging in another, smaller sewer pipe. This one was bone dry and the air smelled positively stale. He gazed at the floor with his ocular implants amplifying the light and saw no footprints in the heavy layer of dust and sediment. All good signs.

Once Crusher climbed through, they continued their journey towards the main cell block, the smaller pipe veering to the right away from the main storm sewer they had been traveling in. A bit over one hundred meters later and they came to another drain grate, this one much more substantial than any of the others and inset vertically into the pipe.

"This has got to be it," Jason said with a low whistle. "It would take Lucky two days to get through this."

"It was made to hold back the worst of the worst," Crusher said, running his hand over the bars. "Twenty enraged warriors can cause a lot of damage." Jason shuddered inwardly at the thought. He was intimately aware of what just a single enraged warrior could do. "This drain looks big enough to just cut the bars and not risk getting burned by the stubs. This one looks like it's held in by more than just four dinky bolts, so I don't think your angle cut trick will work."

"It wouldn't anyway," Jason said. "I can't get this cutter flush against the corner, the flange is too wide. So those are the tunnels beyond there?"

"Should be," Crusher said. "This grate is so large because the pumps used to evacuate the knockout gas were at the other end of this pipe. There isn't really that much water runoff down here."

"Well," Jason said, hefting the cutting tool, "here goes nothing." The alloy the grate was made out of was incredibly dense and the progress was slow. Each bar took at least ninety seconds to get though, and he had to pause often to let the laser cool down.

"Can't you focus the beam more?" Crusher asked while Jason was taking his second break.

"I could, but we can't bend the grate out of the way as I go along, and if I narrow the beam down too much the metal will weld itself back together before I can cut the last one off. I need at least five millimeters of space so we can pop this out," Jason said.

As it turned out, the cutting tool ran out of power when he was halfway through the second to last bar. Nonplussed, Jason pulled out the micro-cutter Crusher had given him and expended the rest of its power getting through the rest of the job. When the last cut was made, Crusher grabbed the grate and, with a surprised grunt, muscled it out of the way. "Heavier than it looked," he said. They peered into the gloom of the tunnel beyond. It had a definite "dungeon" feel to it, Jason decided, as he stepped through the drain, careful not to touch any of the still glowing stubs of bars sticking out.

They moved quickly along the tunnel, ignoring the collection of Galvetic bones and mummified remains as they went. They had a map of the system and were heading straight to the cell Fordix was last known to occupy. Jason knew there were similar places on Earth, but he was still revolted at what he saw and couldn't imagine being sentenced to such a place, crawling around in pitch black and not knowing if the next person you ran into was going to try and help you or kill you.

"This *should* be it," Crusher said doubtfully, looking up the curved chute at what should be the floor of Fordix's cell. Jason switched over from low-light amplification to mid-wave infrared on his ocular implants and inspected the hatch.

"Those should be the drains for the latch mechanism up near the front," Jason said, pointing at three small holes evenly spaced along the edge of the corner.

"Are you going to just cut partially through them and then make us shear off another chunk of alloy with brute force?" Crusher asked.

"We could do that," Jason said, refusing to take the bait. "Or I could just inject the nanobots Twingo prepared for me through the drain and let them chew away the metal." He reached into one of the pockets of his tactical vest and pulled out a long, metal tube. The light on the tube was still green indicating there were at least eighty percent of the specialized little machines still alive.

Unlike the medical nanobots that Doc used on them regularly, or even the ones they always had in their blood stream, creating and producing a specialized variety was difficult and expensive. Twingo had gone through four batches before getting the variety that now rested in stasis within the tube. Jason twisted one end of the tube and a short, stout, needle-like apparatus shot out of the other end and the indicator started blinking green and yellow. When it just blinked a staccato green pattern it meant the nanobots were initialized and ready for use.

He climbed up the smooth walls of the chute, standing on Crusher's shoulders, and waited until the light began flashing only green. When it did, he pushed the needle end of the device as far into the drain as he could get it and pressed the button on the base of the tube twice with his thumb, deploying the nanobots. When the light turned red, he removed the tube and nodded for Crusher to lower him back to the floor.

"Shouldn't be long now," he whispered.

"How will we know if it's working?" Crusher asked. Before Jason could answer, a fine stream of silver steel dust began to dribble out of the drain holes. It was just a trickle at first, but soon the filings began pouring freely from the holes as the nanobots chewed through the heavy latches. "I guess that answers that," Crusher muttered.

They had to wait a full five minutes before the stream began to abate and taper off to nothing. Jason had to give

133

Twingo credit; the solution had been silent and effective. As long as the floor had actually been freed to move, they would likely completely avoid detection while breaking into Fordix's cell.

"As far as prison breaks go, this was pretty damn easy," Jason remarked, getting ready to move up and try the floor.

"I can't believe you would actually say something like that while we're still inside the prison," Crusher answered in a pained voice. He reached an arm out to stop Jason. "I'll go up first. We need to keep him from yelling out in alarm. An alien poking his head up out of the floor may startle him; he's not a young warrior anymore."

"I ..." Jason trailed off as he couldn't think of any reason to refute Crusher's logic. The simple truth was he didn't want to be the anchor man and push the three hundred and twenty pound warrior up the chute. "Fine," he said finally. "Let me get in position and then climb up on my shoulders." He lay down on his back in the chute and then bent his legs until he was basically crouching on the ground. Crusher climbed up part way and also laid on his back while standing on Jason's shoulders.

"Now," Crusher whispered. Jason began to straighten his legs, straining to not only push Crusher's bulk up the incline but overcome the added traction of all the fine steel dust the nanobots had littered the chute's surface with. "Damnit, hold on. Stay how you are," Crusher said, lowering himself back down until he was crouching on Jason's shoulders. "You're carrying the bio sign spoofer." Jason dug around in his vest until he found the little device and handed it up. "I can't reach it," Crusher said.

"I can't get my arms any higher with your giant feet on my shoulders," Jason said, beginning to sweat under the exertion. He felt Crusher try and lower himself more until something forced him to bend his neck forward. He tried not to think about what was resting on the back of his head, separated by only a few layers of clothing.

"Got it!" Crusher whispered triumphantly.

"Good," Jason grunted. "Now get your ass off my head and get the hatch open."

Crusher straightened back up and braced his hands against the hatch. With little effort, the hatch slid back into its recess smoothly and with surprisingly little sound.

"Fordix?" Crusher whispered.

"Who is there?" Jason heard another guttural, Galvetic voice.

"It's me, Felex," Crusher said. "No ... down here on the floor."

"Ah!" Fordix said. "What are you doing here? Are you insane? You come back to Galvetor and then walk yourself into Casguard?"

"Long story," Crusher said. "You remember the Caretaker?"

Jason balled his right fist and punched Crusher in the leg three times as hard as he could manage given the angle he was swinging from. "Oh, right," Crusher said. "We should probably get you out of here and catch up later. Make your bunk up to look like you're under the covers and then put this under the pillow." There was some shuffling around on the floor above him and, finally, Crusher signaled to him that he was coming down.

Jason straightened up painfully as a pair of legs appeared at the open hatch and Fordix slid down the chute to land easily on his feet. He wasn't sure what he expected an aging warrior to look like, but Fordix wasn't it. He could have passed for Crusher's slightly older uncle, but he looked as formidable as anybody he'd seen on the streets of Restaria. Maybe more so. He had noticed that Crusher was quite a bit bigger than the average warrior and Fordix looked like he was only an inch shorter and giving up less than thirty pounds on his friend.

"I am Fordix," the warrior said, approaching and putting his right hand on Jason's left shoulder in the traditional Galvetic greeting. Jason responded in kind.

"Jason Burke," he said. "I'm a friend of Felex's."

"I know of you, Captain Burke," Fordix said with a smile. "Thank you for the risk you're taking. The only thing I can tell you right now is that the risk is worth it."

"It won't be if we get caught," Crusher said. "Captain, hop up here and close the floor back up." Jason and Crusher reversed roles and he slid the floor panel shut as quietly as he could. When the hatch butted up against the stops, he reached back into his vest and pulled another tube of nanobots out. This batch would do the opposite of the first. When they were done, the hatch would be welded shut and the mechanism fused. It was just one extra little step to give them some time to get away. If the floor was loose and sliding and a guard walked in before scheduled, there would be no doubt as to how their prisoner had escaped.

"We're good to go," Jason said. "Let's start backtracking." Crusher pulled out a pair of shoes for Fordix to replace his prison-issue plastic sandals and they were on the move.

The trip back along the drain system took half the time as the trip up. They paused once to grab the rest of their discarded gear near the generator shack, stuff it in a bag they then handed to Fordix, and continued on down the sewer.

"There should be another drain up ahead that will come out in the parking area behind vehicle maintenance," Jason said. "From there it's a straight shot to the east wall."

"I assume we have a plan to make it past the wall?" Fordix asked.

"Sure do," Jason said, "but it is the most risky part of the operation."

*****

"We're coming up on show time," Kage said into his tactical com unit. "Everything set up?"

"*Everything is ready,*" Lucky answered. "*I am moving to the secondary location.*"

"Copy," Kage said. "We'll see you shortly."

"This is the part of the operation that I'm not entirely confident in," Morakar said from the back seat of the nondescript airtruck they were sitting in. "You say you've done this before?"

"More than a few times," Kage confirmed. "Relax, Morakar. You're working with the best right now. Meluuk, if you'd be so kind as to patch me into the local network." Meluuk climbed out of the driver's seat and ran the hard line they'd installed into the junction box they were parked next to into the airtruck. Kage grabbed the cable and ran it into his gear.

"A hard line?" Mazer asked.

"While this may be counterintuitive, a hard line is harder for them to trace than if I access one of the public nodes," Kage said distractedly. He closed his eyes for a moment as his neural implants made connection with his gear. "Tell Lucky I'm ready whenever he is." Mazer grabbed his com unit and alerted the battlesynth that they were now waiting on his signal.

*****

"Go ahead and send Lucky the signal," Jason said. "We're as ready as we'll ever be."

"Here comes the exciting part," Crusher said and aimed an ultraviolet laser over the east wall. He sent two blasts, paused a second, and then three more. By a stroke of luck, the drain they were in had a ladder so Crusher was able to climb up and aim the laser through the gaps in the grate without having to expose himself or stand on top of one of his companions.

"How will we know they got the signal?" Fordix asked. A moment later a horrendous explosion rocked the complex. Alarms started blaring and flood lights turned the night to day.

"There's the signal," Jason said.

"You think?" Crusher said. "How long until we move?"

"Another thirty seconds and then we move," Jason said, watching the timer on his combat computer. "And … now!" Crusher shoved the grate up and over and was up on the surface in less than a second, covering the others with his stun rifle. Fordix went next, followed closely by Jason. As soon as Jason brought his weapon up Crusher replaced the drain grate.

"Looks like the guards are congregating around the west wall," Crusher said. "If Kage did his job, we should be clear."

"Let's get moving then," Jason said and led the pair of warriors in a flat-out sprint across the vast gravel yard that separated the main complex from the outer walls. Just as they stepped from the paving stones of the ancient prison to the gravel, the lights in the east section cut off, their first indication that Kage was on top of his part of the mission. The extended perimeter barrier was meant to give the security forces one last chance to stop a runner before they reached the wall, although it was unlikely even a warrior as strong as Crusher could clear the enormous stone barrier, especially given how weak they would be from lack of exercise and a reduced diet.

"Shouldn't we blow the wall before we get to it?" Fordix asked with concern.

"We're not blowing it, we're going over it," Jason said, pulling his com unit out. "Lucky, we're almost there."

"How can we possibly—" Fordix was cut short as a battlesynth flew up and over the wall, riding his foot repulsors to a gentle landing right in front of them.

"Captain," he greeted Jason curtly before tossing him and Crusher both a device that looked like a truss in the shape of an "X" with straps hanging down. Without another word, Lucky grabbed Fordix, startling the warrior into speechlessness, and fired his repulsors again, sending the pair streaking over the wall.

"You think these will work?" Crusher asked.

"Eh ... fifty-fifty," Jason said, sliding his arms through the straps hanging from the trusses. "Twingo was in a hurry when he built them."

"Here goes nothing," Crusher said. He was holding the "X" apparatus over his head and squeezed the handles. Four ion jets positioned at each end of the four arms ignited and the device shot upwards, taking up the slack on the

139

straps and yanking Crusher straight up with a startled yelp. Jason watched him streak up and over the wall, hopefully to be deposited safely on the other side.

"I hope that wasn't the only one that actually works," Jason muttered, raising his own extraction device over his head. One last look around confirmed they hadn't attracted any attention yet. All total, their rush to, and over, the wall had taken less than two minutes. He squeezed the activation control and was startled as the truss was ripped out of his hands. The jets accelerated until the straps under his armpits yanked him off the ground with enough force to make his hands numb. The jets flung him up over the wall before they automatically angled over to eventually deposit him two hundred meters beyond on the other side.

The jets began to throttle back and he began slowly descending towards a clear landing zone. Just when he thought the extraction was going to go off without a hitch, one of the jets died. The other three put up an admirable fight to compensate and keep his flight stable and level, but they were in a losing battle. Jason began to swing wildly in the straps as his forward speed increased at the same time as his altitude was quickly decreasing.

Jason looked like a pendulum as the remaining three working jets quickly expended their fuel trying to take up the slack of the malfunctioning fourth. When the second jet failed, the remaining two flared brightly for a second before also cutting out. The good news was that he was only ten meters off the ground, but the angle his body was at in relation to the ground meant he didn't have enough time to try and get his feet under him before impact.

He smashed into the turf chest first, angling his head back to avoid shattering his jaw, and rolled across the turf. The straps holding him to the extraction device thankfully failed and he heard the truss bouncing across the ground near him as he kept his limbs tucked and bled off the rest of the speed he'd carried into his crash landing. When he stopped, he took stock of his body and, shockingly, appeared uninjured save for the expected bruises and abrasions.

He rolled over and sat up, located the now-crumpled jet truss, and climbed slowly to his feet. "That incompetent, short, big-eared, blue-skinned little bastard," he muttered as he pulled the straps off his arms and grabbed the hissing device. He checked his position and then struck off to the southeast towards the rendezvous point.

Chapter 14

"So you're sure we're clear?" Jason asked Kage for the third time that afternoon.

"Yes," the Veran said patiently. "The wall breach is now thought to be an accident, and Fordix's disappearance is being investigated with an eye towards the other inmates."

"I don't understand how the wall breach could be an accident," Fordix said. It was their third day in the cramped safe house and nerves were wearing thin.

"There are explosives embedded in the walls of Casguard," Crusher explained. "They were put there so that nobody could cut through or try a surgical breach without setting off an entire section and likely killing everyone involved in the escape or assault. It wasn't a publicized fact, for obvious reasons."

"Interesting. So your battlesynth placed a charge on the wall to set off the explosives as a distraction?" Fordix asked. He seemed unable to grasp the concept of Lucky having a name and an individual identity. After being corrected many times, both Jason and Lucky had given up. Crusher, stuck in the middle, tried to smooth over the insult, but both his friends had been decidedly cold towards his mentor since the escape.

"And Kage has been able to ensure the sensor logs of the prison show a clean yard to the east," Crusher said. "It's like we were never even there."

"Clever," Fordix said, seemingly uninterested in the details and unimpressed by their success. "So how much longer will we stay here?"

"We will be leaving Galvetor tomorrow night, Master Fordix," Morakar said. "With the success of the extraction team, our schedule remains unchanged." Fordix said nothing, just nodded and walked back into the kitchen area.

"Captain," Mazer said softly next to Jason, "I'm going out to inspect our vehicle one more time. Care to join me?" Jason knew the soft-spoken warrior had no interest in the airtruck parked in the detached shelter behind the house, as Meluuk was responsible for all the mundane details like that. So, there must be something on his mind.

"Sure," Jason shrugged. "May as well do something useful while we wait." The pair walked to the rear exit and, after a careful look around, quickly crossed the lawn to the outbuilding. "What's on your mind?" he asked once they were inside.

"Am I that obvious?" Mazer smiled.

"Not especially," Jason said. "But I doubted you really wanted to come out here to inspect the vehicle."

"No," Mazer said, looking like he was trying to pick his words carefully. "The atmosphere inside the house is stifling. I mean no disrespect, but does it seem to you that Fordix is not all that grateful that he's been freed from Casguard Prison?"

"No offense taken," Jason said. "While we're being completely honest, I've not been that impressed with any aspect of Fordix's behavior or demeanor."

"Lucky?" Mazer guessed. Jason just nodded.

"While he runs into this sort of discrimination often, it's never been from someone whose ass he just saved," Jason said. "But I agree with your line of thinking ... he seems very entitled for someone who should be showing nothing but gratitude. Is he in a position of leadership on Restaria?"

"That's just it," Mazer said, now much more comfortable talking freely with Jason. "He's just one of the dozen or so counselors that will guide and advise an Archon as he matures. He has no official rank within the Legions and is more akin to someone like the Caretaker."

"While I don't know him at all and I know even less about your culture, I can tell you that Crusher seems to sense something is off about him as well," Jason said.

"Lord Felex said something to you about this?" Mazer looked skeptical. "Fordix was one of his closest advisers and friends when he was growing up."

"He didn't say anything to me, but I can tell he's uncomfortable and is going out of his way to try and smooth over the tension between Fordix and us," Jason said. "That in itself is *very* unusual behavior for him. For some sick reason he usually enjoys interpersonal conflicts."

"I would not presume to know the Lord Archon as well as you," Mazer admitted. "I had only seen him from a distance when I was very young. I will trust your judgment on this, however."

"So," Jason said, "the million credit question is: do we ignore it as just poor manners, or do we make an extra effort to stay vigilant until we're all safely back on Restaria?"

"I would say prudence demands we stay extra vigilant even after we get back to Restaria," Mazer said seriously. "*Especially* after."

"I like the way you think," Jason said with a smile.

*****

They were all packed into the airtruck, its repulsors humming loudly with such a heavy load, and making their way to an outlying airfield four nights after pulling Fordix out of Casguard Prison. By the time they were ready to leave, the only person still speaking to Fordix was Crusher, for obvious reasons, Morakar, due to his impeccable manners and sense of propriety, and Meluuk, who was subservient to all he met in the warrior caste.

Jason, Mazer, Lucky, and Kage avoided him at all costs; the latter two wouldn't acknowledge him even when spoken to. It would be a relief to get him back to Restaria and be done with it. Jason also hoped that anything after this would entail a diplomatic solution between Restaria and Galvetor and that Omega Force's role in the internal conflict would be over. Best case scenario was the *Phoenix* was wheels-up within the next three or four days. He sighed inwardly … how he wished he actually believed that.

"This airfield routinely services shuttle launches to relieve crowding at Cessell Spaceport," Meluuk was saying as he drove along. "It's actually where the wealthier of Galvetor keep their private craft."

"I remember it from the intel brief," Jason said gently, not wanting to throw a wet blanket on his enthusiasm. "So between you and Kage we're certain that they aren't looking for Fordix?"

"Quite certain, Captain Burke," Meluuk said. "The wall was quickly deemed to be a mishap with aging explosives housed within the wall. In fact, there's talk now of tearing down the rest of the wall and replacing it with something less prone to that sort of thing. The explosion seemed to be the big story and Master Fordix's disappearance is being speculated as criminal cartel activity inside Casguard Prison. The official line is that they took advantage of the confusion in the explosion to get rid of him and were able to somehow dispose of the body."

"That doesn't really make any sense," Kage said. "I had thought it a bit of misinformation being let out into the public, but every internal memo and communication I was able to get a hold of backed up the official story."

"Why are they settling on an answer with so many obvious holes in it?" Jason asked. "Like how they got out of their cell and into Fordix's in the first place, or how they got the body out. There are dozens of reasons that theory doesn't hold water."

"It's the gelten character, Captain," Fordix said from one of the rear seats. "They don't *want* to know what actually happened. They don't want an unsolvable mystery and they don't want to admit to their superiors that they lost such a high-value prisoner without so much as an idea as to where he went.

"It's just one more indicator of the rot at the core of this world. Millions of geltens, all consumed with their own self-interests and unwilling to sacrifice anything for the benefit of all. How is it that Restaria has managed to construct such a precise and focused society with over a million warriors but Galvetor continues to decline further and further when this place has the potential to be a model society?"

They all fell silent after Fordix's somewhat bizarre diatribe. The only reaction was for Mazer to elbow Jason slightly in the side. He gave a slow, shallow nod to indicate that he, too, found the entire thing to be very odd. Even Crusher looked extremely uncomfortable in his seat next to his old mentor.

"Well, whatever the reason, it works in our favor," Jason said, breaking the logjam of discomfort that had halted the conversation in the vehicle's cab. "How much longer?"

"Only a few minutes, Captain," Meluuk said. "You can see a departing shuttle there just above the tree line."

"Ah," Jason said as the ion drive of a small transfer shuttle flared and climbed into the night sky. It took another twenty minutes for them to reach the small airfield and then to drive around the perimeter in order to enter through the private, automated entry gate rather than take the risk of going in through the larger gate manned with gelten sentries.

They would be sure to send out a casual patrol when they detected the far gate had been activated, but the vehicle would be stashed long before they reached it and it was unlikely they'd bother grounding any departing shuttles to satisfy a mild curiosity. That had been the thought of everyone when they'd planned out the mission details. Jason knew that the unspoken truth was that no glorified security guard was going to stand in their way during the final moments of the operation. The loss of life so far had been, thankfully, zero ... but that could change at any time.

"There's our hangar," Meluuk said quietly. "We'll drive directly inside and be out of sight from any overly curious patrols."

"Once we're in, Lucky and I will clear the interior. You remain here with the repulsors running," Jason said. "Under no circumstance can Crusher or Fordix be caught here on Galvetor." Jason saw Fordix stiffen in his peripheral vision and knew he didn't approve of his casual reference to Felex Tezakar by such an undignified pseudonym. He actually got the impression the older warrior was less than happy about Crusher consorting with what he deemed lesser species since his exile.

"Of course, Captain," Meluuk said respectfully. He and Morakar had come to hold the human in high esteem after the prison break had gone off more smoothly than anyone could have dared hope. Crusher's tales of Omega Force's adventures may have helped some too. While those two were able to accept him and acknowledge his worthiness, Mazer embraced Jason as a friend with enthusiasm. For his part, Jason had to admit he enjoyed the company of the younger warrior, though he was a bit on the high-strung side. Fordix, however, seemed to view Lucky, Kage, and him as useful tools and little more. Still … it could be worse.

The airtruck pulled into the hangar without challenge and the high cargo door closed silently behind it. When the lights came up in the building, Jason was surprised to see their ride. It wasn't one of the boxy, underpowered rock jumpers he'd seen flitting around since arriving in the Galvetic System. This was a large, powerful combat shuttle complete with shields, an impressive arsenal, and a slip-drive.

"Subtle," he said.

"We felt that it would be best to be ready for anything at this stage in the operation, Captain," Morakar said.

"I don't disagree," Jason said. "But you may have gone too far the other way. That's an Eshquarian combat shuttle, and a fairly new model used by their intelligence service, if I'm not mistaken. This beast lifting off from here won't arouse any suspicion?"

"We've taken that into account," Morakar said. "It will draw no more attention than any other light craft capable of interstellar flight."

"If you say so," Jason shrugged. "Lucky, let's get to it." The pair quickly exited the airtruck and each began to sweep the interior of the hangar in opposite directions, Lucky with his sensors at maximum acuity and Jason now armed with a powerful plasma rifle.

It took less than five minutes to verify the hangar was empty and another five to climb over the shuttle and ensure it hadn't been tampered with. Jason boarded the fierce-looking craft and began the pre-flight sequence while Lucky went back to retrieve their charges. At his signal, Meluuk, Kage, and the four Galvetic warriors hurried from the airtruck to the shuttle, quickly finding their seats.

Jason revised his opinion of the craft as he continued down his checklist. It wasn't just an impressively powerful bit of military hardware; the damn thing was practically brand new. The elapsed time indicated on the powerplant and the engines was negligible, and the slip-drive had only performed six jumps. He knew at least two of those would have been done by the manufacturer. The ship had to be incredibly expensive and didn't fit into the ragtag image the Order had tried to present when Jason first arrived.

"The airtruck will be picked up by someone else," Meluuk told him. "The person has no knowledge of who we are or what we're doing and there is nothing to connect us to the incident at Casguard."

"Very good," Jason said. "Well done, Meluuk. Could you send Mazer up to the flightdeck when you go back there?"

"At once, Captain," the gelten said before walking back down the short flight of steps off the flightdeck and into the main cargo area. It was a few moments before the young warrior's head leaned forward over the center pedestal between the two flightcrew seats.

"You summoned me, my Captain?" Mazer said with a grin.

"Funny," Jason said. "Let me ask you something … does this seem like a piece of equipment your guys could afford? And if you had a brand new combat shuttle, why were you, your brother, and Connimon skulking around Colton Hub and bumming rides from pirates? You could have easily tracked us down with this thing if you knew where to look."

Mazer's expression grew serious and he looked over his shoulder back towards the cargo area. "These are questions I'm asking myself, Jason," he said quietly. "Things are making less and less sense the further we go."

"Could you ask Morakar?" Jason could see the warrior squirm slightly before answering.

"It's not likely he'd know anything, but that's not the issue," Mazer said. "He's a true believer. He would never question the motivations or methods of the Praetores, and if he caught wind that things aren't what they appear, he may question those things aggressively. I don't think any of Morakar's normal reactions will help us here."

"I'll trust your judgment on that," Jason said. "Let's just all keep our eyes open."

"Who do you want made aware of your suspicions?" Mazer asked.

"You, me, and Kage will be it for now. Suspicions may be too strong a term anyway, let's just say we've been around enough to know when something doesn't pass the smell test," Jason said.

"Thanks for including me, Captain," Kage said from the copilot's seat.

"I didn't have much of a choice. You're sitting right here."

"Your words hurt sometimes," Kage said.

Mazer laughed and straightened up to leave. "I'll let everyone know we're preparing to depart," he said before walking back off the flightdeck.

"In all seriousness, Kage," Jason said once he'd gone, "let's keep an ear to the ground. Also, let's not mention any of this around Crusher just yet."

"Ooo, I love the intrigue," Kage said, rubbing his two smaller hands together as the other two continued readying the shuttle's systems. "Now we're a secret circle within a secret circle."

"Just keep me up to speed on anything you might pick up," Jason said wearily. "But keep your killer instincts in check. Let's not invite trouble by having you slice into any private networks until we're sure there's something there to find."

It only took another fifteen minutes to get the shuttle prepped to roll out. Impressive since it was completely cold when they had first boarded and a testament to how new and modern the ship was. Kage remotely accessed the hangar door control and commanded the massive sliding doors to part while keeping the landing pad lights darkened. Jason brought the repulsors online and lifted the shuttle off its landing skids to an altitude of one meter, then nudged it out of the building with the main drive. Raindrops began to splatter against the steeply raked canopy as the ship emerged fully into the gloomy night and the growing storm.

"We're cleared to lift at our discretion," Kage reported as the main drive began to spool to full power. "They seemed fairly uninterested in our flight plan. The only thing they said was to fly south away from Cessell City before we break for orbit."

"What about once we hit orbit? Do they care where we're going?" Jason asked, somewhat surprised.

"The flight plan stated we were making a courier run to Restaria," Kage shrugged. "Again … I don't think they care. Things on this planet are so boring and routine I'm not sure they have any suspicions even when things are slightly out of the ordinary."

"I'm just surprised that a ship like this doesn't raise a few questions," Jason said. "Here we go." He smoothly brought the throttle up, letting the gravimetric drive absorb the weight of the ship, and swung them around south in an easy, spiraling climb. Once the main drive was fully engaged, the repulsor system put itself into standby. "Prepare the hull for exoatmospheric flight," he ordered.

"It's already done it by itself," Kage said. "This isn't your standard shuttle, apparently. A lot of the systems are similar to what we have on the *Phoenix*."

"Well, if we can't have the old girl for an escape run I guess this is the next best thing," Jason said. "Let's get out of here."

Chapter 15

"Fifteen minutes to the landing site," Kage said as the combat shuttle tore through the upper atmosphere of Restaria. "No issues to report, but there is something odd."

"And that is?" Jason asked.

"I can't get a response from the *Phoenix's* status beacon," Kage said, frowning. "We should be close enough, but there isn't a very well-developed public nexus on this planet. That could be the reason."

"We stashed her pretty far out from Ker," Jason said. "I'm sure it's nothing."

"Probably not," Kage agreed. "Anyway, your landing zone is going to be the unused portion of a vehicle maintenance yard to the southwest and on the outskirts of Ker. It's going to be a tight drop. You'll have to come to a full stop and drop us in nearly forty meters between the buildings that flank either side."

"No sweat," Jason said. "Let's hope our pick-up is on time."

He flew a slow, standard pattern down into the city so as not to attract the unwanted attention of flying in too hard and risk someone taking too close of a look at the vessel. The sparse traffic over Ker was a blessing when it came time to bring them to a stop in midair and quickly lower the shuttle into its cramped parking spot.

"Secure from flight ops," Jason said to Kage, "but after that I have a special little thing I need you to do."

"What's that?"

"Here's what I want..." Jason began, explaining to Kage what he needed done before they disembarked.

*****

"Master Fordix," Fostel greeted them as they came down the ramp, "welcome home."

"Thank you, Praetore," Fordix said with a bow of his head. "While I will be forever grateful for the Order getting me out of that pit, I am disappointed that you risked the life of Lord Felex on such a mission."

"He insisted on going," Zetarix spoke up. "He said his team was more suited for this sort of mission."

"And you agreed?"

"I do not tell the Guardian Archon what he may, or may not, do," Zetarix said stiffly.

"The decision was mine," Crusher said, ending the argument. "This was a tactical decision, my friend. You have information we need and we were the best suited to get you out."

"We should continue this discussion in a more discreet place," Mutabor, the third Praetore, said. "While the escape was a success, it would be a shame to be caught now as we loiter near the ramp of the escape vehicle."

"Indeed," Crusher said. "Kage, lock the ship up and we'll get moving." Kage gave him a mocking salute and went over to the external access panel and set the locking protocols on the shuttle before running to climb into yet another ground vehicle with no windows that would whisk them away to some undisclosed location.

"Have you been able to raise the ship yet?" Jason whispered to Kage as they drove through the heart of Ker.

"No," Kage said, "and Twingo isn't answering his com unit either."

"As soon as we get to where we're going, let's get this sorted out and make preps to get out of here," Jason whispered back. "Now that Fordix is out I don't think we'll be needed."

"Will he be coming with us?" Kage asked, nodding towards Crusher.

"I hope," Jason said, frowning, "but the choice is his, just like it is for all of us." He hadn't really considered that Crusher might stay behind on Restaria and try to reclaim some of his old life, but as he watched his friend become more integrated with the Order, he had to admit that he had his doubts. He didn't want to think about what might happen to Omega Force without Crusher there.

When they finally arrived at the next hidden location belonging to the Order and climbed out of the airtruck, Jason went to where the Praetores had congregated.

"Excuse me," he said. "I don't mean to interrupt, but if there is no longer anything pressing for us, I'd like to collect the rest of my crew and check in on my ship."

"Your crew members returned to your ship shortly after you left," Mutabor told him. "They said they would be more comfortable there and less of a risk of being spotted on Restaria. They were transported out there by one of our members days ago."

"We have been unable to raise the ship, or them," Jason said. "All the more reason to check in on them if you can spare a vehicle."

"It would be unwise for you to move through Ker on your own," Fostel said with a frown.

155

"I'll take them," Mazer volunteered. He'd been hovering around Jason, seeming interested in what was being said. "There's nothing for me to contribute that Morakar doesn't also know."

"Very well," Fostel said after a moment. "But please be quick about it. If their ship is discovered it will raise some uncomfortable questions."

"I will be careful, Praetore," Mazer said with a bow. "Captain?"

"Let me tell Crusher what's going on and then we'll be on our way," Jason said. He was beginning to become anxious over the situation … there was no logical reason why Kage shouldn't be able to at least ping the *Phoenix* and get a status update at this range.

*****

"I could have sworn this is where I parked," Jason said with a humor he wasn't feeling. The four of them were standing in a large, empty field that used to have a DL7 heavy gunship parked in the middle of it.

"This is the right place, isn't it?" Kage asked.

"It is," Jason confirmed, "I can still see the indentations from the landing gear."

"Judging from the way the grass has popped back up in those indentations, I would estimate that the ship has been gone for some days," Mazer said, kneeling down where the nose gear had been sitting.

"Captain," Lucky called from near where the right wing would have been. He held up a customized scanner with a cracked display for Jason to see.

"That's Twingo's," Jason confirmed.

"That would indicate there was some sort of struggle," Mazer said, walking up beside Jason.

"The screen has always been cracked," Jason said, "but he would never just leave his gear lying around outside."

"Maybe they were spotted and had to lift off in a hurry," Kage suggested.

"Doubtful," Jason said. "The grav-drive was in standby. To lift off in an emergency they'd have had to fire the ventral repulsors and that would have chewed the ground up pretty badly. The only disruption I see is where the wheels and the end of the ramp were sitting."

"There is something with a power supply near the edge of the clearing over there," Lucky said, pointing towards the trees to the north. They all walked over and found the remains of what had once been a blaster rifle. It was impossible to determine the origins or manufacturer since it was mangled and charred.

"Whoa! Look at that," Kage said, pointing back into the woods. When Jason looked closely he could see three exploded tree trunks and some heavy scorch marks along the ground that had been obscured by the foliage from their original vantage point. Jason looked back over his shoulder and tried to get a bearing on how the *Phoenix* would have been oriented.

"This is from the tail guns," he said finally. "Something triggered the defensive protocols." A hard, cold knot was forming in his gut. The *Phoenix* was gone without a trace, and so were his friends.

Chapter 16

The four inspected the landing site for another two hours, expanding their search outward, before finally walking back to the vehicle they'd arrived in to head back to Ker. Jason had wanted to find some definitive evidence that Doc had been there as he had with Twingo's scanner. He worked hard to stay focused on the task, but his anxiety about what had become of his friends was making it difficult. So he relied on Lucky and Mazer to approach the problem with a more dispassionate eye, but they turned up nothing past the initial findings of a missing ship and a broken hand tool.

"Kage," Jason began.

"Already forming a plan, Captain," Kage said, his eyes a little distant as his brain ran through parallel probability calculations. "I will need access to a slip-space com node, but if the *Phoenix* is out there and in one piece I should be able to track it down. I can't guarantee how quickly though."

"I'll do my best to leave you alone while you work," Jason said, knowing he tended to hover when he wasn't able to do anything useful to help. "I know you'll crack it faster than anyone else would be able to."

"Captain," Lucky said, "I do not think it would be prudent to announce our trouble to the members of the Order when we return."

"I was about to say the same thing," Jason said.

"Why not?" Kage disagreed. "We could use their resources."

"I agree with Lucky's instincts," Jason explained. "Something isn't feeling right. For starters, where did they get that shuttle we flew back on? That's easily a one hundred million credit ship. I also get an odd vibe from Fordix. No ... for now we play this one close to the chest." The three members of Omega Force turned simultaneously to look at Mazer.

"Hey," he said, raising his hands, "I'm with you guys. I agree that something doesn't quite ring true regarding recent events. I had no idea the Order had access to that type of weaponry either."

"Can you get us a slip-space com node and a secure location for Kage to work from?" Jason asked.

Mazer thought about it for a long moment before nodding his head. "I have the perfect place, actually," he said. "You'll be safe there and it should have any equipment you need to begin your search. What are we going to tell the others when we get back?"

"Why do you ask?" Jason said.

"I'm sure it's occurred to you that there were only a few people who knew the location of your *Phoenix*," Mazer said seriously. "I hesitate to even utter this aloud, but it is entirely plausible that someone within the Order orchestrated the capture of your ship."

"The thought has crossed my mind," Jason admitted. "But I don't want to focus on the worst case scenario until we have more evidence."

"I can understand that," Lucky said.

Kage looked back and forth for a moment until he couldn't stand being silent any longer. "Okay," he said, "why is that the worst case scenario?"

"If the Order captured the *Phoenix* that means we were likely lured here for reasons other than what we were told," Lucky said.

"And it means Twingo and Doc are likely already dead," Jason finished, the lump of ice in his gut becoming heavier.

*****

The drive back to Ker was silent and tense. Mazer, despite his helpfulness, had the demeanor of someone who felt guilty for something he didn't actually do. Jason's mind was racing as he tried to think of who on Restaria would have a motive to take the ship. Not only that, but how? It was obvious the *Phoenix* tried to defend itself at least once, but there wasn't near the amount of carnage he would expect from someone forcibly boarding the gunship. There was also the fact that without the proper code clearances, a forced boarding would result in incremental amounts of damage to the main systems. The harder they tried to get it running, the worse it would damage itself, just short of full destruction.

He also had to consider the possibility that Twingo had been captured in order to gain entry to the ship, but the engineer didn't have the command authorization to unlock the primary flight systems. Not only that, but Doc would be useless to them if their mission was just to steal the ship, so his body should have been lying in the grass when they arrived.

All of his various conclusions were sunk, however, when he remembered the shiny new combat shuttle parked in a nondescript staging yard in the city that was now on the horizon. With access to that sort of firepower, why bother going through the enormous trouble, and danger, of stealing a single gunship? He forced himself to slow his breathing and heart rate. Flying off in a million different directions wouldn't help him find his friends if they were still alive. Since he hadn't heard from them, he had to assume they were counting on him to put the pieces together and come get them.

"This is it," Mazer said. "It was one of our first safe houses. It's been long abandoned since it is quite small, but it should fulfill your needs. There is a food prep area, sleeping quarters, and a full slip-space com suite."

"Lucky, I want you to stay here with Kage," Jason said. "I'll go back with Mazer and tell them you guys decided to stay on the *Phoenix*. Either that will explain your absence or I will get some sort of reaction out of them."

"I'll be fine here by myself, Captain," Kage insisted. "I've had to sneak around in a lot more dangerous places than this and I'll keep my com unit close by. My absence is easy to explain, but Lucky not returning might arouse suspicion." Jason stared at his diminutive friend for a moment, considering the request.

"Very well," he said finally. He pulled a small blaster out of the holster at the small of his back and handed it to Kage. "Be careful and keep me updated on what you're finding. Make sure you encrypt the signal."

"Will do, Captain," Kage said, accepting a code card from Mazer that would gain him access to the safe house. "Don't worry … this is what I do. If they can be found, I'll find them."

Jason nodded once to him. "Go," he said. "Find them and report back to me."

"Is he really that good?" Mazer asked as Kage disappeared quickly up the stairwell that would lead to the upper floor of the three-story building.

"You have no idea," Jason snorted. "He's not bragging when he says he's the best. He's so good that

161

when I found him he was locked up in a stasis cell to be sold to the highest bidder."

"Were you all captured to be sold? Is that how your group came to be?" Mazer asked, pulling the vehicle back into the sparse traffic.

"Not all of us," Jason said absently. "Twingo, Doc, and I were never in stasis pods."

"So Lord Felex had been captured and put into one of those things?" Mazer asked incredulously.

"Don't read too much into it," Jason said. "Crusher's … Felex's mistake was that he assumed everyone in the galaxy operated under the same honor code he had since he'd been born. It was a tough lesson, but one he's learned well. It doesn't matter how powerful a warrior you are when a drink laced with a powerful sedative is served to you."

The younger warrior remained silent for a while as they drove through the heart of the city. "I never considered the hidden dangers out beyond our world," he said finally. "We're so safe here in our isolation and with the legions surrounding us. I have to wonder how well I would do out there on my own."

"You're smart enough to realize that you don't know everything," Jason said. "You'd do fine."

*****

Jason wasn't quite prepared for the changes that had taken place in the few hours they were gone. When he and Lucky were led into the room where everyone had been meeting, Crusher looked to have undergone a complete transformation. He was in some sort of ceremonial armor that was comprised of a sculpted cuirass, black enameled pauldrons, and heavy forearm guards. There were also a pair of armored gauntlets on the table in front of him and

Crusher was standing at the head of the table with the obvious air of command about him.

"Where is Kage?" he asked when they walked in.

"Stayed back on the ship," Jason said casually, depending on Lucky's unparalleled situational awareness to record and analyze any reactions from the Praetores or Fordix. "He said this wasn't really his scene. So what's going on?"

"Captain Burke," Fordix began, "while we appreciate your service, I don't believe that you're needed to—"

"I don't believe I asked you, Master Fordix," Jason said pleasantly. While the exchange may be viewed by those in the room as unbelievably rude, the insult was quite intentional. He wanted everyone in the room as off balance as possible so that Lucky could record any inadvertent slips or odd reactions.

"We've just been debriefed by Fordix about the situation on Galvetor," Crusher said in the silence, giving Fordix a warning glare. "It's more problematic than we thought. I'm afraid now would not be the best time for us to leave, Captain."

"I see," Jason said neutrally, glancing at the maps and documents strewn about the table and allowing his neural implant to record everything for later. "How problematic are we talking?"

"Likely a full-blown civil war," Crusher sighed. "Galvetor has been secretly putting together an assault force to try and capture the legion leadership. After that they will assume command here on Restaria via the oversight committee."

"To what end?" Jason asked dubiously. "There has to be a larger political goal here, a reason for action against the legion's leadership in the first place."

"We're not entirely sure," Morakar admitted. "We were fortunate to learn as much as we have."

"So what will be our next course of action?" Jason asked, maneuvering himself in the room so that he could turn his back on Fordix.

"We're assembling the leadership here in Ker," Crusher said.

"I was under the impression that was something that has not happened in a long time," Lucky spoke up.

"You're correct," Fostel said. "It is highly unusual, but now that Lord Felex has returned, we can unify the Legion leadership under a single banner and plan a more coordinated defense. We would not be able to do this without him."

"Captain, perhaps I could interest you in something to eat," Mazer spoke up from the doorway. "It has been a long day."

"Thank you, Mazer," Jason said with a nod. "I believe I'll take you up on that."

Jason and Lucky followed him out of the meeting room and through the compound to the dining hall. The entire way Mazer wore a frown and carried a hard set to his eyes.

Chapter 17

It was well into the evening when the expected knock came on the door of Jason's room. "Come in, Crusher," he called, getting up from the bed.

"I wish you wouldn't intentionally antagonize him, Captain," Crusher said without preamble. "He gets so agitated it's difficult to get any more information out of him."

"Your friend is an asshole," Jason said simply. "I'm only returning the favor."

"No," Crusher said with a shake of his head. "There's something else going on here. You're intentionally pushing on him. Tell me why."

"So you're giving me commands now?" Jason asked mildly, hoping to change the subject.

"Why are you being so difficult?" Crusher snarled. "Did I not nearly die during the defense of your homeworld? Now that *my* people are in danger, you seem to—"

"The *Phoenix* is missing, Crusher," Jason said, cutting him off.

The big warrior stood frozen for a moment, mouth hanging open and his recriminations dying on his tongue.

"What?!" he was finally able to say.

"The *Phoenix* is gone," Jason said quietly. "We went to check on her and there is nothing but twelve divots where the wheels were and a few blast marks where the tail guns lit someone up."

"What else aren't you telling me?"

"Twingo and Doc are missing as well," Jason said.

"Why am I just now hearing about this?" Crusher demanded, his fists clenched. "Where is Kage?"

"Kage is in a safe location trying to track down some leads," Jason said. "I couldn't tell you until I was able to get you alone."

"You did not trust me," Crusher stated, his voice breaking.

"You know that is *not* true," Jason said hotly. "But I don't know how much I can trust those in the Order. There were only a few people who knew where the *Phoenix* was parked."

"But they have resources we could use," Crusher began. Jason held a hand up to stop him.

"Kage is now plugged in and on the trail," he said. "If the ship is still in one piece, he'll find it. If we find the *Phoenix*, we find our friends. There was no evidence they'd been killed, so I have to believe they were taken captive for whatever reason."

"So what should I do?"

"For now, exactly what you're doing," Jason said, grateful the conversation was going as well as it seemed to be. "There's not much you can do right now, honestly, and we'd just be in Kage's way. Once we have a firm lead we'll act."

"Who else knows the ship is missing?"

"All the remaining members of the crew and Mazer," Jason said.

"Do you trust him?" Crusher asked. Jason decided to treat it like a serious question and not a petty accusation.

"I do," he said. "He's solid. He reminds me a lot of you, actually." Jason intentionally left out the fact Mazer was also harboring suspicions about the true motivations of the Archon's Fist. *That is a really stupid name for a secret society.*

"Try to keep me informed," Crusher said, moving towards the door.

"That's a given, Crusher," Jason said. "I didn't exclude you as an insult. It was simple logistics ... I needed to talk to you without anyone overhearing."

Crusher just nodded. "Goodnight, Captain."

*****

Jason rose early, not having been able to actually sleep, and went in search of Mazer. Unsurprisingly, Lucky had stood watch outside his door all night. The pair moved through the compound towards where Mazer shared a room with his brother.

The young warrior was already awake and had been waiting for them. Jason had approached to within five feet of the door when it swung open and Mazer, already fully dressed, emerged and closed the door quietly behind him.

"I've been expecting you," he said softly. "Let's get to work. What do you need?"

"Let's go check in on Kage," Jason said. "I need to get an update as well as make a secure slip-com call myself."

"I've already secured a vehicle," Mazer said with a nod. "This way." He led them back through the compound and down a spiraling staircase that led to the underground parking facility. Jason noticed how crowded the halls seemed and had to wonder how they were keeping everything secret at this point. It seemed since Fordix was brought back and Crusher resumed his role as the Archon that the Order was much more bold in operating out in the open, at least compared to the dungeon they had been led to upon first arriving.

"How did you know it was us when you opened the door?" Jason asked, mildly curious.

"Lucky's feet make a distinctive sound against the stone floor," Mazer explained. "I knew you were in front because your stride is shorter than any of the warriors currently housed in the compound. I didn't want to wake Morakar. For now, the less he knows the better until we get a firm handle on what is happening with your crew." He looked at Jason with a slightly guilty expression at that last bit.

"I can't thank you enough for the assistance, Mazer," Jason said with genuine gratitude. "I think we'd have been in real trouble if you hadn't stepped up." Mazer seemed to puzzle through the expression a moment before answering.

"It's my honor to help however I can," he said seriously. Jason wasn't sure how to respond to that, so he didn't.

"I assume you want access to the com node in order to alert Captain Colleren of our predicament," Lucky said.

"Correct," Jason said. "She and Crisstof need to be aware of the situation. I don't necessarily want any assistance since the *Defiant* showing up in orbit over Restaria would cause more problems than it would help, but I owe them the courtesy of at least a message."

"I've heard these names," Mazer admitted, "but the ship sounds unfamiliar."

"You probably associate their names with a ship called the Diligent," Jason said. "The *Defiant* is a brand new battlecruiser that replaced the older frigate."

"What happened to the Diligent?" Mazer asked.

"Captain Burke rammed it into another ship as a diversion, destroying both vessels in the process," Lucky stated matter-of-factly. Mazer just turned and stared at Jason with an expression that was part awe, part horror.

"There was nobody on it," Jason said defensively.

*****

"What the shit, Kage?" Jason exclaimed when he walked in and saw the Veran. "I've told you about this ... how long have you been hooked in now?"

"Not sure, Captain," Kage said dismissively. The little Veran was sitting in a padded chair and had no less than six computers running search algorithms simultaneously while controlling and filtering the results with his neural implant and brain. There were infusion packs strewn about from a tea that was a powerful stimulant and at some point he had wrapped a wet towel around his hairless head.

Jason had been there when the doctors on Aracoria had warned Kage that the new implant would heat up if he taxed it too hard and that he must take precautions to not allow it to heat his cranium too much. Apparently he thought a wet towel would wick away enough of the heat that he could press on through the night. Jason knew the little code slicer could be tireless when on the hunt, and with his friends in almost certain danger he obviously wasn't thinking about taking a break anytime soon.

"Is the towel actually working?" Lucky asked.

"It would be better if I had some air moving over it," Kage said. "Don't worry, I'm monitoring the thermal output of the unit. I'm well within acceptable limits." There was something odd about the way he was talking that led Jason to his next question.

"How many partitions are you up to right now?"

"Um..."

"How many?" Jason pressed.

"Five continuous, but I can do six for short bursts," Kage admitted.

"That's it," Jason said. "Shut it down. Now. You're unplugging for at least four hours to get some food and rest. The automated searches can keep running on their own."

"But—"

"Now, Kage," Jason repeated. "I need the slip connection for a bit anyway." He knelt beside Kage's chair and put a hand on his shoulder. "I know you want to find them as much as I do," he said gently. "But finding them may only be half the fight. I need you at one hundred percent … you can't run yourself down to the point that you can't fight when the time comes to go get them."

Kage just nodded and his eyes went blank for a moment as his unique brain began to reintegrate into itself. Without a word, he climbed out of the chair and headed back to one of the bunk rooms.

"What did you mean by partitions?" Mazer asked. "Sounded serious."

"What do you know about Verans?"

"Other than they have four arms and are a dark green color? Nothing," Mazer said.

"Their brains have the ability to divide into what amounts to parallel processing units," Jason tried to explain. "It goes far beyond multi-tasking. Kage can literally think about six unrelated things simultaneously with as much accuracy as he can just one."

"Sounds complicated," Mazer said, clearly not that interested.

"Yeah," Jason agreed. "I sort of just take his word for it … it's a bit beyond me."

He cleared some of the junk away from the desk and began configuring the com node for a long-haul video link. Punching in the code for the remote com node from memory, he waited until he was prompted and then put in the long encryption string that would make tracing the signal that much more difficult. It was another few minutes before the nodes negotiated back and forth and established a solid signal through the ether of slip-space. Jason was never unimpressed that he was able to make a realtime video call from thousands of lightyears away.

The link went from an amber status symbol to a blinking green, meaning the signal had been accepted and he was awaiting a response. He had pinged Kellea's personal com unit so he know it would take her a bit to break away and answer it depending on what hour it was on the ship. There was no way he was going to signal the bridge and have them track her down or, worse, have to explain what the call was about. He knew most of the *Defiant's* bridge crew and wasn't ready for half the galaxy to know he'd lost his ship and a third of his crew.

"Hello there—" Kellea broke off as the video image of Jason resolved. "What's happened?"

"I've lost the *Phoenix*," Jason said with no lead up, breaking the news as quickly and brutally as he could.

"Where did she go down? It says you're still on Restaria."

"No… I mean I lost her. I landed at the outer edge of one of the larger cities for safekeeping. When we went back to check on things the ship was gone without a trace," he told her, watching her expression morph from concern to disbelief.

"Is this one of your pranks?" she demanded. "I really don't have time for this sort of thing, Jason."

"There's more," he pressed on, ignoring her. "Twingo and Doc are missing as well. We know at least Twingo was near the ship when it was taken."

"You're serious, aren't you?" she said. "Since I'm assuming the rest of you are full throttle trying to find them, just tell me what you've found so far. What are you into out there?"

"More than we bargained for," Jason said. "There have been some … things … that would be frowned upon by the authorities. But from what we can tell, the ship went missing well before anyone could have linked us to it, at least without there being an internal leak with Crusher's friends."

"You don't feel you can trust them?" Kellea asked.

"One I can trust for certain," Jason said, "the others are all suspect until proven otherwise."

"And Crusher? How is he handling being back home?"

Jason took a deep breath before answering. "Crusher is actually Lord Felex Tezakar, the Guardian Archon of Galvetor," he said. Kellea just stared blankly at him for a moment.

"Unbelievable," she breathed. "Crisstof had looked for him extensively when word got out he'd been exiled, but nobody knew for certain what he looked like. Looking back, I should have suspected there was something unique about him."

"Yeah, well …what it means right now is that I'm a man short trying to track down Twingo and Doc," Jason groused.

"Who is the one person there you've been able to trust?" she asked.

"His name is Mazer Reddix," Jason said. "He's a warrior from the same legion as Crusher. He's been facilitating getting us the gear we need and transporting us around the planet without being spotted."

"Well, at least you have some sort of support system in place," she sighed. "I'm currently in the Ta'amidil System, quite far from your location."

"Never heard of it."

"I'm not surprised," she said. "Minor system, no sort of trouble that would have attracted your attention. We're here on a relief aid mission."

"Is Crisstof with you?" Jason asked.

"No. We're supposed to pick him up when we leave here," she said. "Jason, I don't know realistically when I can get to you."

"I'm not asking you to," Jason said, holding up his hand. "You can't reposition the *Defiant* every time we get in a pinch. We'll manage. I'm just giving you a heads up in case the worst happens. Anyway … I've got to get going. Lots happening."

"Be careful Jason," she said seriously. "Go get your guys."

As soon as he disconnected, he began to go through the summary file Kage had been compiling as he worked. It was well organized and Jason was quickly able to not only ascertain the overall strategy but get a good feel for the results.

Kage had been thorough. He'd hacked into the few global surveillance satellites there were around Restaria and was able to locate the *Phoenix* from the old data. It barely showed up on the low resolution, wide area scans, but as soon as it was no longer there it gave him a timestamp to begin expanding his search from. He had checked the air traffic control and departure control logs after that to look for any ship leaving that hadn't filed a flight plan. After that he actually sliced into the individual sensor logs of ships that were known to be in the area to see if they may have picked up the *Phoenix* in flight. It all came up empty.

From what Jason could tell, Kage seemed convinced the gunship was still on Restaria somewhere. He left a note in his summary file giving the elapsed time between when the satellite had spotted the ship on the ground to when it would have been within sensor range of ships passing by the area. Jason understood what he was onto: the *Phoenix* would not have been able to go from a cold condition to slip-space capable within that period of time.

"Fuck," Jason muttered to himself.

"That bad?" Mazer asked, walking into the room with Lucky in tow. They'd given him some privacy when he'd made contact with the *Defiant*. Actually, Lucky had made a not-so-subtle gesture that they should leave because of the personal nature of Jason's conversation. *I don't know why he's worried about that now ... he routinely eavesdrops on every conversation I have within a hundred meters of him.*

"It's not good," Jason said, worrying at his scalp with his right hand. "Kage has been able to work some serious magic with the limited resources available, but we're no closer to getting a bead on the ship than we were standing around in that clearing. Well, that's not fair ... we do have a general time of when it would have been taken."

"What's our next move?" Mazer asked. Jason looked up and could see the genuine concern on his face. For some reason, he was greatly comforted by that.

"We let Kage keep at it," he said. "He's never let me down yet and I still think he'll be able to—" A strident beep from the console stopped Jason short as the displays began streaming lines of what looked like computer code, something he had no hope of understanding.

"Move!" Kage shouted, sprinting from the bunk room. Jason practically threw himself out of the chair to make room for Kage since he was already leaping off the ground, intent on getting to the console whether Jason was still there or not. All four of his hands began flying over the touch-sensitive displays as he reintegrated his neural implant into the link. Jason waited patiently. He knew Kage would report the second he was able to.

"That's how they got her," he said quietly after a few more minutes. The screen to Jason's right flickered and the grainy image of a bulky ship came into view.

"What am I looking at?" Jason asked. Instead of answering, Kage began cleaning up the image and zooming it in until he could clearly make out what the odd-shaped craft really was: it was two ships linked together. The larger was some sort of utility ship that had outriggers extending out from its flanks, three per side. Tucked up underneath, its landing gear still deployed, was a DL7 heavy gunship.

"I'll be a son of a bitch," Jason said.

"Huh?" Mazer asked, thoroughly confused at the expression.

"After the defensive systems made it impossible for them to board her, they brought in that rescue ship and lifted her right out of the clearing. It's not something the defensive systems were ever designed to handle."

Mazer peered closer at the image before muttering a curse of his own.

"That's one of our ships," he said finally.

"Are you sure?" Jason asked, hope springing up in his voice. While the ship being taken by a bunch of badass warriors wasn't ideal, it was far better than not having any idea at all.

"Quite sure," Mazer confirmed. "There are three of them still in existence. We were allowed to keep them after Galvetor relocated us here. They were to be used to harvest asteroids and assist in major construction efforts."

"What are they?" Kage asked.

"Exactly what Captain Burke said they were," Mazer answered. "Rescue ships. They were designed to go in and extract damaged combat landers after an assault. That ship is over two hundred years old."

"Is it slip-space capable?" Jason asked with dread.

"Yes," Mazer said simply. Jason's shoulders slumped. The *Phoenix* could be on the other side of the sector by now. "But they're not very fast," Mazer continued. "Slower still when they're hauling a ship."

"That makes sense," Jason said. "The drive would have to expand the slip-space field to accommodate the carried vehicle. So maybe they couldn't have gotten that far after all."

"I'm already on it," Kage said. "I'm accessing all the specs for the carrier ship. I should be able to determine the maximum theoretical distance by accounting for the mass and size of the *Phoenix* in the calculation."

"Now we're getting somewhere," Jason said, grabbing Kage's shoulders and shaking him. "Good job."

"It's not a sure thing yet," Kage warned, "but it's a damn good start." The slicer settled into his seat and began attacking the problem with renewed vigor.

"A word, Captain," Mazer said, indicating one of the unused bunk rooms. Jason followed him in there, nodding to Lucky that everything was fine. *He'll be listening in anyway.* Jason couldn't figure out Lucky's morality at times. He could be the absolute epitome of courtesy and manners, and then spy on your most personal moments without a bit of shame.

"What is it?" he asked once they were in the room.

"That ship means that my people are involved in this somehow," Mazer said. "This means your hunch was right, it was someone within the Order that had knowledge of where your ship was."

"Not necessarily," Jason said. "All someone had to be aware of is that we came to Restaria at all. The ship wasn't

177

that well hidden; it could have been found using the satellite feed just like Kage did. For that matter, one of your rescue ships could have been stolen. There are just too many unknowns, so for right now we keep playing it tight."

"What good does that do?"

"If the people who did this are in the Order's inner circle, and we don't let on that we have the slightest clue as to what happened, they're more likely to relax their guard," Jason said.

"Ah," Mazer said. "Basic counterintelligence."

"Essentially, yes. All we'll—" Jason was interrupted by Mazer's beeping com unit.

"It's text only," the warrior said as he looked at the display. "It's from the Caretaker, she says she needs to speak to us right away. In person."

Chapter 18

"In here," Connimon said calmly, leading them away from the entrance of the parking area. Mazer, Jason, and Lucky said nothing as they followed her into an area of the compound they hadn't been in before.

She led them across the length of the main building and then down a narrow flight of stairs into the sub-basement. Still further into the bowels of the building she went, not speaking until coming up to an unmarked door set into the wall. "I hope I can trust your discretion," she said and opened the door without waiting for an answer.

Inside was a room with bare rock walls, lined with work benches around the entire perimeter. Those benches were loaded up with computer consoles and com units, even a compact tactical slip-space com node. Sitting at one of the benches was Morakar.

"Brother, Captain, Lucky," he nodded in greeting. "Welcome."

"What is this place, brother?" Mazer asked, looking around at the screens that showed various views from hidden surveillance cameras placed around the compound.

"This is my secret," Connimon said. "I only just now brought Morakar down here. I needed to know whom I could trust."

"Maybe you should start from somewhere near the beginning," Jason suggested.

Connimon walked over to an empty chair and sat down slowly, suddenly looking very weary.

"When Lord Felex first learned he was to be exiled, he came to me with a specialized mission," she began. "He said it wasn't to be a command, but that it was important that I accepted. He knew that the circumstances surrounding his fall from grace were suspect, but he didn't have any substantiated evidence beyond that.

"I began with simple observation, keeping tabs on the leaders of the different legions within my role as the Caretaker. Nothing seemed out of the ordinary and for a time I began to think that Lord Felex was mistaken and there was no deeper plot here on Restaria, just the normal ebb and flow of politics from the homeworld. I began to lessen my suspicions and went about my life as I always had."

"Until?" Jason prompted.

"Until I was approached by the three Praetores you met earlier," she continued. "By that time the Order had already been formed and they were slowly recruiting those loyal to the Lord Archon for membership. They knew of my service to him and, despite not being of the warrior class, asked me to continue my work with them.

"At first it just seemed like a social club ... then more like a cult. Even then I thought it nothing more than harmless reminiscing by a bunch of middle-aged warriors with nothing better to do. But then they began recruiting younger commanders, key personnel in logistical positions, political contacts on the homeworld ... it all began to point to a buildup of some kind."

"Let me guess," Jason interrupted. "The talk of insurrection and emancipation began seriously shortly afterwards."

"Correct, Captain." Connimon paused to reflect a moment before continuing. "The hostility began to escalate on both sides with neither really understanding why. The propaganda on the homeworld was to stoke fear of a warrior uprising and dig up the specter of the last confrontation that led to the colonization of Restaria. It was no different here, as rumors of an invasion by the homeworld fomented a general feeling of distrust among the legions.

"Fordix was accused of inciting rebellion and was promptly arrested by Galvetic Internal Security. They came in the middle of the night and abducted him before anyone knew what was happening. This enraged the senior members of the Order and it was then that they tasked me with tracking down Lord Felex. I left with two warriors I trusted the most and set out after you."

"This still does not explain what the current emergency is," Lucky pointed out.

"You know that they've summoned the leaders of the outlying Legions, right?" When everyone nodded she continued. "I've learned that the leaders didn't just come for a meeting with Lord Felex. The warriors are all mobilizing."

"And by mobilizing you mean…" Jason said.

"Exactly what it sounds like. They're preparing for war. Not an exercise or a demonstration … the armories are being opened and warriors armed with live weapons and real armor are now mustering and will be deploying to staging areas surrounding Ker," Connimon said.

"And this is related to Crusher being back in the picture?" Jason asked.

"He is the only one with the authority to command all the legions," Morakar said.

"Which may explain why you were asked to track him down," Jason mused. "Is it possible that this has all been a complicated ruse just to get him back on Restaria so he could unify the Legions?"

"That was my thought," Connimon confirmed. "But we're still without a firm motive or even a main suspect. In other words, this could all be speculation that is far off target."

"My gut tells me it's not," Jason said, "but we should move with caution from here. Let's keep this between only the people in this room until we can get a better handle on what's happening."

"Does this include Crusher, Captain?" Lucky asked.

"No," Jason said, "but only due to the lack of access to him right now I will brief him on everything when I get the chance."

"Do we assume the Lord Archon is above suspicion?" Morakar asked.

"Yes," Mazer said forcefully before Jason or Lucky could answer. "Remember, brother, he had no desire to even speak to us, much less come back with us. Not only that, but he didn't make it easy to find him."

"I agree," Jason said. "Even though the politics of this star system are a little murky for me, I know my friend. He would not be a part of … well, whatever this may turn out to be."

"I also concur," Lucky said. "Crusher has risked his life to fight this type of corruption. He would not be a part of it."

"I was not casting aspersions," Morakar said defensively. "I was just making sure we're all in agreement before we proceed."

"Yeah, we're in agreement," Jason said sourly. "We agree we have no fucking clue what's going on right now."

*****

"*Captain!*" Kage's voice was cutting through Jason's head like a knife via his neural implant. He had asked the code slicer not to do that, so he assumed this must be a unique emergency. Given what was happening around them, he skipped the admonishments and opened the channel.

"What is it, Kage?" he said aloud, knowing it would be picked up and transmitted back. He'd never been able to master transmitting a spoken message without actually speaking aloud.

"*That rescue ship has just reappeared in the system,*" Kage said, talking very fast. "*It's following a normal approach course and is heading back to Restaria.*"

"Can you continue to track it?" Jason asked excitedly.

"*Yes!*" Kage nearly shouted. "*They're simply flying a normal approach and have already been picked up by the orbital control system.*"

"How long?"

"*They'll make orbit in just over three hours,*" Kage said. "*I'll contact you again if there are any changes in course and speed.*" Before Jason could answer, he felt the channel close. While Lucky seemed to know whom he'd been talking to, Mazer was staring at him as if he'd lost his mind.

"That was Kage," he said. "That rescue ship is on its way back to Restaria. We have three hours to prepare an intercept."

"We don't have access to a ship unless we go and speak with the Praetores," Mazer said. "I don't think even Lord Felex could authorize us the use of a ship without too many people knowing about it."

183

"Oh we have a ship," Jason said, winking at Mazer. "We always leave ourselves options. We will need to get an aircar, however."

The trio moved through the facility as quickly as they could without drawing attention on their way back to the parking facility. A suitable aircar was selected and soon, after a quick negotiation with the warrior who had been watching over the vehicles, they were speeding over the streets of Ker. Thankfully, vehicle guard duty in the Legions was much like it was in any other military: a punishment. The bored-looking warrior could not have been less interested in which vehicle they were taking, or why.

Jason was beginning to see the change happening in Ker that Morakar and Connimon had been talking about. The first time he'd come through the city there had been laughter, music, and lively conversation on every block. Now, grim-faced warriors in full tactical armor stomped about, many fully armed. There was even a smattering of physical altercations between warriors of differing units as they left the main metropolitan area and cruised into the sparsely populated outskirts.

When they reached their destination, Mazer looked over at Jason skeptically. "How are we going to gain access to this ship? It's locked up tight."

"Didn't I say we always leave ourselves options?" Jason said with a large smile. "Kage was kind enough to leave us full access before we left." He climbed out of the aircar and walked up to the sleek Eshquarian combat shuttle that had brought them to Restaria from Galvetor. The ship, an incredibly expensive piece of military hardware, was sitting in the same spot they'd left it, only now with a covering of dust and leaves. The fact the Order would just leave it lying about meant they were likely very well-funded by someone; he just wished he knew to what end.

When he walked up close, however, he could see that they hadn't forgotten about it. There were footprints all around the area where the access control panel was located and even some tool marks on the hatch itself as if someone had become impatient and actually tried to pry it open. There were also some impact marks in the hull coating where it seemed once the brute force method failed they began beating the ship with their pry tool. Warriors were nothing if not predictable. He placed his thumb on the glossy black access control panel and waited while the ship began to take biometric readings.

There were a series of beeps and squawks until the rear hatch popped open with a hiss and lowered gently to the ground, creating the entry ramp.

"Gentlemen," Jason said, "after you."

"Welcome, Captain Burke," the ship said as the interior lights of the cargo area came up and the environmental systems began circulating the stale air. "Primary systems are now warming up. Time to flight-ready: seven minutes."

"Nice touch," Jason said as he followed Mazer and Lucky through the cargo hold and up the small flight of stairs to the flight deck. "You know, the *Phoenix* could use some better manners."

"So you had Kage change the command authorization before we disembarked the last time?" Mazer said. "How could you possibly know we would need it again?"

"I didn't have the slightest clue," Jason admitted. "I just know our operations usually devolve into a pile of shit no matter how well planned, and this was one of the worst plans we've had in years."

"So what if we hadn't needed it?" Mazer asked.

"Kage could remotely release the ship anytime," Jason assured him, "and barring that, the original command authorizations would be restored after two weeks with no contact from us."

"Impressive," Mazer conceded. "Will this thing be able to intercept that rescue ship? Even through it's slow it is heavily armored."

"Not an issue," Jason said as he slipped into the pilot's seat. "The term 'shuttle' may be a bit misleading. This is really just a top of the line heavy fighter with an attached cargo bay for inserting troops. The Eshquarians use it for their special operation commandos. Don't worry, we've got plenty of engines and firepower."

"What is our plan, Captain?" Lucky asked as he carefully lowered his bulk into the copilot's seat.

"I don't really have a plan, as such," Jason admitted. "I'm sure something will come to me before we actually get within range of the rescue ship." Both his companions gave him looks that ranged from incredulous to downright hostile. He ignored them both as the engines of the new shuttle were already warmed and spooling up, ready to provide power. Not that he would ever admit it out loud, but he did have to admit that the brand new ship being ready to fly in less than ten minutes had some appeal when compared to a grumpy gunship taking over thirty for a cold start and even then complaining through most of the first hour of flight. But one thing the clever, slick Eshquarian shuttle couldn't match the older Jepsen in was speed or firepower or the ability to take a horrific amount of battle damage and keep coming back for more.

"All flight systems active," the ship said over the intercom.

"Lucky, get on the com and start coordinating with Kage," Jason said. "We'll fly out of here low and try to catch the rescue ship as it comes in over an unpopulated part of the planet."

The shuttle lifted smoothly from its concealed landing site and swung north away from the heavy population centers of Ker. As they flew over the outskirts, Jason could see that troop transports were still rolling into the city. Some warriors looked up as the combat shuttle flew over and a few even shook a fist in the air in salute. A few of the convoys stretched on for miles into the distance. Just the logistics of feeding and housing so many warriors was daunting, and Jason had to wonder why they were being relocated in the first place.

"Your first course corrections are on your navigation display," Lucky said. "Kage would like us to hold there until he is certain the rescue ship will be committing to landfall on that entry vector."

"Copy that," Jason said as the fly-to indicators lit up to direct him. "This is where the fun begins."

Kage had them come to a full stop in what seemed to be the middle of nowhere over an equatorial rainforest. Jason lowered them down until the landing skids were only a couple of meters above the treetops and waited, setting the ship to hold the hover automatically. He let go of the controls and stretched out in the seat.

"Let him know we're here," he told Lucky.

"We have a telemetry link open to him," Lucky said. "He has been monitoring our flight the entire time we have been airborne."

"How much longer?"

"It will be another hour before the ship begins atmospheric entry," Lucky reported.

The larger ship had already filed a plan that would have them entering the atmosphere near the equator and landing at a field in the northern hemisphere on the other side of the planet. The rough idea of a plan began to form in Jason's head as he looked over the topography data stored in the ship's computer. Just as the ship would be descending through forty thousand feet, they would be over what looked like Restaria's version of the Great Plains. The computer highlighted some points of interest, but from what Jason could tell it looked to be mostly untamed wilderness and some enormous corporate farms owned by companies on Galvetor. Those farms were almost entirely automated so the entire region had a population of less than six thousand people. If he wanted to force the ship down before it reached its base, this would be the area to do it. He went ahead and authorized the computer to arm the weapon systems. He was dismayed to see that the expendable munitions racks were empty. Whoever had ordered the ship had had it delivered without any missiles. Thankfully the energy weapons were installed and should be more than enough to force an antique ship hauler out of the air.

"We have confirmation," Lucky said after fifty-two minutes. "The ship is following the predicted track and will pass overhead in four minutes. I am sending speed and heading data to your display that will allow us to intercept the ship just as it overflies the plains region you indicated."

"I've got it," Jason confirmed as a new set of waypoint indicators popped up on his display with the corresponding velocity changes. He advanced the power and sent the shuttle skimming along the treetops, gaining little altitude as they flew along their target's intended flight path.

The incoming ship was traveling at nearly twelve times the speed of sound as it screamed through the thin upper atmosphere and would soon pass overhead of the much slower-moving shuttle. Jason was able to watch the intersecting tracks on his tactical display as he slowly brought up the power on the shuttle's drive.

"The ship has overtaken us," Lucky reported. "You are clear to intercept."

"Power coming up," Jason said in response and brought the drive to full atmospheric power, sending them streaking along the ground after the incoming ship. Mazer had confirmed that the sensor gear on the target ship was as antiquated as everything else on it so there was little risk of detection if they could get up in the drive wake while the ship was still blinded by atmospheric entry.

Jason brought the nose up and allowed the ship to climb sharply toward their intercept point. He watched as the spidery shockwaves appeared along the leading edges of the nose as they transitioned from transonic to supersonic flight. Once past the speed of sound in Restaria's atmosphere, the engine noise decreased dramatically as they were now outrunning the sound of the bellowing exhaust, and the slipstream could be heard against the large, raked canopy.

Soon they were passing thirty thousand feet and quickly closing the distance to the decelerating ship. Jason checked his position one more time before concentrating on the view outside the canopy, trying to get a visual on his target. His neural implant recognized the speck against the sky before his brain could register what he was seeing and boxed it in a flashing red reticle for him. They were running passive sensors to avoid detection, so the next maneuver was critical as they made the final approach to where they would trail the larger vessel until the next part of their plan.

His implants calculated that the ship was four degrees off course and four thousand feet lower than it should have been, so he made his own corrections and continued his approach. There were two timers counting down on his tactical display, one in red that showed when the target was projected to regain use of its sensors after entry, and one in green that told him how long until they were safely tucked up under the drive section given their current speed and heading. Since the green number was lower than the red number, he kept his control inputs steady and concentrated on not overflying his intersect target.

"Mazer," he said as the ship began to loom large in front of them, "what do you think the crew complement will be on that thing?"

"It's hard to say given the unusual nature of its recent actions," Mazer said. "I remember that it takes a minimum of eight crewman to fly it, so at least eight."

"Thanks," Jason said drily. "If you would, take a peek inside that weapons locker on the starboard side of the forward bulkhead in the cargo area and see what sort of toys we're packing along." Without a word the warrior unstrapped himself and went down the stairs. Jason could hear him sorting through the arms locker after a moment of messing with the latch.

"If it is only eight, and we maintain the element of surprise, I should be able to easily neutralize the crew, Captain," Lucky said.

"I'm counting on that since the concealed blaster I'm carrying may not take down a pissed off Galvetic warrior," Jason said. "But we don't know for sure it's only eight and we have no idea if they're armed or armored … or both. I'd rather not leave anything to chance at this point."

"We do have the shuttle weapons still," Lucky pointed out.

"True," Jason said, "but if we vaporize the crew, getting answers out of them will be that much more difficult." Lucky simply turned and gave him a hard look at the sarcastic comment, but remained silent.

"Four blaster carbines and six sidearms," Mazer said, sitting back in his seat behind the copilot station. "No heavy weapons, unfortunately."

"Lucky has the heavy weapons taken care of," Jason said with a smile. "We just need to cover him and keep them from concentrating any defense they may be able to raise at him."

"Sounds like we have it all figured out," Mazer said glumly, staring at the flaring engines of the carrier ship that was now clearly visible now that they'd closed to within less than a kilometer.

"Try not to sound too happy about it," Jason said, looking over his shoulder.

"Sorry, Captain," Mazer said. "But it just occurred to me that those are Galvetic warriors on that ship."

"Is fighting your brethren such an unappealing prospect?" Lucky asked curiously.

"Not at all, my friend," Mazer said. "But the fact that we need to fight them because of what they've done is upsetting. Legionnaires don't just blindly follow orders like common foot soldiers. For them to confiscate your ship and abduct your crewmen means that the situation was explained to them and they agreed."

"I can understand that," Jason said, not mentioning that his crew may not have been abducted, but rather disposed of. "But the reasons they were given may not have been the truth. We *are* looking at the leading edge of what appears to be a significant power play here on Restaria unless I'm way off the mark, and I don't think I am."

"Perhaps," Mazer said, sounding unconvinced. Everyone fell silent after that, listening to the drone of the engines and each thinking about their part in the upcoming action.

"We are nearly to the demarcation area," Lucky said, referring to the zone Kage had marked on the map where the foothills of the mountains flowed into the seemingly endless grasslands of the plains. "We will be clear to engage momentarily."

"Just let me know when," Jason said, straightening in the seat and making the final adjustments on the targeting script he'd set up for the weapons. He began his final approach to the target and closed to within one hundred meters, causing the shuttle to bounce and rock in the wake vortex of the much larger ship. Now that he was so close, he could see what an antique it really was. The huge outriggers appeared to be flight stabilizers that were equipped with what looked like nozzles for a liquid-fueled rocket assist. The other propulsion components looked to have been upgraded at some time during the ship's history since the repulsors and main engines were of different vintages.

"Weapons are locked on and we're in range," he said to Lucky. The battlesynth didn't answer; he just continued to monitor the ship's instruments for a while longer as the shuttle descended with the larger ship and the grasslands rolled along underneath them. It was another ten minutes of descending and decelerating before they crossed the thirty thousand foot mark.

"Jamming transmissions from the target," Lucky said. "Weapons free."

"Firing," Jason answered and activated his weapons script. There was a whine audible on the flight deck as the power surged into the forward plasma cannons. A split second later, three brilliant red blasts lanced out and impacted the starboard engine of the rescue ship. While the damaged engine began to belch out smoke and fire, the shuttle dipped down and lined up along the starboard, ventral surface and strafed the repulsors along that side, leaving only three of the ten operational.

The effect was predictable and immediate as the rescue ship lost almost all propulsion on its starboard side. It began to yaw to the right as the port engine flared to full power and rolled as the three remaining repulsors on that side could no longer maintain level flight. It began to spiral down slowly towards the rolling plains below.

Jason looked at his tactical display and saw the crew of the ship was desperately trying to signal an emergency, but the shuttle's capable countermeasures system was suppressing every transmission.

"They're not losing altitude quickly enough," Jason said, switching back over to manual control for helm and weapons. He slowed down to allow the ships to separate a bit more before diving underneath the stricken vessel and destroying four more repulsors along the port side, this time at the forward half of the ship. The destruction must have overloaded the system because one more of the repulsor emitters exploded outward as the shuttle zipped out from underneath and pulled a hard, climbing turn to the left to get back above and behind the now-doomed rescue ship.

"They're falling too fast," Mazer said in alarm. "A hull full of corpses doesn't do us any good."

"They can still arrest their descent," Jason said calmly. "But now they'll be forced to do it instead of trying to limp back to within range of their base." Sure enough, just as the ship looked like it would lose all its forward momentum and tumble from the sky, the rocket nozzles at the end of each outrigger began to stream fuel vapor before they ignited and blew out gouts of bright orange flame.

As the liquid rocket motors came up to temperature and the fuel mixture was optimized, the exhaust went from hazy orange to a bright blue and then focused into a white-hot stream of superheated gas as the outriggers themselves moved within their limited articulation range to bring the thrust to bear where it would do the most good. Even through the crew must now know that it was inevitable that they would be crashing, they seemed determined to make it survivable.

"Looks like they're going to just clear that next rise and then dig her into the field just beyond," Jason remarked as he flew a lazy circle around the plummeting ship at a safe altitude of fifteen thousand feet. He was reasonably confident the ship would make it down in one piece, but if it impacted too hard he'd rather not get collected in the resulting explosion. Doubly so since it appeared it was carrying a full fuel load for the liquid rocket thrusters.

"Agreed," Lucky said. "Estimated twenty seconds until impact. The speed and rate of decent are within acceptable limits."

"It's still gonna hurt like a mother though," Jason said. Mazer's brow scrunched up as he tried to figure out the meaning of Jason's truncated obscenity. Even from their lofty vantage point it wasn't difficult to pinpoint the moment of impact. The grass began to smoke and burn in the ship's passage as the rocket motors scorched everything in their path, but even the three extra thrusters weren't enough to keep the ship level and the starboard outriggers dug into the soft ground first, causing the ship to spin wildly. Once it lost its forward stability, it fell the rest of the way to the ground, slamming its underbelly into the turf before bouncing up and digging its nose in next. Still carrying a lot of velocity, this caused the ship to actually flip up and over and land hard on its dorsal surface, literally breaking its back. The aft section of the antique vessel sheared away and the forward section continued to slide on its top across the field.

"Holy shit," Jason muttered, a pang of guilt going through him. Despite the Galvetic honor code, he had his doubts that the crew in the ship was anything other than a group of soldiers following what must have seemed like a mundane order: go grab a ship suspected of criminal activity along with its crew. Despite the fact they may be shortly having a shootout with them, he was hoping they all survived the fall from Restaria's sky.

He nosed the shuttle over into a sharp descent towards where the forward section had finally ground to a halt. The repulsor emitters were all dark, the rocket motors were now extinguished, and only heavy jets of steam were still billowing up out of the nozzles.

"Tell Kage part one went off without a hitch," Jason said to Lucky. "We'll be out of the shuttle for this next part so he'll need to keep an eye on when they figure out the ship isn't coming back to base."

"If they didn't detect it dropping we'll still only have a few minutes," Mazer warned. "But the response time after they report it missing may be anywhere from twenty minutes to a few hours. These ships are part of Logistics Command, and with what's happening in Ker it could take some arguing before anyone is dispatched to look in on it."

"I don't think we'll be that fortunate," Jason said as Lucky talked to Kage over the com. "Even as basic as they are, your satellites will be able to see the smoke and wreckage from orbit."

"I just inquired about that," Lucky said. "Kage said there is no satellite capable of surface imaging due overhead within the next hour, give or take a few minutes."

"I retract my earlier statement," Jason said as he eased the shuttle down into the grass. "If they have a bird due overhead in under sixty minutes they're unlikely to dispatch an aircraft to check on a ship that is late to arrive. The obvious answer would be they made an emergency landing or had a mishap." Once he felt the ship bounce and settle onto its landing skids, Jason switched the main drive to "standby" and locked out the command inputs. On the off chance they were overwhelmed by the crew of the rescue ship, he didn't want to make it easy for them to simply fly off in the shuttle.

"Grab your gear," he said, climbing out of the pilot's seat. "Let's try to get this done with a minimal loss of life … especially ours."

Jason and Mazer both grabbed a rifle and a sidearm each. Lucky simply switched over to combat mode, the red glow of his eyes and whine of charging weapons filling the cargo bay of the shuttle. Checking his crew over one more time, Jason popped the rear hatch and waited as it lowered to the ground.

They exited the shuttle single file, Lucky leading since Jason and Mazer had no body armor or personal shielding. They moved around the shuttle in time to see what looked like an emergency access hatch pop off the side of the hull, likely via explosive bolts, and hit the soft ground with a thud. The soot-streaked face of a Galvetic warrior emerged and looked right at them with a look of utter confusion. He then looked over at the parked combat shuttle; his eyes widened in understanding and he disappeared back through the hatchway. They could hear him shouting all the way from where they were standing.

"Damnit!" Jason snarled. "I should have landed behind the damaged section. They didn't even know they'd been shot down."

"We may still be able to salvage this," Mazer said. He moved over to where one of the remaining outriggers was dug into the ground and leapt upon it. Running quickly up the appendage, he made his way to another hatch on the exposed belly of the ship and began manipulating the manual release controls. Jason and Lucky also ran up the outrigger to back him up. "When I open this Lucky should be the first to drop in."

"Should I try and apprehend them first?" Lucky asked.

"I trust your judgment," Jason said. "But *NO* unnecessary risks, they won't be trying to stun you and you know firsthand how hard these guys can be to take down."

"Lord Felex is a special case, even among us," Mazer said. "But yes ... do not engage them to incapacitate if there are more than two in the area. Even ship jockeys like these guys will be able to quickly adapt a strategy against you."

"Understood," Lucky said.

"Are you ready?" Mazer asked. When Lucky nodded, he reached into the recess he was crouched over and cranked the handle within until there were three loud pops and the hatch swung inward, banging against something inside the ship before swinging wildly from its hinge. Lucky tucked his arms in close and jumped in through the hatchway. An instant later there was a deafening *POP* and a blinding flash of light from within the ship.

"Lucky!?" Jason shouted, not yet training his weapon on the opening since he didn't know who was near it, the crew or his friend.

"I am fine, Captain," Lucky called up. "Three of the crew are incapacitated. Two more were stunned, but were able to escape into the forward sections. You and Mazer may come down." Jason hopped through first and made way for Mazer to follow behind him. He switched through modes on his ocular implants until he found a decent combination that could deal with the smoke and darkness.

"What the hell was that?" he asked.

"I set my plasma cannons for wide angle disbursement and fired into the bulkheads at close range," Lucky said. "It creates a sonic shockwave accompanied by a flash that most biologicals find disorienting."

With a somewhat surprised look on his face, Mazer looked at the three warriors that had fallen where they had been setting up an ambush.

"Yeah ... you disoriented the shit out of these three," Jason said.

"Only one of them has—"

"It's just an expression, Lucky," Jason said. "Which direction did the other two go?"

"They retreated towards the forward section of the ship," Lucky said.

"They'll regroup near the bridge," Mazer said. "It's the only place left forward of here with heavy enough bulkheads to make a stand."

"So much for this being easy," Jason grumbled. "Let's go, single file, Lucky on point."

Walking on the overhead of the passageway was a bit disconcerting as well as slightly hazardous. Jason had to constantly check where he was walking because of the darkened lighting fixtures, conduits, and signs that threatened to trip him up as they moved along. They had gone only twenty-five feet when they realized Lucky had no idea where he was going inside the large ship.

"I really don't either," Mazer admitted. "I've only been on one of these a couple times and I didn't really get around all that much."

"This is absurd," Jason said, becoming irritated. "We don't have an indefinite amount of time here, let's just keep moving forward. This thing isn't that big." They pressed on until coming to a ninety-degree bend to the left.

"I know where we are now," Mazer whispered. "There's an identical passageway to this one on the other side. This lateral corridor connects those and once we get to the center there will be a wide, short archway that leads up to the command deck."

"Now we're getting somewhere," Jason whispered back. "Let's move carefully along this passageway and we'll make a decision on the final assault once we get to where we can sneak a peek at the bridge."

As they crept along, Jason could see where the passage to the command deck was from the light that was likely coming in through the bridge windows, or at least where they used to be. Since the ship was upside down and the prow had taken the brunt of the impact that flipped it, the light coming through was fairly weak. They were within a few meters of the opening when they could hear movement in the passageway beyond.

Jason moved to the opposite side of the passage to get a better angle on the entryway, training his rifle on the opening. He selected the stun setting on the weapon since he was nearly certain that they wouldn't be able to rush out in a mass around the corner before Lucky and Mazer would pick them up. He also wasn't sure how many survivors were left on the bridge and he needed at least one left alive and coherent to question. Not only that, it was poor manners to be invited to a planet and begin killing off the inhabitants.

He detected a slight movement ahead, just a change in the light really. Since there was not much smoke in the forward passageway, he switched his vision to straight infrared and saw the shoulder and head of a warrior moving slowly around the corner leading to the passageway they were standing in. He aimed quickly and fired a stun bolt directly into the side of his head, sending him flopping around on the deck. Since the deck was actually the sloped overhead and not the stairs that normally led to the bridge, the warrior's gyrations caused his body to slide back the way he came and out of sight. *Shit.*

"Nobody else has to die today," Jason called out loudly. "We just want to ask a few questions."

"Why have you attacked us?" a strong, deep voice called out. "Who are you and who do you represent?"

"I said *we* were going to ask the questions," Jason snapped back. "You've just come back from hauling a ship off of Restaria. I want to know where it went, where the crew is, and who authorized you to take it."

"We do not answer to you," a thinner-sounding voice called out. "You will get nothing from us." As Jason had been talking, Lucky had moved even closer to the edge of the bridge entry and Mazer had moved to a position between the both of them and was covering the way they came as well as the passageway beyond.

"That's the wrong answer," Jason said. "You have ten seconds and then we do this the easy way."

"Do you fools realize what you've done?" Mazer suddenly shouted. "Were you aware that the Lord Archon has returned to Restaria?"

"We had heard," the deep voice said with less certainty. "It is true then?"

"It is," Mazer said. "Now, what do you think he'll say about the fact you have stolen his ship and taken it off-world?"

This caused an eruption of quiet, frantic babbling on the bridge. Jason caught Mazer's eye and nodded to him in approval. Thanks to his quick thinking, this may be over with nobody dying from a plasma bolt to the chest.

"We did not have any idea that the ship belonged to the Lord Archon," the deep voice called out. "The orders came in through the normal channels."

"What did I tell you?" the thin voice said harshly. "Tell them noth—" The voice was cut off suddenly and there was a strange gurgling sound now coming from the bridge.

"We would like to negotiate our surrender," deep voice said. "How would you like us to proceed?"

"Are you able to get outside from your current location?" Jason asked.

"Affirmative."

"Everyone clear out and muster twenty meters off the prow and wait for us," he continued. "Take no weapons and made no sudden moves when you see us."

"Acknowledged," deep voice said. "We're moving now."

"Mazer, do you know where the flight data recorders are on the bridge?" Jason asked.

"I think I know what you're referring to," Mazer said, "and yes, I do."

"Go grab those and Lucky and I will go out and keep an eye on the prisoners," Jason said.

While the pair from Omega Force made their way to the forward emergency hatch they'd passed on the way to the bridge, Mazer moved cautiously onto the bridge, watching carefully for any traps or warriors that may have been left behind. It took them a moment to figure out how to blow the hatch, but within two minutes of leaving the bridge they were dropping onto the ground and walking around the crumpled prow to see six warriors and one normal gelten standing in various non-threatening poses with one exception: one of the warriors had a clawed hand clamped firmly around the normal gelten's throat and nearly had him lifted off the ground.

"My name is Jason Burke," Jason said, training his weapon causally along the loose assemblage. "I'm an associate of Felex Tezakar and have been tasked with finding his ship. We have confirmation that your vessel took the ship off of Restaria a few days ago. So … who wants to talk first?"

"I am Kade Trask of the 108th Legion," deep voice identified himself. "I will tell you everything that I know. As I said before, we were simply following orders to remove a suspect alien vessel."

"Kade," Jason nodded. "I'm overjoyed that we've decided we can resolve this as rational beings. So what's the story with him?" He was gesturing to the gelten being held with a vice-like grip by one of the other warriors.

"He was the liaison from command that brought our mission orders," Kade explained. "After you shot us down and informed us of whose ship we took, he became somewhat agitated. He tried to destroy the ship with all of us onboard and then ordered us on a suicide mission to rush you and the battlesynth once you accessed the bridge.

"I'm not absolving myself of blame and will stand in judgment before the Lord Archon, but it is almost certain that this is the person you actually want to question."

"Perhaps," Jason said. "Answer me one question and then we can decide how to proceed. Were there any crewmembers on or around the ship?"

"Yes," Kade confirmed. "The vessel had some sort of defensive system active and killed one of our crew. We then apprehended the two beings that were in the area and lifted the ship from above to nullify the ground defense system. Were these two also associates of Lord Felex?"

"Yes," Jason said tightly.

"They are still alive," Kade said.

That simple statement almost broke the dam that Jason had built to hold back any emotions that could threaten his mission effectiveness. He could feel the lump forming in his throat as it sunk in that his friends were still alive.

"One was injured during the initial stages of the operation, but both were handed over alive, although the more belligerent of the two was making things difficult on himself."

Twingo. That means Doc was the one injured.

"This brings up the obvious question," Jason said, pushing his emotions back down and getting back to business. "Who did you turn them, and the ship, over to?"

Kade nodded to the warrior holding the normal gelten, who in turned wound up and flung the much smaller being across the ten meters of separation so that he landed in a heap at Jason's feet.

"He will answer the who and why," Kade said. "We will then fill in any technical details you may need."

The gelten rolled over and looked up at Jason and Lucky.

"Do I really need to make a bunch of melodramatic threats to get you to—" Jason was interrupted by the gelten jamming his hand into a pocket and, lightning fast, shoving something into his mouth and chomping down on it. "Shit! No!" Jason dove at him and tried to pry his mouth open, but it was already too late. The gelten's eyes rolled back in his head and his body was wracked by convulsions so violent that his spine sounded like it may have snapped and he bit off half his tongue. It was over in an instant, and afterwards Jason was staring at a dead and quickly discoloring body.

"Son of a bitch!!" Jason raged to nobody in particular. As his temper rose, so did his adrenaline levels. Ignoring the rushing sound in his ears, he reared back and kicked the body hard enough to send it flying back towards the stunned warriors. Even they, who were raised in a culture of violence, were looking at the smallish, pinkish alien with slack-jawed astonishment. Jason put his hands on his knees and forced himself to calm down. *What the hell is going on with me?* He'd always had a bit of a short fuse, and that was something that was nurtured by his time in the military, but since Doc had been tweaking his DNA the reactions seemed to be much more extreme. When he looked up, Lucky, now out of combat mode, was staring at him with obvious concern.

"The mission logs have been deleted," Mazer said, joining the group. When he saw the body of the gelten crumpled up at Kade's feet, he looked at Lucky in confusion. "So, what'd I miss?"

"Of course they were deleted," Jason said, ignoring Mazer's question and taking a few steps towards the group of warriors. They all took two steps backwards at his approach, still eyeing him with distrust.

"Relax," Jason said, "I'm not going to shoot you or anything. I just don't feel like shouting across this field to talk. As of now you're my only chance of getting my crew members back and finding my ship. Please tell me you know where you dropped the gunship off."

They all looked at each other a moment before answering.

"I do," Kade confirmed. He gestured at the dead gelten before continuing. "He tried to keep the location a secret, but I made sure I knew where I was taking my ship."

"And you can tell me how to get there?" Jason pressed.

"I can do better than tell you," Kade said. "I will take you there myself."

"Why would you do that?" Mazer asked.

"I am hoping that my actions will be taken into account when I stand before the Lord Archon," Kade admitted.

"Good," Jason said. "I like that you're honest about your intentions. I'll tell you what, Kade ... if I get my crewmen back alive, I can guarantee that not only will you not be punished, but Lord Felex will be enormously grateful."

"How can you make such assurances?" Kade demanded.

"Captain Burke and the Lord Archon have a ... unique relationship," Mazer said quickly, shooting Jason a warning look. Jason realized his mistake as soon as he said it, Crusher was no mere warrior to most on Restaria. He was a legend, almost a myth that hovered near royalty and bordered on deity. The fact a strange, unknown alien was claiming to speak for the Lord Archon probably didn't sit well with Kade, especially given the geltens' borderline xenophobia.

"Perhaps I overstated things," Jason said. "All I meant is that Lord Felex trusts my judgment in matters like this. He will, of course, make his own decision." This seemed to mollify Kade somewhat as he considered it.

"That is the best I can hope for," he said after a moment of reflection. He then turned to his crew. "One hour after we are gone, you may activate the emergency beacon and call for a pickup."

"Are we picking up Kage first?" Lucky asked.

"No time," Jason said. "We're leaving. Now."

Chapter 19

Crusher paced the upper floor of the Legion Center in Ker. Every major city in Restaria had such a building—an administrative hub as well as contact point for Galvetor—and each was opulent in its own way. He was decked out in full ceremonial armor, crimson cape flowing down his back. He had worn this exact same armor for most of his twenty-eight years before being sent away from his home. It had seemed completely normal, even natural then. Now he felt rather foolish and juvenile.

The six years he had spent away, five of those with Omega Force, had left him with a more pragmatic turn of mind. Thinking of his crew gave him a pang of self-pity. He had been cut out of the loop. Jason had told him about his friends going missing as well as the *Phoenix* being stolen, but he had received no updates or requests for help. He knew the younger warrior, Mazer, had been seen with Jason and Lucky, but beyond that nobody knew where they were or what was happening. Connimon was avoiding him and he had no idea where Kage had run off to.

Crusher's mood had been bouncing from the aforementioned self-pity to anger at having been left out. He was still part of the team; why were they treating him so differently? He caught a glimpse of himself in a mirror as he was pacing and had to amend his train of thought. He knew exactly why they were treating him so differently.

"You seem troubled, my lord," Fordix said as he entered the room with the three Praetores of the Order trailing behind him. Morakar was also in attendance and took up a discreet position near the entryway.

"What do you know of your brother's whereabouts?" Crusher demanded, leveling a finger at Morakar and ignoring Fordix completely.

"I have not seen my brother or your companions since yesterday morning, Lord Felex," Morakar said in a strong, clear voice. "I am not aware as to where they might be, nor would I care to hazard a guess." Crusher appreciated the direct answer. Since it had been revealed to more and more of the people that he had returned, the near cowering deference to him was becoming aggravating.

"Would you go and see if you can find out what is going on?" Crusher asked in a softer tone. "When you do, report back to me and only to me."

"At once, my lord," Morakar saluted and slipped from the room.

"We have people who could locate them more quickly," Fordix said, walking over to the large, ornate double doors that led out to the terrace.

"And I have Morakar," Crusher said. "I trust him and I would rather not advertise the fact that I cannot keep track of my friends. When are we scheduled to meet with the Legion leadership?"

"Tomorrow at noon, my lord," Fostel said. "They are all in the city with their own honor guard but are still distrustful of each other. They have agreed to meet here at your command." Crusher stared at Fostel for a long moment, unsure as to why the Praetores of the Order were still hovering around now that the secret was being discreetly leaked out.

"It's good to see nothing has changed," he said sarcastically, clasping his hands behind his back. "Not only must we fight the bigotry of our own people and homeworld, we also must fight amongst each other like a pack of wild *kolvkiks.*"

"Perhaps you would do us the honor of addressing the Archon's Fist?" Zetarix said. "I'm sure they would be overjoyed to hear your words one more time before the news of your return spreads far and wide."

"You can talk to them yourself," Crusher said, dropping the stilted, formal manner of speaking. "I'm going for a walk, and then I am going to bed."

"As you wish, my lord," Zetarix said, his voice sounding like he'd been clenching his teeth. Crusher also saw the glare in the other warrior's eyes as he walked by. He stopped for a moment, considered answering Zetarix's challenge, but instead walked from the room. Not even half a decade ago he'd have beaten the other warrior to a pulp for such an outward show of disrespect, and if he died it would have been his own fault. But like his armor and cape, the commonplace things of his past now seemed absurd when viewed from the perspective of who he was now. Where *was* everybody?

*****

Kage was annoyed beyond all measure. He'd finally heard from Lucky and found out that Jason had blasted off with the captured captain of the ship that *he'd* found for them, without first coming to pick him up. Not only that, they'd not bothered to give him anything useful to do … just stored him in the safe house like a piece of unused equipment.

He'd spent the first twelve hours making improvements to the connections coming into the gear the Order had left in the flat so he could begin expanding his search. After climbing up on the roof and patching in three more optical cables, he was able to slice into the automated data traffic center and activate them so he could run all his connections in parallel, essentially turning four optical pairs into one big data pipe.

With the new bandwidth from the local nexus, he began slicing into any and all surveillance systems around Ker to get a real view of what was happening. As Jason had told him, the streets were now crowded with large, armed, and surly looking warriors. They were all eyeing each other with distrust as groups from all the legions roamed the area. He was quickly boring of gelten watching when a striking if somewhat absurd figure caught his eye.

Crusher was walking alone in the gardens area that was between the two towers that made up the Legion Center. He looked as sad and morose as Kage had ever seen another being.

"What have we here," he whispered, taking control of a few of the cameras and zooming in on his friend. He watched as Crusher looked around before sitting on a bench and staring at the ground.

"Aww," Kage said. "Somebody's sad. I better record this." As he began recording the feed from multiple angles, Crusher looked around again before slumping forward and eventually putting his face into his hands.

"Holy shit!" Kage exclaimed with glee. "Is he crying?" He leapt forward and zoomed two cameras in on Crusher's face as close as he could. "Come on," he coaxed, "just a couple tears. Just let 'em fall, big guy."

The alert tone from the slip-space com node interrupted him. He fully intended to ignore it until he saw whom the incoming channel request was from. With some regret, he pulled away and answered it.

"Hello, Kage," Kellea Colleren said. "How are things going?"

"I'm watching Crusher cry in a park. He's wearing a cape."

"Is Jason there?" Kellea asked after staring at Kage for a long moment.

"Nope. He and Lucky went with Mazer to get the *Phoenix* back," Kage said, still trying to look at the other screen. "Oh yeah, I was supposed to send you a message and tell you I found out what happened to her. Anyway, they think they have the location nailed down so they went to rescue Twingo and Doc and bring the ship back."

"Can anything just be normal with you guys?" she asked almost desperately. "If I give you a message, can you get it to him? Kage!"

"I'm listening!" Kage insisted, tearing his eyes away from the other monitor to look her in the eye. "Give the captain a message. Got it."

"Would you like to know what the message is?" Kellea said, rubbing her temples.

"Sure."

"Tell him I was able to break free. I'll be relocating the *Defiant* to Galvetor. I'll be there in four days," she said with slow, exaggerated speech. "Have you got all that?"

"Yeah, I'll tell him," he said. She reached over and forcefully stabbed at the control panel, killing the channel without saying goodbye. "What the hell was her problem?"

*****

"This is the last of the rations we pulled off of your ship, Kade," Mazer said as he brought three pre-made meals up to the flight deck.

211

"We are nearly there," Kade said. He'd been quiet during the entire flight. As it turned out, the rescue ship didn't have a functional slip-space drive. After pulling the *Phoenix* off the surface of Restaria, they had docked inside of a large cargo hauler that took them out of the system. The crew was not permitted to leave the ship, but Kade was smart enough to take a star-fix when they'd exited the craft to deposit the *Phoenix* on the surface. The planet was only a two day slip-space flight for the modern combat shuttle.

Lucky had passed the time by recounting stories of Omega Force's operations, slightly embellishing Crusher's role, to the rapt audience of Kade and Mazer. Jason noticed that his friend was very much at ease in the company of fellow soldiers, even those he just met. He also thought there may have been a certain kinship with the gelten warriors who had been shunned by their own kind and sent to inhabit an unwanted planet away from "normal" society. The downside of Lucky's new pastime was that it caused Kade to become more withdrawn from the shame of what he felt was an egregious affront to the Guardian Archon.

Jason completely understood following orders and not fully comprehending what the ramifications may be. From what he could tell, Kade had no way to see that something was abnormal about the orders coming down to him, and certainly nothing immoral. He made a mental note to talk to him in private. While Kade would only truly feel absolved when Crusher talked to him, there was no need to tiptoe around them in the cramped shuttle like an unwanted pariah.

"The ship says another thirteen hours of flight," Jason said, confirming what Kade had told them. "When we make orbit we'll need to confirm the drop-off location and then we'll wait for nightfall to make our incursion."

"Will you be able to make contact with the *Phoenix* from orbit?" Lucky asked.

"Not from this ship," Jason said. "Once the *Phoenix* goes into defensive mode she also locks out coms. But, if she's not under too much shielding and there's still power onboard, I should be able to ping her with my neural implant, even from orbit."

"What will we do with this shuttle once we have your vessel back?" Kade asked.

"I hadn't really thought about it," Jason said. "This is a nice little ship *and* brand new. It'd be a shame to just leave it on the surface."

"I would be willing to ferry it back to Restaria," Kade said, "if that would be permissible, of course."

"I don't see why not," Jason shrugged. "You're welcome to it if the *Phoenix* can still fly and we manage to escape. What are you going to do with it?"

"I will turn it over to my commander," the warrior answered softly. "He will not be happy my ship was destroyed." Jason almost told him not to worry about losing the rescue ship and that he'd have Crusher intercede. But that would not only be unhelpful, but insulting to a proud warrior who had lost a ship under his command, no matter what the circumstances were.

"Sounds good," he answered instead. "I'm sure your commander would be happy to have something so capable." They all ate in silence for a while longer before a chirping at the console attracted Lucky's attention.

"Incoming message from Kage," he said. "A lot of this does not make any sense, but I think the only relevant part is that Captain Colleren is on her way to Galvetor with the *Defiant*. He is also quite angry about being left behind and is making some implausible threats I am not sure he is capable of carrying out." Jason just rolled his eyes.

"So reinforcements are on the way? Excellent. Message back and tell him I expect him to stay out of trouble," he said. "I wish we had some way to get in touch with Crusher, but it's too risky with us not knowing what is really happening in that inner circle that's orbiting around him now."

"I will relay the message," Lucky said and turned back to the console. Jason closed his eyes and leaned back in the seat.

Hang on guys … we're almost there.

Chapter 20

"Is this planet even habitable?" Jason asked, looking at the data the shuttle was collecting on the dun-colored lump of rock they were orbiting.

"Only in the most technical sense of the word," Kade said. "Due to its proximity to the primary star in this system, the surface is so hot on the day side that it's unsurvivable, and the days are fairly short thanks to a fast rotation."

"I can see that," Jason said, still staring at his display. "Three hundred and forty-two degrees Kelvin at high noon … I can't survive in that without my armor and I'm pretty sure neither you nor Mazer can either. Lucky would be the only one of us still mission capable."

"The heat is only one of our concerns," Mazer said, also looking at the data readout. "The radiation levels are dangerous for extended stays on the surface."

"That means a night assault," Jason said. "While that's normally my preferred method anyway, I have to assume whoever is down there will be expecting that since they'll know as well as we that a daylight assault is too dangerous."

"From what intelligence I could gather, I don't believe they are expecting any kind of assault," Kade said. "They did not believe that we would know where we were due to our isolation within the cargo ship, and they appeared unconcerned about any of your crew that may have been left on Restaria."

"That's good and bad," Jason said with a frown.

"How is that bad?" Mazer asked.

"If they weren't worried about leaving four highly trained mercenaries behind, it means we were likely going to be taken out shortly after the ship was pinched," Jason explained. "This isn't good. Kage and Crusher could now be in serious danger."

"Lord Felex is under constant guard," Mazer protested.

"Yeah, and how many of those guards have been personally vetted?" Jason shot back. Mazer fell silent at that. "I'm not worried about Crusher anyway … God help the poor bastard that gets a hold of him first. There won't be enough left to mail home to his family. No, it's Kage that I'm worried about."

"He will be safe if he remains hidden," Lucky said. Jason just gave him a flat stare. "Ah," Lucky said finally understanding, "we will need to hurry."

"I'm missing something," Mazer said.

"The odds of Kage sitting still the entire time we are away from Restaria are not as good as your odds of surviving a walk on this planet in the daylight," Lucky explained.

They all milled around the flight deck of the cramped shuttle until the terminator could be seen on the horizon and nightfall was draped across their target LZ. Kade had pinpointed exactly where they had deposited the *Phoenix* and had spotted tracks from multiple wheeled vehicles leading off from the site and into the mouth of an enormous artificial cave carved into the side of a mountain.

While Kade hadn't been able to actually see into the cave, it stood to reason they would not have the ship brought somewhere that would require it to be moved long distances, and a cave would be someplace that could be protected from the heat and radiation with some simple, cheap technologies.

"I'm going to bring us in slowly and straight down," Jason said. "We'll be using a lot of fuel since the grav-drive will be working a lot harder, but we won't be spotted by any visual scanners by coming in too fast."

"We're ready," Mazer said.

"Alright then," Jason said, looking around. "Let's get this job done."

*****

"Now who are you guys?" Kage asked, still talking aloud to himself in a futile attempt to stave off madness while he sat alone in the cramped safe house. He was watching as a group of six beings, obviously not Geltens, approached the building he was in. All six were swathed in concealing clothing including loose, billowing outer garments and full facemasks.

They paused outside the main entrance and, trying to be discreet, began unpacking some serious firepower. That was all Kage needed to see and he began running through the egress plan he had developed while hanging around with nothing better to do. The monitors on all the stations began to flash and wash out into static as he ran a localized EMP emitter he'd rigged up over all the processing units. Next, he yanked the bulk storage drives, tossed them in the basin that was in the food prep area, and poured a powerful corrosive agent over them. The reaction was immediate as the drives began to dissolve and noxious gasses began flowing out of the basin and down along the floor.

Step two was to pop off an air duct grate and slip in, traverse the five feet of thin-walled ducting he had already cleaned out, and enter the empty unit next door through another grate he had removed previously. Once he was in the next unit, he reached out with his neural implants and activated all the anti-intrusion devices he'd rigged up, including some fairly powerful explosives.

He grabbed a bag near the door of the unit he was in that contained not only a change of clothes, but a veritable disguise, and casually walked out through the unlocked main entrance. He was nearly to the ground floor when the muffled *whump* of an explosion shook the building and dimmed the lights in the passageway. Shrugging, with a slight smile on his wide mouth, he ducked out into the rear side street and pulled the large hood of his cloak up and over his head.

Kage may not have had the brute strength and fighting ability of the one-half of his crew, but he was what Jason described as "slippery," and he wasn't saying it as a pejorative. His small stature meant people tended to overlook him, and his sharp intellect and cybernetic implants meant he missed very little and was able to run three or four probability chains in his mind simultaneously when deciding what to do. Before Omega Force, he'd been a career criminal and a thief, things he wasn't proud of with his newfound career and sense of purpose, but they had given him a unique skill set. Above all else, Kage was a survivor.

Had this been his old life and an operation had gone belly up, he'd have escaped much as he just had and then disappeared. But there were people relying on him and now that a strike team had just tried to take him out, he had confirmation that the *Phoenix* disappearing was not some bizarre, unrelated event. Someone was out to eliminate them and there was one member of the team who might not yet be fully aware of that. As Kage walked down the street, trying to remain nearly invisible to all the armed and agitated warriors roaming around, he looked up at the Legion Center towers and began to formulate a plan on how to get in. He had to get to Crusher and warn him that he wasn't safe.

*****

"You asked to see me, my lord?" Morakar asked respectfully from the entrance to Crusher's study.

"Yes," Crusher said. "Come in and close the door behind you."

"I'm afraid I still have no idea where my brother may have disappeared to," Morakar said, trying to hide his irritation. "But there have been some interesting happenings on Restaria I'm almost certain he was a part of."

"Oh?"

"One of our three remaining salvage carriers was shot down over the eastern grasslands three days ago," Morakar reported. "The rescued crew said that a modern combat craft crewed by a strangely mixed group, including a battlesynth, were the perpetrators. After that, I went to verify that the shuttle we flew from Galvetor was still where it was supposed to be. It was not."

"So," Crusher said thoughtfully, "the captain shot down one of our ships and then disappeared with Lucky and Mazer."

"And the captain of the salvage vessel," Morakar added.

"Tell me, as I was never very knowledgeable about those antiques, would one of them be able to pick up a DL7 heavy gunship?" Crusher asked. Morakar blinked twice without answering as the implications of what Crusher was asking sunk in.

"It could," he confirmed. "But that would mean whoever stole your ship would be someone within the Legions."

"Or have help from within the Legions," Crusher corrected. "Not necessarily the same thing. All I know is that despite his sometimes rash behavior, Jason isn't prone to acts of senseless violence and destruction unless he's sure he's standing on firm moral ground. He is a little shaky when it comes to standing on firm *legal* ground, however, but if he has information that the ship was used to take the *Phoenix* and possibly our missing friends, he would not have hesitated to act. What sort of insight can you provide of your brother's actions?"

"Mazer is quite young and impressionable, my lord," Morakar said uncomfortably. "He seemed to have an unhealthy obsession with any news we could get about you and your crew, specifically what you were doing out beyond Galvetor. Captain Burke would have had little trouble convincing him to do almost anything."

"Be that as it may, I trust the captain completely," Crusher said after a moment. "I also have no doubt that he will let us know what is going on as soon as he can."

"As you say," Morakar said, bowing his head respectfully.

"There was something more troubling you?"

"I've been out in the city recently, Lord Felex," Morakar said, seeming to choose his words carefully. "I'm becoming concerned about the number of troops in Ker. There are far too many warriors wandering the streets for an honor guard, and they are all armed with tactical gear, not ceremonial."

"You think there's something more at play here than we've been led to believe?" Crusher asked.

"I knew very little as it was," Morakar admitted. "I took it on faith that the Order was being honest. It made sense to bring you home in order to keep the Legions from fracturing and acting as independent units if Galvetor's civil unrest becomes any more serious, but I'm no longer certain that is what we're seeing."

"Explain," Crusher said with a frown.

"What if the goal of bringing you back was simply to consolidate the Legions in order to use their combined strength?" Morakar said. He spoke carefully so as not to betray the Caretaker's trust since she had asked him not to share her suspicions with anyone. But his first loyalty was to his people, the Archon, and so on until, finally, he reached Connimon. He would respect her wishes only so long as it didn't create a conflict with his duty. "Only you have the authority to do that without causing massive infighting among the leadership. A unified Restaria would be a frightening force if someone were to use it as a political tool."

Crusher just stared at Morakar for a long time, thinking. His silence was misinterpreted as an admonishment.

"Forgive my ignorance, my lord," he said. "I'm only a simple foot soldier and should not have presumed to know what—"

"Quiet," Crusher said, cutting him off. "Right now I need people around me who are going to be honest. Don't back down because you think I won't like what you have to say.

"Back to the issue you've raised ... I feel you may be on to something. I've had the feeling there's something at the perimeter of all this that I'm not seeing. If you think you can dig that up then that is exactly what you will do."

"Of course, my lord," Morakar said, somewhat relieved that the Archon wasn't angry with him. "I assume it will be the same arrangement as before; report only to you."

"You assume correctly," Crusher said. "Now get to work … we might not have a lot of time."

Chapter 21

"Captain, we have another incoming message from Kage," Lucky said. "Text only."

"Short version, Lucky," Jason said. "We're about to mount an assault on a fortified position with a handful of people and no heavy weaponry."

"He says we need to hurry," Lucky said simply.

"You can't be serious with that," Jason deadpanned.

"You said short—"

"Just give me the message in its entirety, please," Jason said with a patience he didn't feel.

"A fire team made up of non-geltens attacked the safe house," Lucky said. "They seemed to know exactly where he was. He was able to escape and even take out the assault team, but is now adrift in Ker. He is also concerned that Crusher may not be safe but is having a difficult time getting to him."

"I see," Jason said, hefting the plasma rifle he was planning on carrying. "So it looks like things are now in motion on Restaria, which means we haven't got long here either."

"Indeed," Lucky agreed. "I do not think it will be long before we get a look at the real reason we are here."

"What is that supposed to mean?" Mazer said defensively.

"It means that no matter what you were told, or your intentions, it's almost certain that we've been dancing along to someone else's tune this entire time," Jason said. "Now that someone tried to take Kage out and things within Ker seem to be moving quickly, it won't be long before we'll see who's been calling the shots."

"So you don't think the Order has been on the level about keeping Restaria out of Galvetor's internal politics?" Mazer asked.

"No offense, my friend," Jason said, "but I didn't believe that when Connimon first told us about it. But I don't doubt that's what you were told."

"Gentlemen," Kade said urgently from the rear hatch, "night does not last long, and the longer we sit in here the more likely that we will be spotted."

"Understood," Jason said. "Let's go."

When the hatch popped open, the blast of heat almost knocked Jason down. He immediately began to sweat profusely and watched as the dry air wicked it away almost as fast. This was a dangerous environment, even at night. He had landed on a small outcropping that was above and behind the cave entrance and would allow them to take advantage of what minimal cover there was as they approached what Kade had assured them was the entrance.

He switched his ocular implants to simple light amplifications since the ground was still so hot it was washing out his thermal mode to the point that picking his way carefully around the loose rocks and scrub was difficult. The descent wasn't especially long, but within ten minutes the geltens were panting and struggling and he didn't feel like he was faring much better. Lucky led the way down with his sure footing and imperviousness to the heat. Jason wished, and not for the first time, that the combat shuttle had been better equipped past the standard small arms locker.

Once they were all down through the narrow pass and standing at the cave entrance, Jason got his first good look at the tracks that were all around. While there were the tracks from what looked to be various ground vehicles, there were also larger tracks that could only have come from landing gear. Very large landing gear and, in fact, he could make out six deep ruts that could have very well been made by a DL7's tricycle landing gear.

Without speaking, the team moved to the right side of the cave opening and entered, hugging the interior wall. The passage looked to be mostly natural but Jason could make out tool marks on the walls where irregularities had been smoothed out and a larger clearance cut into the indigenous rock. They had moved into the tunnel about fifty meters when they came to a synthetic wall that completely blocked their way. He reached out with the butt of his rifle and knocked up against it, watching it shimmer as waves from the impact propagated outward.

"This is only an environmental barrier," he said. "It's not made to keep anybody out that's determined to get in."

"Do we try to breach here?" Kade asked quietly.

"Negative," Jason said back. "There will be a crew entrance somewhere near here. This won't be the only way in or out. Spread out along both sides of the tunnel."

They split up and began searching the walls of the tunnel. The structure was sixty meters wide and at least as tall, so it wasn't a necessarily fast search. Unsurprisingly, Lucky found the crew entrance on the left side of the tunnel a short way back from the thermal barrier. It was a small, irregular tunnel that branched off from the main passage and ended in a heavy alloy door.

"I do not detect any anti-intrusion devices or alarms, Captain," Lucky said quietly.

"Let's go ahead and make entry," Jason whispered back. He looked back over his shoulder at the two geltens and made a hand gesture he hoped they would interpret correctly as, '*Be ready when the door opens.*' Lucky turned the handle and the hatch unlocked with a painfully loud *clank* before swinging outward. After shuffling backwards to allow the door to open, the four of them peered inside at what looked like a small antechamber with an identical door on the other side.

"It's an airlock," Jason murmured. "They're going through a lot of trouble to keep the environment on the other side of that barrier stabilized." He nodded to Lucky and raised his weapon slightly as the battlesynth went and opened the second door even as Mazer was closing the first one. They timed it so that the latches moved at the same time and minimized the individual sounds they were making. Jason was impressed. That wasn't something they had prearranged, but the young Galvetic warrior seemed to have a natural instinct of how to operate within small-unit, covert teams. Kade was a pilot and the captain of a ship that had long outlived its usefulness, and it wasn't even a tactical vessel, but he was still a member of the warrior class and would be a force to be reckoned with if things turned out badly inside.

Beyond the second door was another tunnel, this one much longer than the first. They moved quickly down its length until they emerged into a dimply lit alcove that had protective equipment and suits hanging along one side. Jason grabbed one of the suits and held it out at arm's length: two legs, two arms, one head (or at least one neck); all much smaller than an average human adult. A quick look at the others confirmed they were all of a similar size and configuration. While he wasn't foolish enough to judge a species by its size alone, he was mildly relieved that they wouldn't be facing a force of heavy gravity bruisers the deeper they went into the facility. He was about to say so to his team when his neural implant gave him an alert. He was surprised to see it was an incoming message and hoped it was one of his crew before authorizing his wetware to accept it.

STATUS

DEFENSIVE PROTOCOLS ACTIVE

EMERGENCY POWER: 72%

Jason blinked in surprise as the message scrolled across his field of view. It wasn't exactly one of his crew: it was his ship. The *Phoenix* rarely initiated contact with him on its own, but the fact he got a message at all was heartening. "The ship just contacted me," Jason said. "She's on emergency power, which is dwindling, and the defensive protocols are still active."

"So that means it's still operational?" Mazer asked.

"Likely, but not guaranteed," Jason shook his head. "Hell, the computer core could be sitting plugged into a power source by itself and send that message. But it detected my tracking signal so I'm inclined to believe it's still intact."

"What about Doc and Twingo?" Lucky asked. Jason tried to query the ship, but got nothing useful in return.

"They're not onboard," he said. "Other than that I don't know. She just keeps giving me the same status message in response to anything I ask. The range may still be too great or there's some interference somewhere in here." He turned and waved for them to follow him out of the alcove and they emerged on the other side of the synthetic barrier. Jason tried to estimate how long the tunnel was they'd just come out of and figured that the ship-sized airlock must be nearly one hundred meters long. The main tunnel led off further into the mountain and appeared abandoned. "Let's get moving while it's still night hours. We may be able to catch them by surprise."

They picked up a brisk pace, hugging the left side of the tunnel, and each incredibly thankful for the cool, dry air on the inside of the barrier. It was another few hundred meters before they came upon the first thing of interest. It was the remains of a DL7 gunship, stripped down to the frame spars; the slag from the cutting tools was in random, solidified pools all around it.

"That's not the *Phoenix*," Jason said, taking a closer look. "This ship was completely original. Let's keep moving." They moved quickly by the dismantled vessel, the members of Omega Force deliberately avoiding the grim sight and trying not to ponder what may be happening to their own ship.

Past the first gunship the cavern opened up into a chamber so large the artificial lights couldn't reach the ceiling and even the walls barely reflected their glow. "This entire mountain must be hollow," Mazer remarked as they crowded up against the wall, out of the light.

"Let's hope not," Jason said. "Otherwise any of our normal escape methods will bring the top down on our heads." He reached out with his neural implant again and pinged the *Phoenix*. This time the ship was able to fully receive his burst transmission and respond.

STATUS

CORE: OFFLINE

WEAPONS: OFFLINE

MAIN ENGINES: OFFLINE

FUEL STABILITY: 4 HRS UNTIL COMPRESSOR FAILURE

HULL INTEGRITY: 100%

He looked around in the gloom at all the ships littering the cavern floor. There was another early model DL7, a DL9, a pair of DL6s and even the dilapidated hulk of an Mk XII transport. All of them were Jepsen Aerospace ships of various vintages and similar configurations. Most of them looked to be in various stages of disassembly, although butchering would be a more apt term for the damage being inflicted to these spacecraft.

But Jason wasn't looking at any of these very closely. The reason for that was tucked far back in the corner, only her nose sticking into the weak cone of light: the *Phoenix*.

"There she is," he whispered, "back in the corner."

"It looks like your ship is intact," Mazer said.

"I think whoever is running this Jepsen chop shop is waiting for the emergency power to run down to the point that the weapons and internal shielding will fail," Jason said. "I just received an updated status and the main reactor is offline."

"What is the status of the *Phoenix's* emergency power?" Lucky asked.

"Low seventies," Jason said. "But we have a bigger problem. In four hours the power will drop to the point that the compressors will fail and the fuel load will vaporize and get vented."

The *Phoenix*, like most modern starships, used liquid hydrogen as fuel in its antimatter reactor. It required a series of compressors and chillers for it to remain a stable liquid, and if those failed the hydrogen would boil and vent harmlessly out of the exhaust ports. The only issue after that would be a starship with an empty fuel tank. Jason was equally worried about trying to get the core started with less than ninety percent emergency power, but he kept that fear to himself for now.

"We seem to have plenty of time to get to the ship and begin the startup sequence," Lucky said.

"No," Jason said, raising a hand. "We need to get to Twingo and Doc first. If we get the ship started then they will either use them as hostages or kill them outright."

"Do you know where they're at?" Mazer asked.

Jason reached out to the ship again with his link. The answer was good and bad news.

CREW STATUS

CAPT. BURKE – FULL MISSION CAPABLE

FIRST OFFICER CRUSHER – UNKNOWN

SECOND OFFICER LUCKY – FULL MISSION CAPABLE

MEDICAL OFFICER "DOC" – INJURED, NON-LIFE THREATENING

CHIEF ENGINEER TWINGO – INJURED, CRITICAL

COPILOT KAGE – UNKNOWN

"The ship isn't able to get a location fix," Jason said. "But they're both injured … Twingo seriously. We need to move. We'll keep going along this wall and down towards what looks like a set of temporary buildings. I'm guessing those are quarters for whoever is running this little operation."

The small team moved out, skirting along the edge of the lit area and relying on Lucky's sensors to warn them of any danger in their path. The work area was vast and it was taking them longer to move around the perimeter than Jason would have liked, but he would be of no use to Twingo if he walked into an explosive booby trap or headlong into a heavily armed patrol. Knowing his friends were alive renewed his energy and focus, but also knowing one of them was gravely injured fueled his impatience.

They had moved right up against the cheap, temporary buildings when the first sounds of life reached their ears. It was a pair of voices coming from one of the doorways closest to the floor where the ships were parked. Apparently this was the night watch, and they weren't very concerned about security within their facility.

"Your turn," voice one was saying.

"Don't you know any better games?" voice two answered.

"Nope," one said. "Just roll them. Our shift is almost over anyway."

"How much longer do you think we'll be stuck in this horrible place?" one complained. "After that last ship is torn down I can't imagine we'll have to stay much longer."

"Unless they bring in more Jepsens," two said.

"Don't even say that," one said. "That last one was bad enough. Whoever owned it must have supplemented the emergency power cells."

"Maybe," two said with indifference. "It would go a lot easier if that little bastard they captured with it would give up the security codes. I've never seen someone so small take so much punishment."

"Torture is an inexact science," one said. "You may have overdone it. He has to be convinced that there is a way out for him. If you make him believe that he'll die no matter what, he has no incentive."

"I was tired of his stonewalling," two said. "I guess it doesn't matter anyway since I doubt he'll live through the night. We'll have to start on the other one after that, I guess."

Jason had heard enough. He could feel his blood pounding in his veins as his heart began to race. His vision began to gray out around the edges and there was a loud rushing sound in his ears. "Captain..." he heard Lucky call, but he seemed far away.

He circled around and slipped in through the doorway, looking down at the two seated aliens. He vaguely registered that he knew this species and that they thrived in hot climates, their green, pebbled skin reminding him of certain lizards on Earth. They looked up at him in complete shock, their game forgotten.

"Who are—"

The voice Jason recognized as number one was cut off as he took two strides into the room and backhanded him hard enough to send him flying out of the plastic chair and into the wall on the far side. Jason continued the crossing motion until he was turned and facing the second alien who was still too shocked to move, much less reach for his weapon.

Jason grabbed him by the throat and lifted him easily out of the seat. The alien's survival instincts finally kicked in and he tried to pull a stubby sidearm out of a waist holster, but Jason saw it and grabbed the offending hand and slammed it into the table until he felt the bones break. The alien howled and Jason picked him up as high as he could reach before slamming him bodily down into the table and pinned him flat, his hand crushing the throat just enough to dissuade any further resistance.

He heard a grunt followed by a sharp impact and looked up in time to see Mazer standing over the other alien with a balled fist. Jason nodded to him and turned to his captive.

"Now ... are you going to tell me what I want to know? Or am I going to have to try out some of that inexact science your friend was talking about?" he asked in Jenovian Standard.

"I'll talk," the alien wheezed.

"Where are the two captives you were just talking about torturing?"

"This building, one level up."

"How many guards?"

"None, they're secured to the walls," the alien said, trying to shift his body to get the pressure off his throat. Jason tightened his grip and lifted him by the throat and waistband before tossing him across the room into a heap by his partner.

"Lucky, with me," Jason snapped. "Mazer, watch these two. Any sign they try to call for help ..."

"Kill them," Mazer finished with a savage snarl. "Gladly."

Jason and Lucky sprinted from the room and back out into the open cavern. He'd spotted the external stairwell leading up the next level when they'd initially approached the building. He tensed and launched himself up the stairs, landing only two steps from the top. As soon as he cleared out of the way, Lucky followed suit, easily clearing the entire flight and landing next to Jason with a surprisingly soft impact.

"I detect no security systems or possible traps," Lucky reported. Jason grabbed the locked handle and twisted it until the metal crunched and the latching mechanism gave way. He put his shoulder into it and burst into the room … he was not prepared for what he saw.

Doc was huddled in one corner, chained to a bar that ran the length of the back wall. His left arm was obviously broken and his face was swollen and malformed. His clothes were in tatters and he'd obviously not been near soap and water for days.

Twingo was unrecognizable. The damage to his face due to multiple beatings looked severe, and Jason couldn't fathom how he was getting air into his lungs. His right ear had been cut off and it looked like they'd gone to work on his upper torso with the same knife. He appeared to have multiple fractures in his extremities and his rib cage appeared to no longer be symmetrical.

"Lucky, cut their restraints," Jason said quietly. Doc's head came up at his voice and he looked at the two in disbelief.

"Captain?"

"Be still, Doc," Jason said gently. "We're getting out of here."

"Twingo … get Twingo," Doc mumbled, falling forward as Lucky cut his restraints. Jason went over to his best friend and waited for Lucky to come over and use his laser to cut the chain holding Twingo's left arm to the bar.

"I'm going to try and get underneath him," Jason said. "I'll carry him. You help Doc." When he glanced over, he could see that Doc had already struggled to his feet and was trying to come over to help with Twingo. As gently as he could, he slid his friend out away from the wall until he could crouch down and ease both his arms up under his torso. Then, with excruciating slowness, he straightened his back and carefully pulled each leg up underneath him until he was standing with the smaller, blue alien cradled to his chest.

"Jason," Twingo tried to speak through his ruined jaw. "I didn't tell them anything." Tears streamed freely down Jason's cheeks as he looked down at his friend.

"I know you didn't, buddy," he said quietly. "Now don't worry about anything, I'm getting you out of here."

"The ship ..."

"Shhh ... She's fine, Twingo," Jason said as he moved towards the door with Lucky and Doc in tow. "You did good, they were never able to board."

They made it down the stairs with no incident and walked around to where Mazer was standing in the doorway of the room the guards had been lounging in. When he saw Twingo's condition, his jaw clenched and his eyes flashed. He looked at Jason, the unspoken question hanging between them. Jason nodded once, his eyes reflecting the young warrior's anger. Mazer turned and walked back into the room. Shortly thereafter there was a muffled scream that was abruptly cut short with a wet *snap*. A moment later there was a sharp Galvetic roar, and then another sickening crunch of bones. Without a look back, Mazer and Kade walked out of the room and fell in behind the members of Omega Force as they walked across the cavern floor towards the *Phoenix*. Jason reached out with his implant yet again to talk to his ship.

COMMAND ACKNOWLEDGED

DEFENSIVE SYSTEMS DEACTIVATED

MAIN CARGO HATCH AND RAMP OPENING

MEDICAL BAY PREPARED FOR WOUNDED

Even from their distance of over fifty meters, Jason could hear the whine of the actuators as the rear ramp of the *Phoenix* lowered into place. One thing he hadn't counted on was the sudden harsh glow of the cargo bay lights shining out into the cavern, now quite obvious since the tail of the gunship was outside of the internal lighting the salvage crews had been using.

Walking as quickly as he dared with his grievously wounded friend, Jason eased up the ramp and was halfway up the stairs to the crew entry hatch when he heard Lucky close the rear pressure doors and raise the ramp.

"*Phoenix*, reinitialize external defensive protocols," Jason called out. "Ten meter perimeter."

"Acknowledged," the computer's emotionless voice said.

When he got to the infirmary, he realized that there was an oversight that they'd never corrected in all their time owning the vessel: there was only one medical table.

"Shit," Jason muttered as he gently deposited Twingo onto the bed and stepped back. Doc, limping heavily, walked in behind him.

"I can handle this, Captain," he said. Despite the obvious pain he was in from an unset broken arm and multiple blunt force wounds, Doc walked over without hesitation and began commanding the automated systems to begin Twingo's emergency treatment. Jason felt humbled at the courage the pair had shown, and were still showing, throughout what must have felt like a hopeless situation.

"Captain Burke," Kade's voice said quietly behind him.

"Yes?"

"Although I am only trained in rudimentary field aid, I believe I can be of assistance to your medical officer," Kade said. "I can at least be his hands since he is quite injured himself."

Jason thought about it before nodding in gratitude. "Thanks. That will help a lot I think."

"If I may ask," Kade continued, "are you fully capable of cold-starting this vessel with less than three-quarters of your emergency power and no chief engineer?"

"That's a good question."

Chapter 22

"Morakar!"

Morakar stopped and looked around. This was the second time he'd heard the urgent, somewhat high-pitched voice whisper his name. He was walking down one of the side streets that led away from Ker Commons, a square in the middle of the city, and had been getting the feeling for a while that he was being watched.

"Over here!"

He looked over and saw a diminutive figure gesturing for him to approach the darkened area where the storm runoff would normally flow between the buildings. The figure was clad in loose-fitting black garments and had a hood pulled far up over his head. Suspecting a trap, Morakar approached with caution. Even though it was exceedingly rare, there were some species that took the chance of engaging in criminal activity within the cities of Restaria. They normally didn't live long enough to regret their decision once they were caught.

As he drew closer, he saw that the being was gripping the edge of the building with two hands, and then adjusted his clothing with yet another hand. Morakar relaxed his stance immediately and walked quickly over to where he was being beckoned.

"Kage," he said in greeting. "I am happy to see you were unhurt in the explosion at the safe house. What happened?"

"I barely made it out unhurt," Kage corrected. "There was a six-person assault team that was just getting ready to breach when I slipped out through the adjacent unit."

"There were no bodies when Internal Security arrived," Morakar said, looking at Kage dubiously. "You are certain about being attacked?"

"I know what the hell it's like to be attacked," Kage snapped. "Likely far better than you do, if we're honest. My little party favor couldn't have killed all of them; the survivors must have grabbed the bodies and moved before security showed up. You at least had to have found where I destroyed all the equipment."

"There was nothing in the report," Morakar said apologetically. "If you left behind damaged equipment they may have grabbed it along with the bodies of their fallen cohorts. What species were they?"

"I couldn't tell," Kage said. "They were wearing masks and concealing clothing. Far too small to be geltens, though. Damn! That's one of the main reasons I've been following you … if I knew the species then I would have a much better place to start trying to find out who is attempting to kill us."

"Us?"

"There is no way this is unrelated to the disappearance of Twingo and Doc, not to mention the ship," Kage said. "Unfortunately we've pissed off so many people this may not even be related to anything happening on Restaria or Galvetor. It could have been someone that happened to track us here. Remember the stealth ship that tried following us from Colton Hub?"

"It does make sense," Morakar admitted. "Have you warned Lord Felex yet?"

"That's the next thing on my list after finding you," Kage said. "There was no way I could get to him inside Legion Center with all that security."

"He is schedules to address the legion leadership within the hour, so there will be no time to reach him before then," Morakar said. "In the meantime, let's adjourn to someplace a little more inconspicuous and compare intelligence."

"Preferably someplace where I can grab something to eat," Kage agreed and followed the big warrior out of the square.

"Actually, I have something a bit more entertaining in mind," Morakar said speculatively as a lieutenant of the 8th Legion strolled by, obviously intoxicated.

*****

Crusher paced back and forth in the small chamber just off of the main assembly area, his formal armor creaking and rattling with each movement. His annoyance with the attire was beginning to reach critical mass. How he had ever worn the ridiculous outfit every day of his previous life was a mystery to him. He did notice that his temper and irritation seemed directly proportional to the lack of information about his friends. He had sent Morakar out a day ago and had yet to hear anything back.

"We're almost ready for you, my lord," Connimon said as she poked her head in.

"Please enter, Caretaker," Crusher rumbled. She moved apprehensively into the small antechamber, as the current foul temperament of the Lord Archon had become somewhat legendary in recent days. When she had fully entered the room, he continued, "What do you make of the current troop buildup in the city of Ker?"

"I'm certain I don't know what you mean, my lord," she said smoothly. She was good. Crusher would have accepted the lie at face value had he never left Restaria. But being around the scum of the galaxy, not to mention world class liars like Twingo and Kage, he was able to detect the slight narrowing of the eyes and the involuntary twitch of her mouth. Whatever was going on, she didn't trust him with the information.

"Of course," he said. "Just some random reports I've been receiving. Nothing firm." He listened for a moment as the three Praetores addressed the assembled crowd. "Do you think this is wise? Will a unified Restaria be enough to stave off the unrest on Galvetor?"

"Perhaps for a time," Connimon said carefully. "But we're being inexorably pulled into the larger galaxy around us. A purely isolationist policy may no longer be practical for our worlds. You, more than any of us, should be able to appreciate that given your recent past." Her tone of voice told Crusher she was trying to suss out his feelings on the issue rather than making a declaration of her own.

"That is not for us to decide," Crusher said firmly. "We've been the guardians, the last resort, and the main deterrent for any potential enemies for as long as we have a written history of our kind. I will not throw away a millennium of tradition and tip the balance of power to any one political side."

"Of course, my lord," she said, almost sadly.

"We are ready for you, Lord Archon," Fordix said from the doorway. Crusher hadn't heard him approach and wondered how long he'd been standing there.

"Very well," he said with a deep sigh. "Let's get this over with."

When he emerged onto the raised stage, a thunderous roar rose from the crowd, such a noise that it could have drowned out a starfighter's engines. Crusher stood in the center and let them view him. Though there had been rumors and sightings, this was the first time their

241

Guardian Archon had been before them in an official capacity in over a decade. He could feel the energy in the room. It was intoxicating, electric. He raised his arms, trying to signal for silence so he could begin his prepared remarks.

As he slipped back into his old role, the thrill of being on stage soon fled and was replaced with an old familiar ache. With his new perspective gained from his time with Omega Force, he now knew that ache to be self-loathing.

Chapter 23

"We have three hours until daylight, Captain Burke," Kade said. "They will undoubtedly be starting their dayshift soon."

"I'm aware of the time, Kade," Jason said patiently. "This cannot be rushed, however, unless you want to be atomized in less than a millisecond if it goes wrong."

The warrior said nothing, but did turn and leave the engineering bay so Jason could continue his work uninterrupted.

Starting an antimatter reactor that had been shutdown was a touchy thing. First, there had to be enough power available to engage the isolators: magnetic constrictors that prevented the antimatter from coming in contact with the conduit walls and destroying most of the ship. Then the antimatter generators had to be brought online, and they used a tremendous amount of power. They would convert hydrogen atoms into anti-hydrogen and send them through the antimatter manifold, along the short conduit, and into the injector housings. At the same time, hydrogen atoms from the same fuel source would prime the injectors on the other side of the core. When the controller fired the injectors, hydrogen would meet anti-hydrogen and the resultant atomic annihilation would release a tremendous amount of energy the converters would then use to power the ship. Once it was all up and running, the reaction was self-sustaining and quite stable; any problem and the small amount of antimatter on hand would be jettisoned.

One problem, however, was the fact that if there was less than eighty percent emergency power, all the needed subsystems could not be safely operated. A deep space combat vessel wasn't without more than one backup, but now Jason had to figure out the best way to employ them without the help of his engineer. He looked over the myriad of individual control panels and indicators, sighing in disgust. Twingo always made it look so easy.

"Computer," he said. "Are the two emergency fuel cells charged?"

"Affirmative."

"If both fuel cells are activated to supplement Main Bus A, will there be enough power to start the main reactor?"

"The power level would not be within acceptable safe limits to attempt a main reactor start sequence," the computer told him dispassionately.

"What would the available power be up to? Give me the answer in a percentage based on emergency power cell outputs," Jason said.

"Eighty-seven percent."

"What are the power levels needed to start the main reactor given it starts on the first attempt? Tell me the accepted minimum and the absolute minimum."

"A nominal reactor start needs ninety percent to be within acceptable safety limits. Absolute minimum is eighty-five percent," the computer droned.

"How long would it take to bring the backup fusion reactor online?"

"Two hours and twenty minutes would be required for the backup fusion reactor to begin supplying power."

"And how long after that before we could start the main reactor?" Jason asked, knowing it was a useless question.

"An additional three hours would be required."

"Shit," Jason muttered. "At least an absence of choices means it's impossible for me to make the wrong one … start both emergency fuel cells and apply the power to Main Bus A. Decouple Main Bus B from emergency power cells and alert me when peak power from all three sources has been reached."

"Acknowledged."

He left Engineering and walked up through the darkened interior of his ship towards the bright lights of the infirmary. He looked in through the transparent double doors at his friends. Doc, his arm now set and in a sling, was dozing in a chair with a tablet computer grasped loosely in his good hand. His face was partially covered with med-patches that were addressing the swelling and soft tissue damage to his face.

Twingo almost couldn't be seen under the coverings and various apparatus that Doc had brought to bear to save the little engineer's life. Not wanting to disturb them, Jason went to the bridge where Mazer and Kade were standing watch, looking out the canopy at the cluster of buildings and waiting for signs of life from the morning crew.

"Anything?" he asked, slumping into the pilot's seat.

"All is still," Kade said. "There are not even any lights in the building we are assuming is their sleeping quarters."

"Let's hope even if they find our handiwork they won't put two and two together and get four," Jason said absently as he brought up a few of his displays.

"Isn't two and two actually four?" Mazer asked, confused.

"It sure is," Jason said, not bothering to clarify the idiom. The two warriors shrugged at each other and went back to their watch. Jason accessed the infirmary through his multi-function display and called up the computer's assessment of Twingo's condition. The explosive breath he blew out when he read it startled both geltens, but he hardly noticed them. It was right there in plain text what the computer thought Twingo's chances were:

Prognosis: Full recovery after nano-treatment.

So Doc's medical nanobots would work their magic and his friend would eventually make a full recovery. The sense of relief he felt nearly overwhelmed him. He drilled down into the report a bit further and saw that the ear his torturers had cut off would need to be cloned and reattached. It was all fairly standard treatment for everything else including a short bout of physical therapy once he was ambulatory again. The list of significant injuries was daunting, though. Those scumbags had really worked him over.

"Emergency power is now at eighty-eight percent," the computer's voice broke into his musings. "Fuel cell backups are now at peak power output."

"Acknowledged," Jason said. "Activate antimatter containment system. As soon as containment is stable start primary antimatter generator."

"Confirmed," the computer said. "Antimatter containment activated. Time until primary antimatter generator start: five minutes."

"I'll be in Engineering, guys," Jason said as he hopped out of his seat. "Keep a look out and call on the intercom if things get interesting." He took the steps off the command deck four at a time and jogged through the common area until he made it to the port engineering bay. More displays and indicators were now active and the familiar ambient noise of the area was picking up as the ship came back to life. He watched the indicators carefully as the magnetic constrictors were charged and stabilized and the entire antimatter containment system reached peak efficiency. The coolant lines hissed and frosted over as they kept the superconductors within the antimatter conduits chilled down to cryogenic temperatures.

"Activating fuel flow pumps," the computer reported. "Antimatter generation from primary source will commence in approximately twenty-five minutes." The ship had dual redundancy when it came to its antimatter generators, but with such limited power available for a restart, Jason didn't dare try and bring them both online at the same time. Once the main reactor was providing power he would be able to bring the rest of their systems up individually. He watched as the manifolds were charged with antimatter and the countdown the computer provided marched towards zero.

They were coming up to the most dangerous part of the mission, or at least the part where they would be the most vulnerable. When the main reactor started there would be a lull until it produced enough power to bring the primary flight and weapons systems online. At the same time, the procedure would have exhausted their emergency power to the point that the defensive systems may not have enough juice to ward off a committed boarding party.

"Computer, open an intercom channel to the bridge," he said as that last line of thought crossed his mind. When he heard the confirmation chime, he continued. "Mazer, I want you and Kade to rotate down here one at a time. I'm opening up the armory and I need you to grab some more substantial hardware than the pop guns that were on that shuttle."

"Acknowledged, Captain Burke," Mazer's voice floated from the speaker in the ceiling.

"Computer, unlock and open the armory," Jason said. "My authorization."

"Acknowledged," the computer said. "Armory now unlocked."

He went back to monitoring the antimatter levels in the injector assembly. When Mazer walked into the engineering space, Jason simply pointed to the heavy blast door to his left that led into the armory. Mazer veered off without a word and smacked the control to open the door. An excited hoot floated out from the open doorway as the warrior walked around in a circle, taking in all the weaponry Omega Force had collected over the years.

"Just grab something that makes sense to repel boarders," Jason called. "I don't want holes in my hull."

"No problem, Captain," Mazer shouted back. "You know, with all these toys have you considered an assault on the enemy's position while we have the advantage of surprise?"

"Jesus, he even sounds like Crusher," Jason mumbled before raising his voice again. "Of course I did … I ruled it out. Enough people have almost died in this debacle already. We're relatively safe in here and we have no idea what sort of force they can marshal out there." As Mazer was still poking around in the armory, Lucky came into the engineering bay to stand beside Jason.

"Where the hell have you been?" he asked.

"I have performed a complete security sweep of the ship," Lucky said calmly. "It appears as if our initial assessment was correct: nobody has boarded the ship since we disembarked on Restaria."

"That's good to know," Jason said. "It'd be a shame if we managed to survive this long to be taken out by a planted explosive as we leave."

"Have you thought about what will happen before the reactor has enough power for us to lift off?" Lucky asked as he took a look at all of the indicators.

"I've got our geltens drawing weapons from the armory," Jason said. "The fact they were waiting for the power to drain until they tried to board leads me to believe their main goal was to take the ship intact, so we'll set up a defense in the cargo bay if it comes to that."

"Why do you think they took the ship in the first place?" Lucky asked after a moment. Jason was well aware of Lucky's borderline obsession with what the synth Deetz had said before he died and didn't want to get into yet another conversation about it. But the cavern floor being littered with the carcasses of other, similar Jepsen ships did give him pause.

"I'm not sure," he said, unable to think of anything that Lucky wouldn't be able to see through. "It could be just a group of salvagers." He could feel the battlesynth's eyes boring into the side of his head as he refused to look over.

"I know you do not actually believe that," Lucky scoffed. "Those other ships look like they have been dissected, not salvaged. Someone is looking for something." Jason sighed heavily.

"Perhaps," he conceded, hoping to end the conversation. "But let's concentrate on getting out of here and then we can revisit your long running conspiracy theory."

"I fear I will be proved correct in the end," Lucky stated emphatically.

"Fine," Jason said, "but we already know there's nothing on this ship. She's been stripped down to the spars and built back up by the Eshquarians. Half her major components aren't even Jepsen manufacture." He was spared any further comments by Mazer walking out of the armory. Both Jason and Lucky did a double take as he emerged sporting two enormous plasma rifles. He was also wearing Crusher's body armor, ill-fitting as it was on the smaller warrior.

"Why two rifles?" Jason asked, ignoring the pang the visual created. It felt wrong that they were in the middle of a dangerous op and Crusher wasn't there with them.

"What do you mean?" Mazer asked, confused. "For when the first overheats."

"Overheats?" Jason asked, looking at Lucky. "I've never had one of those overheat and I've drained the power cell in a single salvo multiple times."

"Really? All the plasma weapons we have overheat and shut down if you maintain a rate of fire that's too high," Mazer said, looking over the weapon in his right hand.

"I saw your weapons," Jason said sympathetically. "They were well-maintained, but about two generations behind our stuff. Save yourself the weight and just grab one but take as many power cells as you can manage."

Mazer just shrugged and walked back into the armory.

"It is strange seeing him in Crusher's armor," Lucky remarked.

"Yeah, it is," Jason said, already knowing what the next question would be.

"Do you think he will still be a part of our team when the immediate crisis on his planet is over?"

"I don't know, buddy," Jason said finally. "I've been trying not to think about it too much."

The maudlin mood was broken up by Mazer walking out of the armory with an enormous smile on his way back to the bridge.

"Injector assemblies fully charged," the computer reported. "Manual input required for reactor initialization."

Jason moved over to the main control panel and began to enter the commands that would authorize the computer to begin the antimatter reaction. He watched as the chamber integrity was checked again and the pressure was confirmed to be as close to a complete vacuum as the equipment was able to achieve. Once the final checks were complete, the control panel indicated that he could initialize the reaction. He pressed the blinking green icon on the panel and held it for three seconds. The icon disappeared and the panel reconfigured itself for the familiar normal operation mode he was used to seeing it in.

For a few moments it seemed like nothing was happening, but soon the deck began to vibrate as hydrogen met anti-hydrogen and the pressure within the reactor chamber began to climb. The computer slowly began to increase the fuel feed until there was enough energy coming from the reactors for the converters to begin generating power for the ship.

Jason watched as the converters began to supply power to Main Bus A, albeit at an alarmingly slow rate of increase. He looked over the instrumentation one more time before stepping back.

"Computer, once power levels reach sixty percent, re-engage Main Bus B," he said. "Do not begin recharging emergency power cells until I say. Keep all external lighting and indicators off and wait for my command before powering up specific ship systems."

"Acknowledged."

"Let's head up to the bridge," Jason said. "We can monitor the reactor progress from there and begin to figure out our overall strategy." They passed Kade in the common area as he was on the way down to the armory.

"This way, correct?" he asked.

"Lucky can show you," Jason said, nodding to the battlesynth.

"If you would follow me," Lucky said, turning around and walking back the way he had just come. While Jason's gut told him Kade wasn't a threat, it also didn't make sense to turn him loose inside an enormous weapons cache right next to one of the ship's main engineering areas. Thankfully Lucky had picked up on his inflection and escorted the gelten without question.

When he arrived on the bridge, more of the stations were active and there were dozens of winking status lights, each vying for his attention. A cursory inspection showed that most of these were just warnings that a particular ship function was not active. He sat down at the bridge engineering station and promptly smashed his knees into the console.

"Damnit! Short little bastard," he muttered, unlocking the seat and shifting it around so he could sit comfortably. The station was one of the few on the bridge that was fully active and he could see that the reactor was still steadily climbing in power and, in turn, the power available to the ship was increasing. Still far short of being able to even think about bringing engines online, but enough that the reactor was now self-sustaining and their depleted emergency power cells were no longer the immediate concern.

"Won't they be able to see all the light from your displays, Captain?" Mazer asked, staying at his post near the canopy.

"They can't see in," Jason said distractedly. "The canopy has an active layer that makes it opaque from the outside."

"Nice," Mazer said. "We've got a little activity. Two targets, same species as our friends, walked out of what we think is the bunkhouse and have walked into another building. The lights have come on in that building but that's been it so far."

"So we're probably looking at the cooks," Jason said, moving up beside Mazer. "I'm always amazed at how much alike we all are. We're separated by millions of years of evolution, unfathomable distances, and who knows how many other differences … but we all want breakfast as soon as we wake up."

Mazer made a snorting laugh at the unexpected commentary. "They haven't been down to the guard shack yet, obviously," he said. "They also don't appear overly concerned that the two haven't made an appearance yet."

"I think our first impression was right," Jason said. "These guys are either complete amateurs or wildly complacent considering how many expensive, rare ships they've stolen. Maybe we should have gone for a frontal assault after all."

"We're doing the right thing," Mazer said after considering it a moment. "Like you said, we're not sure what they have hidden in that complex and it's big enough to house dozens of troops. Besides, slaughtering sleeping soldiers is not one of my preferred methods."

"Nor ours," Jason said. "There's no way they won't find those two bodies before the *Phoenix* is ready to leave. There's an outside chance that they'll think it was an inside job and suspect one of their own."

"That's not going to last long," Mazer said. "Once they check on their little torture chamber they'll know something is going on."

"Maybe," Jason said. "Either way, we may be fighting our way out."

"Main Bus A at sixty-one percent capacity," the computer said. "Main Bus B coupling." There was a *thunk* under their feet as the load contactors for Main Bus B reset.

"About time," Jason said and jogged over to the pilot's seat.

"Good news?" Mazer asked.

"Very," Jason said. "All the power on this ship is multiplexed so that things can be rerouted and closed down in the event of battle damage. The two main buses are tied into the MUX and each can independently power all systems. When coming up from a cold start and needing as much capacity as possible, we'll run the reactor hot and split the output between the two busses so we can get the ship fully operational without stressing Main A or blowing out any power junctions."

"All of that sounds … interesting," Mazer said, indicating it was anything but. "I'm sure Twingo will be impressed you've been able to get everything running without him."

Jason winced at that. "Actually, he's going to be livid *and* an absolute nightmare to be around when he gets back on his feet," he said. "I've bypassed about a dozen safety checks and have been relying almost completely on the main computer to handle the details of the reactor start. By the time this is all done it will probably take him a week just to find out if I've damaged anything beyond repair."

Mazer went back to his watch as Lucky and Kade walked onto the bridge and Jason went about bringing up individual systems. He was again relying on the computer to fill in the gaps as he gave it broad, general commands. First up were the repulsors. There was no way the grav-drive was going to be available, and even starting the process of charging the emitters would bring everyone in the cavern running towards them. He also began charging the capacitors for the weapons, but held off for the moment in priming the fuel flow regulators for the main engines. That would be his last step, since the process emitted a loud, screeching whine accompanied by fuel vapor being vented out of the nacelles.

He went over everything he'd just done one more time just to make sure he hadn't inadvertently created some conflict that would blow the ship up. As he'd hoped, there was nothing he'd done so far that would ruin the illusion that the *Phoenix* was a lifeless hulk, so he just waited and watched as the power levels continued to creep up. In a situation like this, power was life.

"Looks like we've got some action, Captain," Mazer called. His voice was urgent, but calm. Jason climbed out of his seat and looked out over the cavern. Their handiwork had been discovered and four of the aliens were standing around the doorway of the guard shack, obviously agitated.

"Shit just got real," Jason said, this time completely confusing Mazer, who now wore a mildly disgusted look. "It's just a matter of time before they discover Doc and Twingo are missing, and then they'll know exactly where to start looking."

"How close is the ship to being combat capable?" Lucky asked.

"Not close enough," Jason said grimly. "We need to keep them out of that upper room. We need a distraction."

*****

"This is OUTRAGEOUS!! Release me!"

The warrior strained against the thick alloy straps holding him fast to the chair, which was itself anchored to the floor.

"You would be wise to start answering my questions," Morakar said calmly. "I want to know why there has been a full deployment to Ker. What are you preparing for?"

"I will answer nothing. You have no authority to detain me. When I get free I will make sure you are severely punished for this." The warrior had refused to give his name, but Kage had run his biometric scan through a database he'd sliced into and found out he was high enough in the rank structure of the 8th that he should be well aware of why they'd deployed in force, and with full gear, to Ker.

"I don't have much motivation to keep you alive then, do I?" Morakar asked, smiling humorlessly. "As I said, answering me would be your best—" A knock at the door interrupted him. "Too late," he said. "Open the door, Kage."

Kage walked over and unlatched the heavy door and allowed it to swing open. Meluuk walked in and nodded to them both.

"Who is this?" the bound warrior demanded. "I'm to be intimidated by some overgrown gelten?" Nobody answered him or even looked in his direction. They stood silent as another, much larger figure entered the room.

"Not him," the figure said in a deep rumble before pulling the hood of his cloak back.

"Lord Archon!" the warrior practically wailed. He tried to bow, but the restraints held him tight. "Whatever offense I have given, allow me to give restitution. If not, I will take my own life."

"Oh shut up," Crusher said disgustedly. "Nobody is going to kill themselves. But you are going to answer Morakar's questions about the troop buildup within my city."

"His first name is Zellon," Kage said quietly, handing Crusher a data pad. "He's one of the 8th Legion's lieutenants and reports directly to the Primus. Am I saying that right?"

"Close enough," Crusher said before looking back at Zellon. "Well?"

"I don't understand, my lord," Zellon said, looking around the room in genuine confusion. "Is this some sort of test?"

"My patience has never been very good," Crusher said as he stepped forward. "Lately it's been wearing even more thin. I'm going to assume you're not a complete imbecile, so we will start from the beginning. Why are there so many troops deployed here?"

"Those were our orders, my lord," Zellon said crisply.

"From whom did these orders originate? Who authorized the 8th to mobilize?"

"You did, my lord," Zellon said. "I saw the orders myself, signed by you. We were to discreetly disguise fully operational units within our honor guards and deploy to Ker for a ceremony in which it would be revealed you had returned." Crusher stood up and exhaled loudly, rubbing the back of his neck.

"Unbind him," he said to Morakar. "We are going to continue this discussion as civilized beings. Try anything stupid, and I'll tear your throat out myself." Zellon said nothing as Morakar released the straps, but the look on his face said that he didn't doubt Crusher's threat.

"To be clear, I gave no such order," Crusher continued once Zellon was free. "So obviously someone with access to my encryption seal has been issuing orders that I can make no sense of. What was your mission to be?"

"There are one hundred combat landers hidden beyond the foothills outside of Ker. All I know is that within two days we're to board them for a live operation," Zellon said.

"Those landers don't have slip-drives," Morakar said. "Was someone else going to pick them up and transport them to the area of operation?"

"I intend to find out," Crusher growled. "One more thing: Why was part of my crew captured, my ship stolen, and another of my crew attacked?" He didn't really believe a lowly lieutenant would have those answers, but it was worth a shot.

"I am unaware of any of those incidents, my lord," Zellon said.

"Do I really need to tell you this is a conversation not to be repeated?" Crusher asked him.

"Absolutely not, my lord," Zellon said emphatically, eager to ensure he survived the conversation at all.

"Very well, you're free to go," Crusher said. "But there is one more thing … you are now an active asset of mine. Anything you learn beyond what you've already told me and you're to report directly to Morakar Reddix. Is that clear?"

"Perfectly clear, my lord," Zellon said, standing and bowing his head deeply.

"Go," Crusher said. The warrior wasted no time edging around the people standing in the cramped room and making a hasty escape. Not wanting to risk the Lord Archon changing his mind, he could be heard running full speed down the darkened corridor. "Well isn't this an interesting development," Crusher said after he'd gone.

"This is getting confusing as hell," Kage said. "Who would know how to fake your digital signature?"

"I think the answer is simpler than that," Crusher said. "With me gone there was ample time for someone to gain access to my office and acquire my encryption codes. It would be safer than trying to fake it and getting caught."

"So what do we do now?" Morakar asked.

"You two make yourselves scarce," Crusher said. "I'm going to go have a little chat with the Praetores of your Order."

*****

"Lord Felex," Fordix said mildly, "do come in." The comment was made after Crusher flung the door to his offices open hard enough to damage the handle when it smashed into the wall.

"What do you know of troops being deployed within Ker that are on active assignment?" Crusher asked, ignoring the quip. "Did you know a hundred of our combat landers are also loitering in the area?"

"Since when do you concern yourself with the day to day operations of the Legions?" Fordix asked.

"Since when have you decided you are allowed to not answer my questions?" Crusher countered, not in the mood for a "teachable moment" from his old mentor.

"You seem quite agitated by this," Fordix said, still not directly answering the question. "What is this special interest in what appears to me to be simply a routine troop movement?"

"And again you seem to completely—" Crusher's words died in a strangled curse as he stiffened in shock and fell to the floor without even an attempt at catching himself. He couldn't move his limbs at all and his jaw was clenched shut, but he could still move his eyes. They tracked to the right to see Connimon walk around him, an odd apparatus in her hand. She looked down at him sadly before addressing Fordix.

"The device has a firm grip," she said, looking at the small disc with six barbed legs that she had pressed into Crusher's neck. "Nearly all of his voluntary functions are disabled."

"Can he speak?" Fordix asked, also walking up to gaze down at Crusher.

"No," she said. "Even the eye movements will eventually be suppressed. If the device stays attached too long it will begin to shut down his involuntary functions as well."

"There was no other way," Fordix told her gently. "Leave the control with me and continue your preparations." She nodded without speaking, seeming quite distraught. She handed the long-handled device she'd been carrying to Fordix and quickly left the room.

"She really is a gentle soul," Fordix said as Crusher's eyes blazed at him with unbridled hatred. "I can see it was wise for me to have you ... disabled. I'd thought a few times of approaching you, asking for your help even, but you're far too high-minded for that. You simply can't grasp the bigger picture, can you? That's been one of your greatest weaknesses all your life. I do regret this most undignified ending for you, but you're far too dangerous to confront directly."

Fordix walked behind Crusher and lifted him up by his armpits, dragging him over and propping him up into a slouching position in a large chair.

"There," he said. "We'll want to get that done before your arms and legs stiffen up too badly. This really isn't anything personal, Felex, but from that look in your eyes I can see you'll never look at it that way. Which, unfortunately, means I can't leave you alive when I leave here.

"To be honest, you've surprised me a bit. The old Felex wouldn't have been concerned with anything out of the ordinary. Only your own ego and glory drove you. Forgive me if I sound disrespectful, for I have nothing but the highest regard for your position ... but I've been less than enamored with you personally. All those years of raising you, advising you, trying to make you into something you had no interest in being: a real leader for our people." Fordix began to pace the room, his speech becoming more agitated as emotions pent up for decades overcame him.

"You were the most gifted warrior born in generations," he continued, almost seeming to forget Crusher was even sitting there. "Size, speed, power, instinct ... you were the epitome of what a Galvetic warrior could be. Yet you failed miserably in your most important task. We have been under Galvetor's boot for centuries and you did nothing but strengthen that hold. So many of us hoped for so much when it became apparent that you would be the next Guardian Archon. Our chance to be free of the homeworld's stifling influence was at hand, and then you betrayed us all by agreeing with nearly every accord passed down by a corrupt ruling body bent on keeping us subjugated.

"Now our chance to end this virtual slavery is at hand. With the infighting on Galvetor about how much outside influence they should accept or exert, we were able to convince certain members of both political sides that the Legions would be open to supporting their cause. They will welcome us with open arms, and by the time they realize we're not there to participate in their petty squabbling it will be too late. We will remove the current, corrupt government and negotiate a new existence with Galvetor. If they refuse ... well, we'll already have ten thousand warriors in the capital." Fordix walked to the wall-length window and looked out over the city, idly twirling the device Connimon had given him in his left hand. He looked back at Crusher with an emotionless gaze.

"I knew you'd never agree to this," he said. "You would never have come back if you suspected that your only role in this operation was to provide the Order with a unified Legion. I'm not sure if it's a lack of courage, a lack of conviction, or simply a lack of moral fortitude, but I knew you could never be trusted to act in our best interests. You've been a puppet of Galvetor your entire life, a dancing fool, and you took to your role gladly. At least in this, your last act, you will have done something to help your people."

He walked over to the large desk that was in the center of the office and picked up a short, wickedly curved sword. He dropped the device he'd been carrying on the desk in its place. He pulled out a com unit and spoke into it, ignoring Crusher as he paced the office. "This is Fordix, you're clear to begin the operation. Good luck and I will meet you there shortly." He flicked the device off and slipped it back into a pocket.

"As I said, this is not the warrior's death I would have preferred for you, but I'm also not a fool. Challenging you to single combat is a death sentence for anyone stupid enough to try. So instead, this will have to do." He walked up and placed the blade's tip low on Crusher's chest and then slid the sword in with one smooth motion. Even with his current paralysis, Crusher's body tensed up and began to move on the chair.

"Recognize the blade?" Fordix asked as if he were discussing the weather. "It's the one I gave you at the ceremony that installed you as Guardian Archon. If there is an afterlife, I hope you'll have understood I did what I had to by the time I meet you there."

Fordix walked from the room, swinging the door shut with a loud boom. Crusher rolled eyes downward, looking at the ornate handle of the sword still sticking out of his chest. He could feel his blood flowing from the wound. He looked up to the ceiling, unable to believe this was truly how his life would end ... stabbed with his own blade by the person he had looked to as a father figure all his life.

Chapter 24

"It looks like we're patched into their com system," Jason said from the sensor station. He'd been negotiating with the integrated communications systems of the facility the *Phoenix* was stashed away in and, with the help of the main computer, it looked like he could command some rudimentary overrides. It was a stroke of luck that the security on their networked systems was as nonexistent as their physical security of the facility itself. Their over-confidence, or gross negligence, had given him the opening he needed.

"Not a moment too soon," Mazer said, still watching anxiously out the canopy. "They've seemed to calm down a bit and are now methodically searching the other buildings. It's just a matter of time before they discover their captives are missing."

"We're nearly ready," Jason said, hopping back into the pilot's seat. "What I find bizarre is that the cause of death on their two friends isn't exactly something you'd expect to find if one of their own did it. One neck snapped like a twig and a crushed throat with accompanying claw wounds? I'd have expected them to look for intruders immediately."

"When things are so outside of the expected, the correct conclusions are rarely reached first," Kade said.

"Everybody ready?" Jason asked. All three on the bridge gave him an affirmative signal. "Computer, open an intercom channel to the infirmary." When he received a double beep confirmation, he continued, "Doc, we'll be lifting off momentarily. This will be a thrust lift with no grav-drive assistance so it's going to be rough. Are you guys secured down there?"

"We're as ready as we're going to get," Doc's voice came back. "But I'd take it as a favor if you initialized the internal gravity quickly after takeoff. Twingo won't be able to handle too many high G maneuvers without it."

"Understood," Jason said and closed the channel. "Computer, are the repulsors primed to fire on my command?"

"Affirmative."

"Initiate com override, all channels and full volume," Jason ordered. "Stand by for audio source."

"Channel open. Standing by," the computer affirmed.

"Queue song from Burke Personal Audio," Jason said, "AC/DC, Thunderstruck."

"Audio file located. Queued."

"Play file," Jason said. As the opening licks to *Thunderstruck* began blaring out of every speaker in the facility, including computer stations and personal com units, he was surprised at just how loud a racket it was creating. He took advantage of the noise immediately. "Bring all weapons online and begin charging shield emitters," he said as he reached over to his engine management panel, switched the four big main engines to "pre-start" and allowed the heaters to kick on and the fuel system to purge.

When the bass drums began pounding out of the speakers as the heavy metal song built in intensity, the residents of the cavern began milling around in the open, some clamping their hands over their ears, all looking at each other in utter confusion. A few tried to disable some of the offending audio sources, but the override was too complete to simply switch it off. Jason looked up and saw his Galvetic friends were not immune to the pounding rhythms as Mazer's foot began to tap in time with the music and Kade's head was shallowly bobbing as well.

"What is this?" Mazer asked finally.

"AC/DC," Jason said, "it's from my homeworld."

"Is this a battle song of your people?" Kade asked.

"You know, I guess it sort of is," Jason said. "I know it's likely sparked more than a few fights in its time."

"It's outstanding," Mazer said.

The *Phoenix* was really showing signs of life now as power surged into her systems and indicators were turning green all over Jason's status board. "You two will want to get strapped in now," he said. "It's nearly too late for them to try and board." As the two warriors grabbed two of the chairs at bridge stations and strapped in, the final indicator lit up to tell Jason he was cleared to lift at any time. He knew with the cooling loops now active, the vents for the heat exchangers were likely letting off a visible steam from the top of the ship. Confirmation of this came as a handful of the aliens pointed at the *Phoenix* and began walking towards it as the punishing guitar riffs assaulted their ears, which Jason hoped were extremely sensitive. He waited a few more seconds as they got closer and the song's intensity began to peak.

You've been … thunderstruck…

"Fire repulsors!" Jason barked. The *Phoenix* was instantly engulfed in dust and smoke as the ventral repulsors exploded to life and began to lift the gunship off the cavern floor. Tools, stands, and other equipment were blasted away from the ship and right into their would-be boarders as the ship slowly continued to rise. Only one looked to be still alive, but he was quickly obscured as the debris cloud from their liftoff rolled across the cavern floor. The vibrations were horrendous without the grav-drive to dampen things out. He reached over and flipped the main engines to "standby" but left them there. The repulsors were doing enough damage; the massive plasma engines would begin throwing debris around that would be dangerous for them as well as anyone stupid enough to still be outside.

He flicked the hat switch on top of the control stick and began easing the ship out over the main floor area using the maneuvering thrusters. They were just enough to get the big ship moving but not so powerful that any overcorrection on his part would slam the ship into the wall. Next, he retracted the landing gear and finished activating all the weapon systems. Looking down, he saw that the power levels were holding steady and even continuing to climb a little bit.

"Are we going to fire on our friends out there?" Mazer yelled over the roar of the repulsors, nearly deafening inside the enclosed space.

"No!" Jason shouted back. "I'm not going to end this mission by bringing down a mountain on our heads when we're almost out of here." During his slow maneuver out to line up with the exit tunnel, Lucky had come over and sat in the copilot's seat and began configuring the panels to how he wanted them.

"I can operate our weapons and sensors from here, Captain," he said.

"Excellent," Jason said, "I'll need the help." He let his friend take over getting their defensive and offensive systems ready and concentrated on avoiding all the obstacles strewn about the cavern floor while at the same time trying not to overfly anything that the repulsors would turn into a missile. They were entering the area where it choked down to the entry tunnel, and if something were hurled at the rock wall with enough force it could come back and damage the ship.

His tactical display lit up with a warning and the rear sensor feed showed that the workers who weren't injured or killed during their initial ascent were now pursuing them and firing small arms into the tail of the ship. The light anti-personnel weapons could do nothing but leave faint scorch marks on the hull. Jason just hoped they weren't bringing up something more substantial in the meantime.

Once they entered the tunnel, the buffeting from the repulsors really picked up within such a confined space and Jason began to become quite concerned about the jostling on Twingo. He commanded the internal gravity system on and that seemed to help somewhat, but it was still an extremely rough ride. He would have liked to pick up the pace but he was concerned not only about the resonance damaging the *Phoenix* but possibly collapsing the tunnel as well.

"It looks like we'll emerge just at daybreak," Jason yelled. "It'll be hot as hell, but survivable. Do you still want that shuttle, Kade?"

"Yes, Captain Burke," Kade answered.

"Then get down to the cargo bay if you can," Jason said loudly. "I'll stop near the shuttle and activate our transit beam for ten seconds. After that you're on your own."

"Thank you, Captain," Kade said as he handed his plasma rifle to Mazer.

"Good luck," Jason called as the older warrior hurried by and off the bridge.

"Captain, we are now within range of the airlock barrier," Lucky said.

"You're clear to engage with the plasma cannons at your discretion," Jason said, squeezing the trigger on the stick twice to give the computer command authorization to allow Lucky to fire the weapons. A second later, the tunnel ahead was brilliantly lit up as the plasma cannons in the leading edge opened up, bathing the entire bridge in red.

The barrier appeared to be made of a flexible material that was stretched tight across the opening. When the first plasma bolt slammed into it and burned a section away, the entire surface snapped and retracted into the walls of the tunnel. The remaining bolts continued through and took out the outer barrier in the same manner.

"Well that was easier than I thought it was going to be," Jason admitted as he increased his forward speed and flew them out of the mountain and into open air. He breathed a huge sigh of relief as the ship had a big open sky above it again. The tension of weaving it through such tight confines without the fine control of the grav-drive had been nerve-wracking. He keyed open an intercom channel to the cargo bay. "You're up, Kade. I'll be opening the troop hatch in a few seconds." He closed the channel without waiting for a response, eased the ship over to near where they had left the combat shuttle, and climbed to a safe altitude to allow the warrior off the ship while the repulsors were still providing primary lift. "Lucky, open the belly hatch and deploy the transit beam," he said.

"Copy," Lucky answered and his hands danced across the controls to allow Kade off the ship. Jason counted off thirteen seconds in his head, more than enough time for Kade to be out of the ship and clear.

"Close her up," Jason ordered, reaching over and switching the main engines to "active." There was a short whine followed by the always comforting *boom* of the mains igniting. He grabbed the throttle and advanced it, sending them climbing up into the brightening sky of morning. "Lucky, begin taking sensor sweeps of the surrounding area and arm two thermobaric missiles, maximum yield," he ordered.

"Scans of surrounding space show no threats," Lucky reported. "Missiles are armed. What is our target?"

"We're going to give our friends back there a little parting gift for all the hospitality they showed our crew," Jason said as he accelerated along the ridge line and swing them around into a tight turn to face back the way they'd come.

"Missiles set to traverse the tunnel and detonate in the center of the cavern, staggered trigger," Lucky reported. Jason looked and saw the two weapons pop up on his tactical panel as available. He selected them both and opened the forward weapons bay doors as they flew back towards the mouth of the tunnel entrance.

When he was within two hundred meters, he braked to a halt and allowed the ship to settle into a hover. He could see a group of workers desperately trying to repair the barrier as the sun continued its inexorable march into the sky. They looked up at the hovering gunship, seemingly undecided if they should retreat, continue working on the barrier, or open fire with their pitifully inadequate weaponry.

He watched the combat shuttle lift and clear the area and decided to make their choice for them. He squeezed the trigger and held it as two missiles were ejected off the racks and streaked away from the ship, going supersonic as they entered the tunnel.

The results were more energetic than Jason had predicted. First, a blast of debris, including the barrier repair crew, was ejected from the tunnel at tremendous speed. Then the mountain itself began to sag along the southern face and, ever so slowly, the peak began to sink as the entire mountain seemed to collapse in on itself. With a look of grim satisfaction, Jason swung the nose of the *Phoenix* away and began to climb up out of the atmosphere, her main engines roaring over a now truly deserted planet.

They made orbit quickly and were joined in formation by the Eshquarian combat shuttle piloted by Kade. He said he would be happy to stay until the *Phoenix* was capable of slip-space flight, so Jason had Lucky and Mazer prepare a sealed transit box of provisions to send over to the shuttle since he knew they'd eaten everything on board during the trip out. Once they were gone, he told the computer to maintain a high level of alertness and inform him if the sensors picked up anything entering the system. The stealth ship near Colton Hub was still firmly in his mind as he walked off the bridge and towards the infirmary.

"I see you've been busy," Jason remarked as he walked in. "How do you feel?"

"Since my injuries were fairly light compared to his, I'm doing quite well," Doc said. His arm was still in the sling, but Jason could see that the bone had already been knitted by the medical nanobots and the swelling in the limb was reducing significantly.

"I'm glad to hear that," Jason said. "And Twingo?"

"I'm not going to lie; he's still in a lot of danger," Doc said. "But I believe he's out of the most critical stage. He couldn't have handled the shock of a full nanotech treatment despite the computer trying to inject them behind my back every ten minutes. I've been doing targeted treatments over the last couple of hours using nanobots with strict programming. I've been able to repair the worst of the damage to his circulatory system and have been supplementing his oxygen supply to make sure his brain isn't in danger."

"I'm going to have to try and get the slip-drive powered up and active without him," Jason remarked, "so we won't be pushing it on the way back to Restaria. I'll try to keep the flight as smooth as possible so you can keep at it."

"I'd appreciate that," Doc said. "But what I could really use is a more completely equipped facility. Unfortunately there isn't one to be found on Galvetor or Restaria that doesn't cater mostly to geltens."

"Then you'll like this next bit of news," Jason said. "The *Defiant* will likely reach the Galvetor System about the same time we do."

"That *is* good news," Doc agreed. "Their sick bay rivals some planetside hospitals I've been at."

Jason nodded and turned to leave. "Good work saving his life," he said. "Keep me updated and I'll leave you alone to your work."

"Thanks for coming after us, Captain," Doc said seriously before Jason reached the door.

"It's good to have you guys back," Jason said quickly before leaving, not wanting to become overly emotional in front of Doc. He went down to Engineering and checked on all the systems before pulling up another terminal. Thankfully, Twingo had insisted on training up others on the crew about certain aspects of the ship in case they were ever in a situation exactly like the one they found themselves in.

He began by performing a full diagnostic of the hardware and then powered up all the control and safety systems. Twingo had also written a few scripts that could be executed to perform batch commands and bring up certain parts of the system in the correct order without him having to remember each little step. Once everything looked good and the computer agreed that the system was fully prepped, he initiated the charging sequence for the emitter coils. After a flurry of activity, during which there were bangs, whines, hisses, along with chatter from the control panel, he could feel the slight tug of the gravity shifting in the aft part of the ship as the emitters charged and began to form small gravitational eddies. It would all normalize once the drive was fully charged and stabilized, so he left Engineering and made his way back to the bridge to wait.

Like most of the major systems on the DL7, the slip-drive emitters were new and state of the art, so the charging time would be a fraction of what it had been when they'd been flying the original Jepsen equipment. But the delay still rankled him now that he had his ship back. He wanted to get Twingo to a proper medical facility, grab Kage, figure out what Crusher was doing, and then blast out of the Galvetor System as fast as the *Phoenix* could carry them.

*****

Kage and Morakar were walking slowly along the halls near the Archon's offices in the now-abandoned Legion Center. They couldn't figure out why it seemed everyone had left, and had sent Meluuk to the other tower to see if the story was the same over there.

"Even the normal sentries aren't at their post," Morakar said quietly. "This is quite strange." They moved along the halls for a while longer, having not met anyone other than a single cleaning bot and a young male gelten administrative assistant who had forgotten something in her office. She was unaware of anything out of the ordinary, so they let her go on her way.

Morakar was also unable to raise Fordix, the Praetores, or even the Caretaker on their com units. He knew Lord Felex had gone to confront the Praetores about what was happening within the city of Ker, and the fact they could no longer raise any of them was of great concern to him. He and Kage had been steadily working their way up the tower, looking for any signs of life as they went.

"This is just getting plain creepy," Kage said after they'd cleared another floor and were walking up the outer stairwell to the top floor. Morakar halted so fast that Kage walked into the back of him. "What is it?" The Galvetic warrior was sniffing the air, drawing in deep breaths slowly and blowing them out through the side of his mouth.

"Blood," he said simply. "gelten blood. Come on." They raced up the stairs, following Morakar's sense of smell, and ended up in front of the ornate door of the actual office the Guardian Archon used to execute his duties. Rearing back, Morakar kicked it near the handle and sent it flying inward.

"I don't think it was locked," Kage remarked as he squeezed in past the big warrior and looked around inside the office. "Oh shit!" Morakar turned to see what Kage was looking at. Still propped up in the chair was Crusher, his eyes closed and an enormous blade sticking out of his midsection.

Kage moved over to his friend and checked for vitals. "He's still alive, but it looks like he's lost a lot of blood."

"The blade looks like it just missed his heart," Morakar said. "Beyond that I can't tell." Kage reached out for the knife handle, but Morakar grabbed his hand firmly. "Don't. That may be all that's keeping him from bleeding out right now. Who could have fought the Lord Archon and won with such a decisive blow?"

"Nobody," Kage said, turning Crusher's head to the left to expose the small disc still affixed to his neck. "This is interesting indeed. These are only used by Eshquarian Intelligence as far as I know and aren't available for general sale."

"What is it?"

"It's a neural disruptor," Kage said, taking a close look at the device. "It can be programmed per species and then can inhibit any signals you want. It looks like someone paralyzed Crusher and then stabbed him through the chest."

"So we're looking for someone he would have trusted," Morakar said.

"Right now I'm looking for a way to disable it," Kage corrected. "These are almost always rigged to either explode or kill the victim if tampered with. See if you can find the deployment tool … it will look like a long silver baton." As Morakar searched the room, Kage leaned in and extended his hand. Thin tendrils of nanobots extended from his fingers and began probing around the base of the device. He explored the inner workings of the inhibitor using his neural implants and the connection provided by his specialized nanobots and was able to conclude that the device was indeed set to kill Crusher if anyone tampered with it.

"Is this it?" Morakar asked, walking over with a silver-handled device he'd picked up off of the desk in the center of the room.

"Yep," Kage confirmed, "bring it here." He slowly inspected the device before releasing his nanobots once again to infiltrate the device and explore around. While the neural inhibitor was rigged, the remote used to deploy it was not. Kage was able to gain access to the relatively primitive logic inside the wand and command it to disable the inhibitor on Crusher's neck. As soon as he did, his friend pulled in a long, ragged breath and arched his back, moaning loudly.

"Easy, big guy," Kage said, placing a hand on Crusher's chest. "You've got about a meter of sword sticking out of you so let's not making any sudden moves." Crusher had already lapsed back into unconsciousness and didn't answer him.

"I don't understand how he hasn't bled out yet," Morakar remarked, inspecting the wound up close.

"It's the nanobots in his blood. He's carrying a load of general medical bots that will automatically detect trauma and do what they can to stabilize him. The whole crew is, actually," Kage said. "I'd guess whoever stabbed him wasn't aware of our unit's standard operating procedures or they'd have never left him alive like this."

"I have a very bad feeling about who may be responsible for this," Morakar said. "What should we do now? I'm not sure who in the city we can trust, but he obviously can't be left like this."

"Let me get to the com node here and I'll try to get in touch with the captain," Kage said, standing up and looking around the room.

"What com node?" Morakar asked. Kage was making a beeline for what appeared to be just another bit of paneling not unlike the rest that covered the walls. He messed about for a bit, digging at the edge, before the panel rose up into the ceiling and a fully equipped slip-space com node slid out from an alcove.

"This one," he said with a smile. "I could feel it in here the moment we walked in," he said, tapping a finger against his oversized cranium and winking at Morakar. He went about configuring the unit, a surprisingly modern piece of equipment by Restarian standards, and allowed the transceiver's slip-space field to form around the antenna, which was located somewhere else in the building.

Once the field had stabilized and the com node indicated it was ready, Kage began to input the destination address and the encryption standards he knew from memory. It took a few minutes before the other com node negotiated with the unit he was using and opened a channel.

"Kage?" Jason's voice came from the speaker. "Where are you?"

"I'm in Crusher's office," Kage said. "I was playing a hunch … I'm assuming you're sitting on the bridge of the *Phoenix* right now?"

"Correct," Jason said. "We've reclaimed the ship intact and are currently in slip-space heading back to you. Twingo was very badly wounded, Doc was beat up but looks like he's recovering quickly. I'm guessing this isn't a social call."

"Crusher's been stabbed through the chest with what looks like a ceremonial short sword," Kage said grimly. "He was propped up in a chair in his office when Morakar and I found him. His nanobots are keeping most of the blood flow staunched, but he's going to need serious medical care soon and we don't think there's anyone here in Ker we can trust." He could hear Jason blow out an exasperated sigh.

"I started the core myself, so I'm a little leery of pushing the engines too hard," Jason said. "I can risk seventy-five percent slip … that puts us there in under five hours."

"If we can keep him calm that long it should be enough," Kage said as Morakar shrugged with uncertainty. "By the way, prior to being stabbed he was paralyzed with one of those tricky neural disruptors that Eshquarian Intelligence likes to use."

"That's an interesting development," Jason said. "I plan on putting down right in the square in front of Legion Center. What sort of reception can I expect?"

"Probably none," Kage said. "The city is more or less abandoned. I'll explain more when you get here. I'm killing this connection to see if I can raise the *Defiant* ... they may be closer than you guys."

"Copy that," Jason said. "We'll see you soon."

The channel cut off and Kage began to reset the node for another connection. He began punching in the connect codes that would open a channel to the *Defiant's* unsecured node since he didn't have the encryption codes for a private channel to the ship's captain.

The com station began its automated cycle to open a connection over such vast distances. The *Defiant* was also in slip-space, so that made it all the more challenging. Kage set the unit to alert him if it was able to make a connection and went back to check on his friend. He hoped Crusher was as strong as he seemed and was able to hold out until help arrived.

Chapter 25

Jason leapt out of the pilot's seat and ran down to the infirmary, stopping just before the door so that he didn't burst in like a wild man and startle either of his wounded crewmates.

"Doc, we have another problem," he said as he walked into the room.

"That seems to be something we don't have a shortage of," Doc said blandly. "What's happened?"

"Kage just made contact. Crusher's been stabbed through and through with some kind of sword. He said the nanobots you put into all of us are keeping the bleeding to a minimum, but he and Morakar are unable to get proper medical help," Jason said, raising his hands in a helpless gesture.

"How far out are we?" Doc asked.

"I just cranked our speed up," Jason said. "That makes it just under three hours until we hit Restaria's atmosphere."

"If anybody can hold out, it's him," Doc said, getting up out of his seat. "I'll get a kit together. It it's just an impalement, an emergency infusion should be able to not only stabilize him but repair the damage on the spot depending on what was pierced along the way."

"I'll keep you updated on our ETA if I decide I want to risk coaxing more speed out of the engines," Jason said. "Right now everything looks nice and stable and the computer is reporting everything well within limits."

"Thanks," Doc said distractedly as he moved about the small infirmary. "By the way, Twingo woke up for a few seconds. He knows he's on the *Phoenix* right now. As soon as I told him that he fell into a deep, natural sleep. That's the best thing for him right now."

"That's a good sign," Jason said. "I'll be up on the bridge." He quickly made his way back to the pilot's seat and looked over the instruments. Even though it had been a risk, he'd pushed the engines up to eighty percent after talking with Kage. Looking over his indicators, he was reluctant to push them any harder without an actual engineer looking things over. They'd be no good to anyone if a variance between the two engine emitters tore the ship to atoms. Crusher would just have to hang on a little longer.

Instead of fretting over things he couldn't control at the moment, he busied himself making sure the rest of his ship's systems were ready for whatever might meet them when they emerged in the Galvetor System. Even though he wasn't fully confident in his engine configuration, the main reactor was now at full output and the defensive and offensive systems were at full readiness.

*****

"You'll want to look at this," Kage said tightly. Morakar and Meluuk, who had joined them after searching the other tower, left Crusher's side and joined him at the computer terminal that was next to the com station, the latter of which was still trying to contact the *Defiant*.

"It's the capital," Morakar said with quiet awe. "That's why the landers didn't need to have a carrier ship, they were only flying across the system to invade Galvetor."

"What does this mean?" Meluuk asked as he also stared at the monitor.

"It means the warrior class has once again betrayed its people," Morakar said in a pained voice. "We've overthrown the rightfully elected government on the homeworld and I can't imagine that it was for a legitimate reason." The news feed on the monitor showed the capital city on Galvetor in complete chaos. Fires burned brightly, citizens were running in panic, and armored warriors patrolled the streets, sometimes opening fire on sporadic resistance by the city's law enforcement.

There was no accompanying commentary with the feed, only randomized scenes of the destruction. The scene abruptly changed to the capital building itself, and whatever doubt there was about a violent coup was erased when they saw the Praetores of the order, along with Fordix, walking among the elected officials of Galvetor's government. All were restrained and on their knees.

"Is there sound with this?" Morakar asked. Kage messed with the controls on the terminal a bit until Fordix's voice could be heard clearly over the din of the chaos outside the chamber.

"—too long this body has been corrupt, inept, and blind to the fact that Galvetor can no longer survive on its own without outside assistance. Some of you recognize that, most don't, but either way you waste away the years with endless debates and public polling instead of being decisive leaders.

"Yet during all this debate and lecturing by supposed enlightened intellectuals, not one of you has thought that the banishment of the warrior class was something that should be reconsidered. No one has felt that a unified gelten race would be advantageous as we move forward. More importantly, as you've all squabbled about how Galvetor would benefit greatly from trade alliances, Restaria is forgotten except when used as a bargaining piece ... slaves to be sold to the highest bidder to fight their battles while the spoils flow right back here to the capital. This is why we have—"

"Turn it off, Kage," Morakar said wearily. Kage killed the feed and looked over at his companion. "It's the same old argument wrapped in a different set of lies," Morakar said. "Many here bemoan the fact we've been forced to live on Restaria, but conveniently ignore the fact that the reason we are here is because of an attempted overthrow of an elected government. For all of Fordix's righteous indignation, he's simply proving why those that put us here were right in the first place."

"This seems like it's been planned for some time," Kage remarked after a moment.

"Yes," Morakar agreed. "All of this would have had to have been well in place even before they asked my brother and me to find Lord Felex. This also makes me wonder if there aren't some co-conspirators on Galvetor who arranged for Fordix's arrest. It was the perfect excuse to draw the Lord Archon back to Restaria."

Before Kage could answer a dull rumble started shaking the building and began growing in intensity. He ran over to the large windows that overlooked the square and was rewarded with the sight of the *Phoenix* coming through the lower cloud layer, extending her landing gear before coming to a not-so-graceful landing that crushed some benches and sculptures under the massive wheels.

"Things are now looking up," he said, suddenly in much higher spirits. He saw the ramp descend and then Doc, Mazer, and Jason raced out of the ship and into the building. Lucky could be seen walking down to the edge of the ramp to look around before walking back up into the cargo bay to stand guard. From Kage's vantage point, the engines looked like they were still running.

It was nearly five minutes later when the three exited the lift and crowded into Crusher's office. Doc was the only one who didn't recoil in horror when he saw the blade still sticking out of their friend. He moved over quickly, pulled out a handheld scanner, and began taking readings of not only the wound but Crusher's overall health. After a few grunts and tsks he straightened.

"It was close, but this isn't necessarily that bad," he said. "Whoever did this missed his heart, but still did a fair amount of damage. The good news is that it isn't anything the nanobots I've already programmed can't handle." He went through his bag and pulled out three large auto-injectors full of the microscopic little machines and lined them up. He pulled the end off of the first one and injected its entire contents near the wound itself. Jason peered over his shoulder and could see the silver tendrils running underneath Crusher's skin on their way to the edge of the wound.

"Now comes the tricky part," Doc said. "The timing needs to be pretty close or we could have a real mess." Just when the swarm of nanobots looked like they might actually make contact with the blade, Doc grabbed the handle and pulled it out in one swift motion. Crusher's eyes popped open and a gurgling moan escaped his lips before he fell back, his breathing shallow and fast.

The wound did not bleed much as the nanobots poured down into the cavity and instantly began stitching tissue back together and removing any necrosis that had begun around the edges. "Help me lay him flat," Doc said. Jason, Mazer, and Morakar picked Crusher up, kept him level, and then gently put him on the floor. Doc then used the other two auto-injectors and pumped the big warrior full with a veritable army of the specialized nanobots. Jason had been on the receiving end of one of these treatments and he knew there was massive discomfort associated with the near miraculous recovery.

They waited while Crusher slept and his wound healed right before their eyes. Doc began an intravenous drip to help his patient replace the lost blood and fuel his recovery. Soon his skin lost the cool, clammy feel and his breathing began to return to long, deep breaths. It was nearly ninety minutes after the first injection when he opened his eyes and looked around.

"Captain," he said, his voice strong and clear. "You're back."

"Not a moment too soon, it would seem," Jason said, walking over to kneel beside him. "What happened?"

"This has all been a setup," Crusher said. "Everything was to get me back here to get all the legions under a unified command. When I asked Fordix about the troop buildup he stuck a sword through me for my troubles."

"Where is the Caretaker?" Mazer asked.

"She was involved as well," Crusher said. "She's the one that paralyzed me before Fordix stabbed me." The look of sadness on the faces of both Mazer and Morakar was profound. "What has been happening? How long was I out?"

"Shockingly, you've been sitting in that chair with a sword sticking out of you for almost a full day," Jason said. "I have no idea how that's even possible, but either way it looks like you're on the mend. Things aren't so good on Galvetor. The warriors with Fordix have taken over the capital and have been sending out releases about the new order they intend to build. It seems none of them has really thought it through past the initial takeover, though. I'm seeing a lot of talk and posturing and not a lot of action from him or the Praetores."

"That's not surprising," Crusher said, groaning as he sat up. "They're as children … full of idealism and conviction, short on planning and logistics. Slogans are no substitute for a well thought-out plan. Speaking of which, what's our move?"

"You're asking me?" Jason said in mock surprise. "You're the Guardian Archon here."

"This is no time for pettiness, Captain," Crusher said. "We need to do this the way we always do: as a unit. We're vastly outnumbered on Galvetor."

Jason bit down his sarcastic retort. It seemed like Crusher was quite humbled from this latest betrayal and he didn't need Jason taking cheap shots at him.

"I assume you would like me to put you in a room with Fordix?" Jason asked.

"You know me so well," Crusher said with a huge genuine smile that would have terrified any human child.

"Oddly enough, we may have the element of surprise," Jason continued. "Even with ten thousand warriors they're going to be stretched fairly thin. What do they have for close air support?"

"Nine of those Eshquarian combat shuttles," Kage replied. "They had ten but you guys stole one."

"They're no match for the *Phoenix* even with experienced flight crews," Jason said. "So I'm thinking the good ol' frontal assault may be our best bet. Even in your weakened state we have more firepower than we're used to … assuming the Reddix brothers would care to join the party."

"I'm in," Mazer said.

"Me too," Morakar said.

"I would like to participate as well, Captain Burke," Meluuk said.

"I appreciate that, I truly do, but I have something more important for you to do," Jason said, looking at Doc. "Twingo can't make this trip. We're going to secure the medical facility that's on the second floor of this building and you're going to wait here with him."

"Captain—"

"Please, Doc … we can't leave Twingo here by himself. The medical facility should be able to keep him stable until the *Defiant* makes orbit," Jason said. "Meluuk, I'm going to outfit you from our armory and I need you to make sure they stay safe until we return or my associate comes to pick them up. This isn't just someplace to tuck you out of the way, I'm trusting you to protect my family."

"I will not let you down, Captain," Meluuk said with a deep nod of his head.

"Now that we have a loose plan, are we ready?" Jason asked. "Okay then, let's get Twingo loaded up on a med platform and make sure he's safe and then we can get in the air."

"One thing," Crusher said, holding up a hand. He pointed directly at Mazer before continuing. "Is that my armor?"

Chapter 26

The peace and quiet of the beautiful Restaria day was shattered as the *Phoenix's* drive throttled up and she lifted smoothly from the surface and thundered off towards the sunset. They'd managed to move Twingo without incident and had Doc set up in a private corner of the well-equipped medical facility to monitor his progress. Meluuk was given an arsenal of powerful weaponry and posted near the only entrance. Jason silently urged the *Defiant* to hurry up and make it into the system. He was anxious to get Twingo's more exotic treatments started such as the cloning of the parts his torturers had chopped off.

He sent the *Phoenix* on a sharp climb up out of Restaria's gravity well and began the chase of Galvetor around the system's primary star. He wasn't pushing the ship too hard since the damage was already done on the gelten homeworld. Instead, he was letting the ship loaf along to give Doc's treatments more time to get Crusher ready. His friend was moving around the bridge, swinging his arms and bending at the waist to keep loose before they made landfall.

"Kage, I'm going to clear out as much of their air support as I can before we deploy, but you'll be left alone in the ship once we hit the ground," Jason said. "The shields should be more than enough to protect the ship from those shuttles, but I don't want any collateral damage to the surrounding city. After we're off, clear the area if you feel like it's getting too hot."

"Count on that," Kage said. "Air to air combat isn't my strong suit."

"Neither are smooth landings, simple level flight, and not hitting obstacles on takeoff," Crusher said as he continued marching around the bridge.

"At least I can make it all the way through a mission without getting stabbed with my own knife," Kage retorted.

"Mission isn't over yet, little man," Crusher said. The back and forth was like thousands of identical interactions Jason had been witness to, or participant in, since he'd joined the group. At the moment it was oddly comforting.

"Take over, Lucky," Jason said, hopping out of the pilot's seat. "I'm going to go get dressed for the party."

"I'll go with you," Crusher said. "I need to get my gear together, too."

"Mazer and Morakar, you guys can go down once we're back and grab whichever weaponry tickles your fancy," Jason said. "There are some generic sets of body armor down there that should fit you. We don't have enough time to fabricate anything custom. Sorry."

"I'm sure we will be fine with whatever is already in on hand, Captain," Morakar said. Jason looked at him a moment before nodding and walking off the bridge. He seemed to be taking the duplicity of Fordix and the Order a lot harder than his brother was.

"I didn't get a chance to say it before, but good job getting Twingo and Doc back, Captain," Crusher said as Jason pulled his armor out from its alcove and began running a quick diagnostic on it. "Glad the ship was in one piece too."

"Yeah, our timing was more luck than skill," Jason said. "We were almost too late for Twingo. This entire op has been a cluster fuck. While we were chasing the ship halfway around the sector, a hit squad almost took out Kage and then you got skewered by your closest advisor."

"I'm sure there's a lesson in there somewhere," Crusher said after a few tense moments.

"Yeah? What's that?"

"How would I know? I'm just the dumb soldier who got stabbed with his own sword," Crusher said. "I'll see you back up there." He grabbed his gear and stomped out of the armory, leaving a slightly confused Jason alone to try and climb into his powered armor without assistance.

After some undignified contortions, he was able to climb up into the unit and power it up. A moment later, it closed around him and he stepped down off the rack. He grabbed his railgun, two plasma sidearms, and a few grenades before walking out of the armory. This was the first time he'd worn the unit since the modifications that Doc had done on him. The results were unexpected and a pleasant surprise. Before, there was always a barely perceptible mismatch between his movements and the armor's, but the enhanced capabilities were worth that slight inconvenience. Now the powerful suit felt as natural as wearing a well-worn glove. In fact, he barely noticed it was there by the time he was climbing the steps to walk onto the bridge.

Lucky made to get out of the pilot's seat but Jason waved for him to stay. "You may as well get as much seat time as you can," he said. "I'll take over right before we hit Galvetor's atmosphere."

"Of course, Captain," Lucky said and settled back into the pilot's seat. Mazer and Morakar walked off the bridge as Crusher stepped back in, carrying two large sandwiches with him.

"How come he gets to eat up here?" Kage demanded.

"He's too big to say no to, he's armed, and he doesn't leave sticky fingerprints all over my consoles," Jason answered without looking up. "Anything else?"

"Yeah, there are three capital ships that just came out of slip-space at the edge of the system," Kage said.

"Seriously?" Jason asked incredulously. "Put them on the main display." The sensor tracks for the three ships was imposed over a diagram of the system and displayed on the main canopy. "Can we ID them yet?"

"No," Kage said. "The range is too great and they're running silent, no transponders. They're not all that big, however. Smaller than destroyers, possibly frigates."

"ConFed ships?" Crusher asked.

"Not likely," Jason said. "ConFed Fleet wouldn't deploy three frigates alone like this, and they don't sneak into systems without their transponders blaring their affiliation loud and proud. Are they going to be a problem?"

"Not at their current speed and heading," Kage said. "We'll make landfall in another hour; they won't even make orbit for another twelve."

"It'll be all over by then, one way or another," Jason said. "Flag them, have the computer track them, but this doesn't change our plan."

"Lord Felex, we have a request to make of you," Morakar said as he and Mazer walked back onto the bridge.

"Yes?" Crusher asked.

"We would like to claim the Praetores when you challenge Fordix," Morakar continued. "We would like to clear our name of this treason."

Crusher pretended to consider it carefully, turning his back on the brothers and giving a Jason a half-smile and a wink before turning back.

"Granted," he said, "with conditions. While this act will clear your names, I may need you further when this is all over. I expect you to be available and enthusiastic for whatever task I put in front of you."

"You can count on us, my lord," Morakar said with a bow, speaking for them both.

Chapter 27

"We're getting pinged by the automated orbital control system. Seems like the standard automated message," Kage said, sounding disappointed. "What sort of hostile invasion is this? They don't even change the outbound message to warn everyone of the regime change? Or at least declare victory?"

Jason just rolled his eyes. "Just keep tracking those shuttles," he said. "How many have you picked up?"

"Six out of nine," Kage said. "The other three may be on the ground."

"Feed all the airborne targets to my tactical display," Jason said. "Let's tighten it up, full combat mode." He and Kage quickly went about bringing the ship to full power and energizing all the tactical systems.

"Weapons up, shields up, tactical sensors up," Kage read off his status board. "We're ready to kick some ass."

"Strap in everybody," Jason said. "We're going to be hitting the upper atmosphere at speed and making a combat descent."

"What does that entail?" Mazer asked with trepidation as he strapped into the seat.

"I wouldn't want to ruin the surprise," Crusher said humorlessly, looking like he'd rather be anywhere else.

The normal procedure when approaching a planet would be to allow the ship to be captured by the gravity and perform a series of deceleration orbits in order to enter the atmosphere at a safe speed. With a ship as capable as the *Phoenix*, there were a few more interesting options available. Jason angled the nose up a bit and let the ship's shields slam into Galvetor's mesosphere at a velocity that would tear most other ships apart.

As the *Phoenix* skipped off the upper atmosphere, she created a series of enormous shock waves that could be heard on the ground like thunder. Jason angled the nose back down and throttled up, pushing the gunship into a violent dive that slammed everyone on the bridge against their restraints. The coronal discharge of superheated gases cascaded around the shields as the ship bucked and fought her way down into the lower atmosphere.

"Here comes the rough part," Jason said.

"How is that possible?" Mazer shouted.

Jason snap-rolled the *Phoenix* over onto her back and pulled hard. Vapor poured off the flight control surfaces as the air compressed against them. The ship continued to pull around until the nose was aimed straight at the bright lights of the capital which was practically right below them. He throttled up again and put the ship into a powered dive, passing through high-supersonic speeds as they closed on the ground at a terrifying rate.

"Kage, lock up the six flyers with low-yield high-explosive warheads," Jason ordered.

"Only have a line on four of them," Kage said tensely.

"Give me those then," Jason said and began to pull up out of the dive. When they were at fifteen-thousand-feet altitude, he yanked back on the stick and pulled the throttle all the way back, forcing the grav-drive to compensate. It reversed its fields and yanked the ship to a near standstill in less than a few seconds, but thanks to the drive working in conjunction with the active deck plates, the occupants barely felt a tug instead of being splattered against the canopy.

Leveling the nose out, Jason put them into a much slower spiraling dive around the outskirts of the capital. When the four icons in his field of view indicating the airborne shuttles turned green, he squeezed off four missiles to chase after them. Even if they missed, which was unlikely, it would give them something to think about other than taking pot shots at the *Phoenix* as she unloaded the ground assault team. As the missiles streaked away, he pulled the nose around to tighten their turn and put them in line with the enormous structure that was the Senate Hall.

"Two more airborne threats on the board," Kage said. "They just lifted off from our primary target and are on an intercept course."

"Accommodating of them to fly within range for us," Jason grunted and pushed the throttle up to meet the charge. The first few shots of the engagement came from the shuttles as their ineffective fire splashed harmlessly against the *Phoenix's* shields. Jason lined the first target up and let loose with a salvo from the main plasma cannons, destroying it instantly. The rate of closure was too fast to bring the nose around on the second target, so he eased in as close as he could and let the point-defense blasters rake the side of the other ship. Jason glanced down at the sensor feed to see the ship billowing smoke and spiraling down to make a hard crash landing on the street below.

"We'll have to time this carefully, Kage," Jason said as he swung the *Phoenix* around to hover just over the roof of the building. The sensors were unable to give a complete picture of the inside and where the occupants were, but they were fairly certain their entry point would be over an empty space. He targeted their chosen spot with the reticle and squeezed off an extended salvo with the ventral plasma cannons, disintegrating the roof in an explosion of fire and smoke. Jason quickly slid the ship around over the opening, opened the hatch in the belly of the ship, and then activated the transit beam that would carry them to the surface.

"Let's go!" he yelled, grabbing his railgun and affixing it to the back of his armor at the anchor points. He slid his sidearms into their respective holsters as he ran down the steps and through the common area, three Galvetic warriors and one battlesynth hot on his trail. Kage was already in the pilot's seat by the time they reached the crew entry hatch leading to the cargo bay.

Crusher insisted on being the first through the hatch, followed by Jason, then Lucky, then the brothers. Once they were all in, the transit beam retracted back through the roof and they heard the *Phoenix* throttle up and fly off. They were in a darkened chamber that looked like it could have been used for legal proceedings.

"Company," Crusher said as the sounds of running boots could be heard approaching the huge double doors. Lucky switched to combat mode and Jason detached his primary weapon and brought it around. With the railgun slaved to his armor's targeting computer, there was no need to raise it to his shoulder, so he let it rest at his hip and waited. "Shoot to kill," Crusher said grimly. "They'll do no less."

A moment later, five heavily armed warriors blew into the room and deployed into a loose skirmish line, scanning for targets. Jason took the first one from the left, center mass with a high-velocity shot from his railgun. The warrior's light armor may as well have been tissue paper. Lucky mowed down two with his arm-mounted cannons and the brothers took out the last targets.

"Let's move," Crusher said. "Quickly, they'll be concentrated in the main audience chamber."

They let Crusher take point again and moved out in a single file line. The halls of the building were shockingly empty and they didn't encounter any further resistance until they reached the large ornamental doors of the main audience chamber, and even then there was only three additional troops posted. They killed two and disabled the third, moving silently to the door to listen beyond.

They could just make out the muted babble of the senators, now hostages, and could hear Fordix's booming voice still making proclamations in grand, theatrical tones. Jason just shook his head. *That man loves the sound of his own voice.* He detached a high-explosive grenade and held it up to Crusher. The warrior considered it for a second and then nodded. Jason slaved the detonator to his armor and then balanced the grenade between the decorative door handles.

"In three … two … one," Jason said before triggering the grenade and blowing the doors inward, stunning everyone in the large chamber with the over-pressure. Crusher was up and through the door before the debris had even hit the floor. Lucky was right behind him followed closely by Jason. The Reddix brothers, lacking any protective headgear, were shaking off the cobwebs before bringing up the rear.

"All Legionnaires STAND DOWN!!" Crusher bellowed from the ruined doorway.

There was a lot of confusion, but nobody was raising their weapons, so that was a promising start.

"NOW!"

At this, individual soldiers began lowering their weapons and looking at each other, shrugging.

"Crusher, up by the dais," Jason said. He could see Fordix and the Praetores of the Order moving slowly towards the rear exit.

"Block the exits!" Crusher shouted. "The three Praetores, and Fordix, are not to leave this room."

Six troops immediately moved to block off their retreat. Seeing he would not be leaving, Fordix drew himself up and turned to face Crusher.

"Felex," he said. "I see you are far tougher than I gave you credit for."

"Not especially," Crusher said calmly. "You're just an incompetent warrior, much as I remember from my youth. You missed my heart by nearly ten centimeters."

This set the entire room to buzzing. The other warriors in the room were now training their weapons on Fordix and the Praetores, indicating where their loyalties still lay.

"So what now, Felex? You just kill us and everyone goes back to the way things were?"

"Of course not," Crusher said, dropping his weapons and flexing his arms. "You've ruined centuries of peaceful coexistence with your stupidity. After I kill you, we will have to find a new path."

"You would face me in single combat?" Fordix said, his voice actually hopeful. "Even with such a grave injury?"

"You are in for an unpleasant surprise," Crusher said, continuing to close in on his old mentor. Fordix dropped his own weapons and began stretching and walking down off the dais. Jason looked at the older warrior's confident, even indulgent smile. *He thinks he actually has a chance.*

"There's a certain symmetry to—" Fordix's pontificating was cut short by Crusher's deafening roar right before he launched himself across the short distance separating them and crashed his closed fist into his former mentor's skull. Fordix's head snapped back and he flew back a few steps, collapsing to the floor. He struggled to rise, his motor functions slightly off from the devastating blow. When he looked at Crusher approaching, his condescending smirk was replaced with shock and fear.

Fordix came in with two wide-armed, telegraphed strikes that caused Crusher to tuck his arms in and easily block. He then lashed out with an open palm strike that caught Fordix in the side of the head and knocked him to the floor again. Crusher pressed his attack and lunged in with another closed fist strike that crushed bone and drove his opponent's head into the polished stone floor with tremendous force.

"It's over," Fordix wheezed as he raised his hands in defeat, blood running from his nose and ears. Crusher slid a long, curved blade from the sheath on his back.

"It was over before it started," he said and plunged the blade into Fordix's chest. He leaned in and whispered into the older warrior's ear, "That's where the heart is, by the way."

As soon as Crusher stood up, Mazer and Morakar raised their weapons and quickly dispatched the Praetores of the Archon's Fist in a blaze of plasma fire from the modern firearms they'd taken from the *Phoenix's* armory. Fostel, Zetarix, and Mutabor hit the ground, their bodies smoking.

"Who is in command here?" Crusher demanded.

"You are, my lord," a warrior said from the perimeter of the room.

"I mean who has tactical authority," Crusher clarified. "Who is running the ground campaign?"

"I am," the same warrior said.

"This operation is over," Crusher said calmly. "It was never actually authorized. All troops are to stand down and muster in the square near the Senate Hall. They are to stay isolated and are not to provoke local law enforcement until we get this mess straightened out."

"Lord Felex Tezakar," an elderly gelten said, approaching the group. "It was my understanding that you accepted banishment from Galvetor and Restaria both, yet here you are."

"Your understanding is correct, Senator," Crusher said in a neutral tone.

"I will assume you had returned to try and head off exactly the kind of violence between our kinds that we've seen here today," the senator continued. "Such an action would be viewed by the Senate as an acceptable breech of the conditions of your exile."

"Correct again, although I hadn't expected any of this magnitude," Crusher admitted. "Otherwise you'd have never known I was back. I would have handled things on Restaria without the meddling of the oversight committee or the intervention of Internal Security."

"What are we to do now?" another senator demanded. "We can't go back to the way things were. Our citizens will demand action."

"No," Crusher said slowly, "we can't go back to the way it was. We'll need to find another way to live with each other, but that will be largely up to this body."

"I think it will need to be up to all of us this time. No class can feel they were cheated when it is done," the first senator said. "Will you help us?"

"As always, I will do whatever is in my power to help my people," Crusher said. Jason's heart sank at those words. Before he could ask his friend to clarify, Kage broke in on the com channel.

"Captain, those ships have increased speed," he said. *"They'll be here within the hour."*

"Understood," Jason said. "Come pick me up."

*****

"Do we have any better resolution on who these guys are?" Jason asked as the *Phoenix* shot up out of Galvetor's atmosphere.

"No," Kage said. "They're still running silent, but we've gotten better scans on their configuration and power output. They appear to be on the small side for a frigate class vessel and have power readings we would expect to see from a ship that small."

"I guess we can rule out coincidence that they've just happened to show up during an attempted coup and then just happened to accelerate once that was put into doubt," Jason groused.

"True," Kage said. "So did Crusher really just beat down Fordix in three hits?"

"Well, he stabbed him through the chest too," Jason said. "To be honest, it was a bit anticlimactic. Fordix was fairly well organized up to the point the Galvetic Senate capitulated without a fight, but after that he didn't really seem to have much of a plan."

"I wish he could have refrained from the death by combat stuff," Kage complained. "Fordix likely had much more information available about who took the *Phoenix* and who these guys are coming at us."

"Agreed," Jason said with a sigh. "Not to mention where they're getting all the badass Eshquarian hardware. Too bad the Reddix brothers took out all three Praetores shortly afterwards."

"I'm beginning to get the sense the gelten species may be a tad overemotional and more than a little short-sighted when it comes to things like this," Kage said. "But hey! This is fun … just the two of us, flying out to meet the enemy head on."

Jason gave him an irritated look, but decided not to answer. He'd left Lucky on Galvetor to make sure there was a non-gelten presence to keep order between the thoroughly confused warriors milling about and a population that was getting over the initial shock and replacing it with anger.

"Looks like they're turning to meet us," Jason said, looking at his tactical display. They'd flown a course directly away from Galvetor and tangential to the incoming fleet's projected course to see if they could get a reaction.

"They're also powering weapons and raising their shields," Kage said urgently. "Weapons look like standard fare. The shields don't appear to be all that special either, but there are three of them so we'll need to keep our distance."

"Yeah, don't want to get caught in a crossfire situation with three capital ships, no matter how small," Jason said. "Looks like it's stick and move until we can figure out who they are. Bring everything up to full power. No use hiding what we have now. Target all three ships, I'll prioritize from here."

He pushed up the throttle and brought his course around for a direct intercept. Being so outmatched in combined firepower, he decided to make the first pass at high subluminal speeds and then use the gunship's far superior maneuverability to their advantage.

"We're locked on," Kage said. "We'll be in range within two minutes."

Jason activated the link between the ship and his neural implant, effectively making his entire field of view the tactical display. He didn't bother with visual spectrum overlays; at the range and speed that space battles happened, there wasn't much to see. At the last possible moment, Jason shifted their course to starboard by ten degrees and put their nose on the right-most target, opening fire with the main guns when the computer indicated they were within range.

The engagement was over in a split-second as the *Phoenix* shot by the ship they'd hit and was well into its first turn before the enemy could return fire. They felt a few bumps as ineffective point-defense fire impacted harmlessly against their shields.

"The ship we just hit took a fair amount of damage down its port flank," Kage reported, reading the sensor data from the opening shot of the battle. "It must be worse than it looked, bogey is breaking formation and accelerating for a mesh-out point."

"I didn't think it was that bad," Jason said. "I'm guessing they're not here for anything other than the intimidation factor, since we only landed two shots and they're bugging out. I guess their heart just isn't in it."

He accelerated along their current course before swinging around hard to line up on the engines of the next target. As he pulled in towards them, they matched his rate of acceleration and began to turn away from Galvetor, heading out of the system. After thirty seconds, Jason broke pursuit and swung back around to take up a defensive position near the planet. With multiple targets, he would play a completely defensive strategy and not engage them too far into the system, thus leaving the planet unguarded for the other ships or those he hadn't been aware of.

"They're still pulling away hard," Kage said in confusion. "That ship we hit has started to slow down; it looks like they weren't meshing out after all."

"They're regrouping near the edge of the system," Jason said. "I think that was a feeler to see who we were. The next engagement won't be so easy."

Jason actually pulled the ship to a full stop relative to Galvetor and kept rotating to keep their nose on the enemy as they paced the planet around the primary star. After fifteen minutes, they found out why the three smaller ships had broken off their attack.

"Three more slip-space signatures near the edge of the system," Kage said. "Stand by while the sensors resolve them."

"Looks like they had reinforcements hanging just outside of sensor range," Jason said.

"You're not going to like this," Kage said, his voice pitching up an octave. "Two cruisers and a destroyer just joined the three frigates."

"We're sure they're warships?" Jason asked.

"Yeah, power output confirms it," Kage said. "I've been trying to raise them on the com since the frigates turned and ran, but no response so far."

Jason almost admonished him for taking such an action without asking him, but he let it slide since it was something he should have ordered himself in the first place.

"Phalanx formation around the destroyer," Jason said. "Predictable. But when you're only facing a single gunship with an entire fleet, I guess you don't need to be too creative."

"Here they come," Kage said as the formation began to accelerate back down into the system. "Is it too late for me to stay behind with Lucky?"

"Why so defeatist?" Jason asked. "They look like they're forty-year-old ships."

"And that makes a difference?"

"Let's head out and meet them," Jason said. "We'll see how this goes. If we can't get them to turn off again, we'll regroup near Galvetor and hope the geltens have some sort of planetary defense."

"You think we'll be in any shape to retreat after going head to head with a destroyer battle group?" Kage asked, looking at him as if he'd sprouted a second head.

"We've had worse odds," Jason argued.

"With the element of surprise and the fact we were too stupid to know better," Kage said. "A slow march across the system isn't exactly subtle." Even as Kage whined on about their impending defeat, he was optimizing the ship's systems for the upcoming engagement.

"I just wish I knew who the hell they were," Jason said to himself. The com silence from what appeared to be an invasion fleet was unnerving. Were they here to support Fordix's coup? Or was this something else? "Well," he said loudly to Kage, "I'd been saving these for a special occasion, but warm up the XTX-4s." Kage brightened up noticeably at this. In the aft weapons bay, the *Phoenix* was carrying five XTX-4 antimatter "ship killer" missiles. They could be fired at extreme range and had a type of specialized slip-drive that would "pulse" and cause the missile to skip in and out of real-space on its way to the target, making it impossible to track or shoot down. Their size meant that five was all the gunship could carry in a single weapons bay. Their expense was unholy, and it was illegal to even have them onboard in many systems.

Thankfully, they were almost impossible to detect when not powered up and the cost wasn't really an issue since Omega Force had technically stolen them. They were onboard the *Diligent,* Kellea Colleren's former command and Crisstof Dalton's former flagship. They had been in the ammunition magazine when they had raided the ship to use it as a kinetic kill weapon.

"XTXs coming online, ten minutes until they're ready to fire," Kage said.

"Plenty of time," Jason said. "We'll see if they can read and understand what the change in our energy profile means. If they know we're carrying these things, I would assume they will either retreat or open communications."

They waited a bit longer as the ships still maintained their rate of acceleration. They were two hours apart and closing into range of the XTX-4s when the enemy broke com silence.

"We've got incoming on the open channel," Kage reported. "Audio only."

Jason nodded for him to patch it through.

"*We are here to provide logistical support and relief to the new government of the Galvetor System,*" the voice said simply in Jenovian Standard. "*Please state your intentions.*"

"I'm not sure if you've been made aware, but there is no *new* government on Galvetor," Jason said. "I've also never seen six warships deployed for relief aid. So … state *your* intentions, if you please."

There was a long pause as the intruders no doubt tried to contact someone on the planet to verify what Jason had said.

"While we're at it," Jason continued, "how about you tell us who you are and who you represent."

"*We are under no obligation to answer your inquiries,*" the voice said after a moment. "*We suspect you have illegally displaced the rightful government of this sovereign world and will take steps to remove you.*" The channel closed and they refused to reopen it after repeated attempts by Kage.

"It looks like they're determined to do this the dumb way," Jason said with a sigh. "Feed the targeting data to our missiles. Obviously leave the frigate we already hit for us to handle afterwards."

"Whatever investment they made in Fordix's plan must be important for them to take a risk like this," Kage remarked. "The ConFed will view this as an invasion unless they're able to kill us and quickly install a puppet government."

"It won't do any good without the Order's leadership," Jason said, watching the timer on his tactical display. "Crusher is back in charge and the Legions will tear these guys to shreds the moment they make landfall. The entire thing was a house of cards built on Fordix's attempt to deceive the warrior class."

As he watched the ships march towards them on the display, the entire scheme became clearer in his head, but the ultimate motivation eluded him. Was Fordix really such a blind idealist? Or was there a more corporeal benefit involved? The pessimist that he was, he figured it was the latter.

"Oh shit!" Kage exclaimed. "New contact just entered the system. It is very big and very fast."

Jason's heart sank at the news. There were seven big ships and he only had five big missiles.

"*This is Captain Kellea Colleren of the battlecruiser* Defiant," the familiar voice broke in over the open channel. "*To the six warships in this system; you will come about and identify yourselves at once.*"

Sure enough, the sensors resolved the new contact into the sleek and powerful battlecruiser that was Crisstof's new flagship and one of the most powerful warships in private hands. It was only Dalton's myriad contacts within the ConFed and regional governments that allowed him to have such a vessel without being affiliated with any sanctioned military.

"Well, this just got interesting," Kage said. "Inbound fleet is turning away from the planet. It looks like they're stalling for time and trying to put distance between them and Captain Colleren. We're more or less being ignored now."

"In a situation like this, that's the best I could hope for," Jason said. As he watched, Kellea ordered her ship to cut off the attacking fleet and accelerated so fast that it forced their hand; they turned hard away from Galvetor and began getting separation from each other in order to make the transition to slip-space.

"Damn, that ship is fast," Kage marveled. "I'm glad she's not chasing us."

"Me too," Jason said, marveling at the acceleration the enormous ship was able to achieve. A battlecruiser was the second largest warship class, if one were to discount carriers. The *Defiant's* tonnage was more than that of the six ships she was chasing combined. "We may need to start looking into a drive upgrade soon if ships that big are hitting those speeds within a gravity well."

"Truly."

"Damnit!" Jason said suddenly. "Shut down the XTXs! Quick, before the *Defiant* gets close enough to scan us."

Kage didn't ask any questions as he lunged forward and began powering down the weapons and getting them back into a dormant state. He was well aware where they had gotten the very expensive and very illegal ordnance. He was also privy to the fact Jason had played dumb when asked point-blank about the missiles by both Crisstof and Kellea when he had debriefed them on the *Diligent's* destruction.

"*Phoenix, this is the* Defiant," Kellea said over a private channel. "*The immediate threat has left the area. We will be taking up position in orbit over Galvetor and assessing the situation.*"

"Copy that, *Defiant*," Jason said. "We'll meet you there."

"When she says '*assessing the situation*' it sounds more like '*seeing what you guys have done this time,*'" Kage said. Jason winced but chose to remain silent.

Chapter 28

"May I talk to you, Captain Burke?" Mazer asked in a serious tone. They were walking among the troops still left on Galvetor as the lifters were coming and going, taking them back to Restaria. It was two weeks since the attempted coup, and the aftershocks of that political neutron bomb were still being felt. The system was in complete disarray, but it had also opened a dialogue that had been long overdue between the residents of Galvetor and the warrior class on Restaria.

"Of course," Jason said, motioning over to an area that was sparsely populated. "What's on your mind?"

"You've heard that the restriction on leaving the Galvetor System is being lifted?"

"I'd heard," Jason said carefully. "You think there will be many of your people wanting to leave?"

"That's what I wanted to talk to you about," Mazer said. "There are many of us, mostly from the 7th Legion, who want to see what's out there. Living vicariously through the Archon's adventures is no longer enough. For the first time, we're being given the opportunity to see it for ourselves."

"Have you thought about the realities of space travel?" Jason asked. "The reality is that it's mostly riding around in a cramped ship for extended periods that are interrupted with spurts of planetside action."

"We are aware of what it entails," Mazer said patiently. "This is not something that has come from rash thinking."

"How many warriors have approached you?" Jason asked.

"One hundred and twenty-two," Mazer said. "That number may fluctuate more or less by a few heads."

"Damn, an entire company of you," Jason whistled. He realized the enormity of his responsibility. An entire company of Galvetic warriors would be a powerful weapon in the wrong hands. He also had to consider the safety and well-being of the warriors themselves. He would not turn them loose to be cannon fodder.

"I was hoping that possibly one or two of us might join your crew, Captain," Mazer said, interrupting his thoughts. Jason took a moment to consider it, but realized ultimately that a loose mercenary unit like Omega Force wouldn't likely be a good place for a few young, wide-eyed warriors looking to prove themselves. Someone would probably be killed and he wasn't entirely sure it wouldn't be him.

"Let's hang off on that," he said to his friend, an idea coming to him. "Let me talk to someone and get back with you. Stay here in the area, I'm going to try and set up a meeting."

"As you feel is best, Captain," Mazer said, saluting and turning to rejoin his friends.

As Jason walked through the assemblage, he did notice that most of the warriors not only recognized him, but saluted him as well. He felt profoundly honored to have earned their respect. Lucky and Kage had left a couple days ago with the *Phoenix* to pick up Twingo and transport him to the *Defiant* to continue his treatment. The gunship was still sitting in the hangar bay of the battlecruiser, so Jason walked over to the officious-looking gelten and bullied him into borrowing one of the combat shuttles that were still parked on the grounds and being used to support the troop movements.

*****

"So what do you make of it all, Captain?" Crisstof asked. He and Jason were sitting in the *Defiant's* observation lounge sharing a bottle of some incredibly expensive distilled spirit, doing their customary mission debrief that seemed to happen whenever Omega Force got itself tangled up in something he needed to fly in for and smooth over with local governments. "Was Fordix acting alone?"

"I really can't say one way or another," Jason admitted. "My newfound insight into the gelten racial character leads me to believe that he could have been, but obviously he was being supported by someone outside. All the Eshquarian hardware and the six ships waiting to swoop in as soon as Galvetor fell could mean he was just a pawn. Or he could have been using them to accomplish his own means. In other words, I have no idea."

"It's unfortunate Lord Felex killed him before any of that could be determined," Crisstof remarked.

"I told him that," Jason said with a shrug. "But if he was going to recapture control of the situation, he had to prove to the Legions that he was still worthy of leadership. He actually seems fairly disinterested in the details now that the Order of the Archon's Fist has been disbanded."

"Have you spoken to him about his future?"

"No," Jason said glumly. "Crusher will do what he wants to do … that's always been the agreement between us in Omega. Anybody can leave at any time. Hell, I almost did after the incident on Earth. But, whatever he decides, we'll carry on. Lucky actually has a line on two other battlesynths that could be convinced to join up."

"The obvious choice would be Mazer," Crisstof remarked.

"It would be," Jason said, "and he's asked. But he needs some experience outside of life in the Legions within a more controlled environment ... and yes, I know that's incredibly hypocritical of me to say given my own background."

"Which brings me to why we're talking in the first place," Crisstof segued smoothly. "An entire company of Galvetic warriors stationed on the *Defiant*? This is your solution?"

"Look, they're going to leave anyway," Jason said. "They might scrape up enough for a ship of their own and who the hell knows what sort of trouble they'll get themselves into. Or, they may be snatched up by someone looking to use them as shock troops to terrorize anyone they feel like.

"This way, you can keep an eye on them and in the meantime you'll have the most capable company of Marines the quadrant has ever seen on your ship. I really feel this is important, Crisstof. You'd be ushering in a new era for this species by taking these warriors out and letting them see the galaxy a bit without it taking advantage of them."

"I fear you have become as skillful at manipulating me as my captain," Crisstof said ruefully. "Not to worry, Jason. I've already given the order and their barracks are being configured down on one of our many empty decks. They'll even have their own training facilities."

Jason leaned back in relief. "Thanks," he said simply.

"So no word of the Caretaker?" Crisstof asked after another quiet moment.

"It seems she simply vanished," Jason said. "No mean trick on a planet as locked down as Restaria was. I can't even find any definitive proof she went to Galvetor with the Legions, so I have to assume she's either hiding on the other world or had an escape plan."

"What do you think her role was? Besides incapacitating Crusher."

"I don't think that was part of her plan. After debriefing everyone involved, I'm beginning to thing she was acting towards her own goals while playing along with Fordix," Jason said, taking another sip. "She had been feeding information out to both sides in what seems like a clumsy attempt to move people the direction she needed them.

"This leaves a few more loose ends than I care to think about. She could have been working for another player we haven't been able to identify, she could have been trying to warn Crusher about Fordix's plan, or she could have been part of an unrelated scheme. If we think about the theft of the *Phoenix* and the attacks on my crew, the third option seems to be the most likely."

"I thought you felt the incidents involving your crew and ship were related to the machinations of the Order," Crisstof said.

"I did say that," Jason admitted, "but now I'm not completely certain."

"I'm sure everything will come to light in due time," Crisstof said with a small shrug. "You can drive yourself insane trying to chase around ghosts that may not even mean anything."

"You're not telling me anything I don't know already," Jason said with a laugh.

"Now, I heard a nasty, unfounded rumor that when we meshed into the system a peculiar weapon signature was detected on the *Phoenix*," Crisstof said, setting his glass down. "I assumed there must have been some sort of anomaly with our sensors."

"Sounds like it," Jason said, also setting his glass down and standing up. "I'd get a tech team on that pretty soon. Inaccurate sensor readings are bad news on a starship. Anyway, I'm going to check on Twingo and then I'm due for dinner with the captain. Goodnight."

Jason hustled out of the lounge as fast as decorum would allow, missing the older man smirking at his back.

*****

"You're looking good as new, buddy," Jason said expansively. "If anything, the new ear looks even better than the original one."

Twingo actually laughed, holding his chest in pain as he did. He was walking on his own with the aid of a low-tech solution Jason had fabricated for him: a cane.

"It feels good to be up and about," Twingo admitted. "A little more rest and I'll be ready to undo all the damage you've done to my engines."

"It's going to take you a while," Jason admitted.

It had been three weeks aboard the *Defiant* and now his friend was ready to go; Mazer's warriors had just come aboard and were settling in. Mazer had been promoted to captain and made the company commander in a ceremony performed by Kellea. Jason had pinned his rank insignia on at the younger warrior's request. They all had new uniforms to reinforce the fact that they were no longer Legionnaires, but Marines on a battlecruiser and under the command of Captain Colleren.

"I heard we're a man light," Twingo said sadly.

"I wasn't able to get a hold of him," Jason said. "I know he's busy, so I guess that's our answer. We'll get by."

"We always do," Twingo said and shuffled off into the cargo bay with Lucky helping him along. Doc and Kage were already aboard and there was really no reason they couldn't depart. Jason thought about going to see Kellea one more time, but they'd already said goodbye after spending an entire day together, and she was up on the bridge anyway. Even though she had relaxed a bit since he'd met her, he wouldn't compromise her authority by making an unannounced personal visit while she was on the bridge of her ship as its commanding officer.

He looked out over the hangar deck at all the starfighters, shuttles, and tenders the battlecruiser was carrying, thinking back on waking up with Kellea that morning in her quarters. It had been their first time experimenting with any sort of real intimacy, and it turned out his fears of incompatibility, both physically and emotionally, were unfounded. With her dark complexion and dark, upturned eyes, she could have passed for an exotically beautiful human woman with her hair down. The slight differences in the shape of her ears and the ridge that ran up the back of her neck were the only obvious giveaways. Jason discovered it was the differences he found most endearing. He shook his head with a smile and walked back into the cargo bay. His hand hovered over the controls to close the ship up when he heard footsteps coming up the ramp.

"What the hell?! You were going to leave without me?"

"I thought you were staying here," Jason said with a shrug, hiding his surprise at the other's appearance on the

Defiant. "We couldn't get a hold of you and I didn't want to put you on the spot."

"I see how it is," Crusher said, looking visibly angry. "You'll move planets to find Twingo but can't take a shuttle ride down to the surface to check for me."

"You know that isn't true," Jason shot back, his own anger rising. He forced himself to calm down before he continued. "What about your own people? Don't they need you?"

"I'm exactly what they don't need. Not anymore," Crusher said, his temper also deflating. "I'll be the last of the Archons. Galvetor is moving into a new age and normal geltens and warriors will have to find their own way and new traditions."

"So you'll just leave them to it? Isn't that a little dangerous?"

"My last act as Archon was to appoint Morakar as the warrior class's representative in the Senate," Crusher said.

"I bet he wasn't happy about that," Jason said with a laugh.

"Which is exactly why it was always going to be him," Crusher said.

Jason looked at the bag he had with him as well as the well-worn body armor leaning against it. He'd obviously come with every intention of staying with the crew.

"You sure it can go back to the way it was?" he asked. "There's only one captain on this ship."

"My job here is done," Crusher said as he picked up his belongings. "I'm ready to come home."

Jason slapped him on the shoulder and hit the controls to close up the ship. The pair made their way to the stairs leading to the crew entry hatch.

"I can't believe you were going to leave me behind."

"Oh, for fuck's sake, you big baby … all you would have had to do was call, the ship can fly both ways."

Epilogue

"So tell me what you found."

"When we arrived, we had to dig down through an apparent cave-in, but the ship wasn't there. All we found were scraps of other Jepsen spacecraft. Some were the same model, others just of similar design."

"Very interesting. What else?"

"We confirmed the ship was in the area and was involved in some sort of political upheaval on the planet."

"That follows a certain pattern, so at least we know it was the right ship."

"So what does it all mean? Why steal and scrap all those Jepsens?"

"Isn't it obvious? There's another player in the game. Someone else has learned of what makes that ship so special, but they're not so well-informed that they know exactly which ship it is. Where are they now?"

"They were last seen flying away from the Galvetor System. We lost them soon after."

"I assume you know what to do then?"

"Yes. We have already dispatched teams to track them down. It shouldn't be long."

*****

"Please! I did everything you asked!"

"And yet here I sit without the thing I want most in the universe. You understood the deal when we approached you."

"But it wasn't my fault! I couldn't have known the crew would be so hard to control."

"Ah … but we warned you, Connimon. I believe I was quite explicit in that you should be very careful around them. But I do take solace in the fact that neither of us is getting what we wanted in this bargain: Galvetor and Restaria are even now signing new accords and forging a new relationship. Your little revolution is over, so you'll have no need for our fleet in any case."

"Since we both lost, can I just leave and we can put this whole unpleasant incident behind us?"

"Oh, no," the voice chuckled mirthlessly. "I am sorry, my dear, but this is just business."

A shot flared from a blaster pistol in the darkened cargo hold and the Caretaker's body slumped to the ground.

"Dreadful beasts," the assailant muttered before walking over to the intercom. "Send someone down to clean this mess up and let me know when we're clear to leave. I wish to be off of Restaria as soon as possible."

"The battlecruiser and the gunship both made the transition to slip-space an hour ago. There is no indication they were able to penetrate our cloaking field."

"As soon as the hold is cleaned up, you are clear to launch. I will be in my quarters trying to think of a way to break the bad news to *him.*"

*****

Thank you for reading *Omega Force: Return of the Archon.*

If you enjoyed the story, Captain Burke and the guys will be back in:

Omega Force: Secret of the Phoenix

Follow me on Facebook and Twitter for the latest updates;

http://www.facebook.com/pages/Joshua.Dalzelle

@JoshuaDalzelle

Made in the USA
Las Vegas, NV
30 January 2022